A WICKED WENCH

A WICKED WENCH

Anne Herries

Severn House Large Print
London & New York

This first large print edition published in Great Britain 2005 by
SEVERN HOUSE LARGE PRINT BOOKS LTD of
9-15 High Street, Sutton, Surrey, SM1 1DF.
First world regular print edition published 2004 by
Severn House Publishers, London and New York.
This first large print edition published in the USA 2005 by
SEVERN HOUSE PUBLISHERS INC., of
595 Madison Avenue, New York, NY 10022.

British Library Cataloguing in Publication Data

Herries, Anne
  A wicked wench. - Large print ed.
  1. Great Britain - Social life and customs - 18th century - Fiction
  2. Love stories
  3. Large type books
  I. Title
  823.9'14 [F]

  ISBN-10: 0-7278-7468-3

Printed and bound in Great Britain by
MPG Books Ltd, Bodmin, Cornwall.

One

Gervase Winston, Marquis of Roxbourne, paused in the doorway of the busy posting inn, staring at the young woman being assisted from the travelling carriage which had just that minute arrived. She seemed to be having some difficulty, and for a moment he was afforded a glimpse of a pair of neat ankles clad in white stockings. He smiled to himself, his attention caught.

The carriage itself was a shabby affair, clearly having seen better days, and the woman's gown was plainer than those worn by the more fashionable ladies in town. But, as he looked closer, Gervase saw that there was nothing plain or ordinary about the woman herself.

By heavens she was a beauty! His hot gaze intensified as he saw that the neckline of her gown was lower than modesty would suggest proper for the daughter of a well-to-do farmer, which by the look of her she most likely was. He could clearly glimpse the tempting mounds of her breasts, enhanced rather than concealed by her charming lace fichu. He would vow that skin was softer than silk, as luscious as the ripe peaches he sometimes picked from the south-facing wall in the gardens of Roxbourne House.

Yet it was her face that fixed his attention on her, for she was as fresh as dew, seemingly innocent until one looked at those cherry-ripe lips – and her eyes! It was the eyes that gave her away, for they were green and bold, and now that she was aware of him staring at her, they met his gaze with a proud challenge.

Only a few wisps of hair escaped from the tight-fitting white cap she wore beneath her severe black hat, but they were a fiery red and curled becomingly against her cheek and neck. He drew his breath in sharply as he pictured that hair unfurled and lying against the pillows of his bed. She would be as passionate as she was lovely. He knew a swift desire to bed her, and planted himself squarely in her way as she approached the threshold of the inn.

'Will you not stand aside and let me enter, sir?' The sound of her voice sent tiny shock waves down Gervase's spine. He had ever the eye for a beautiful wench and the taste to indulge his pleasures, but few women had assaulted his senses as this one did.

'Whither so fast, mistress?' he enquired, giving her the arrogant, mocking smile that had brought him many a wench's favour.

'Will you not stay to pass the time of day?'

Her eyes went over him, and from their cool expression clearly found him lacking. Gervase smiled inwardly. This proud beauty needed taming! He had met others who pretended to resist, but in the end they succumbed to his charms, which, he was honest enough to admit, were not always apparent at first glance. His features were too harsh, his complexion too dark to be considered handsome by those whose tastes ran to pretty fellows, but there was something supremely masculine about him. He was tall, large-boned, but carried no excess fat, giving the impression of raw physical strength and a will to match. Men did well to fear him, and women were fools to love him for he seldom gave of himself, although he was generous with money, which he had in abundance.

'I pray you, let me pass!' There was an imperious tone in her voice, and he recognized that her speech was too cultured to be that of the farm wench he had taken her for.

'What is it, Arabella?'

A man and another young woman had come up to them. The man was clearly a country squire, fallen on hard times by the look of his stained coat and shabby boots, neither of which was fit to be seen abroad in Gervase's estimation. The other young woman might have been the first's sister, though her looks paled by comparison. She was pretty but insipidly fair, with blue eyes and a mouth too sweet for Gervase's liking.

'Oh, Nan, this *gentleman* does not wish to let me pass,' Arabella replied, looking at the other woman. 'Perhaps Father can persuade him, for it seems that I cannot.'

'What? Eh? What was that, Arabella?' Sir Edmund Tucker stared at the fellow blocking the doorway in some bewilderment. 'What do you mean by this? Stand aside and let my daughters pass if you please, sir. No call for offence, what?'

'I was merely admiring the view,' Gervase replied smoothly, his eyes dwelling for a moment on the plump mounds peeping above Arabella's bodice. She had laced herself tightly to show off her tiny waist, and the boned bodice pushed up her breasts so he felt that with the merest persuasion they would pop into his welcoming hands. 'I have gold in my pocket, sir. If your daughter's wares are for sale I would gladly pay some guineas for a few hours of her time.'

'Damn your eyes, sir!' Sir Edmund roared. 'I am insulted. If it were not that I believe you have been too freely imbibing the landlord's good wine, I would demand satisfaction.'

At this, Gervase threw back his head and laughed, his large frame shaking with mirth at this quite ridiculous suggestion. The gentleman now glaring at him so fiercely was at least a foot less in height and his stature was lean to the point of emaciation. Any duel between them would be mere seconds in duration and there could be only one outcome.

'Think yourself fortunate that I do not care to be insulted by your tone, sir,' he replied easily. 'It is too pleasant a day for quarrelling – and mayhap I spoke too hastily.' He took off his hat and made Arabella a sweeping bow that served only to mock her. 'Forgive me if I mistook the signs, my lady. I shall bid you adieu and allow you to continue your progress unheeded ... but 'tis a crying shame such beauty should go untasted.'

His last words were said in a low voice meant for her ears alone and brought an angry flush to her cheeks. She brushed past him, for he had given her barely enough space to pass, though he stood aside for her sister. She gave him a shy, uncertain smile and hurried after Arabella. Their father glared at him in passing but was too wise to repeat his earlier threat.

Gervase smiled as he walked across the cobbled yard towards his own travelling coach. There were puddles and fresh horse droppings to negotiate, but the yard was kept reasonably clean by the industry of a young lad busily sweeping. Seeing Gervase's approach, the lad rushed to clear a path for him. Gervase threw him a coin, which he caught neatly and grinned as he dropped his broom and opened the door of milord's carriage – a far more elegant conveyance than that of the country squire, with the Roxbourne crest emblazoned on the side in colours of blue, gold and crimson. Inside, a young man was leaning lazily against the squabs, his eyes half closed as if asleep, but it was merely a pose as his first words revealed.

'Who was the brazen beauty?' Jack Meadows enquired and yawned, apparently indifferent. 'I thought for a moment that we were in for a short delay.'

'Had her father taken my offer I might have dallied more than an hour or so,' Gervase replied, smiling at his friend. 'I swear there is fire in that wench, Jack.'

'Which will no doubt be wasted on the bovine fool for whom she is destined,' Jack remarked with a wry twist of his lips. His features were as pretty as milord's were harsh, his hair as fair as milord's was dark, his eyes a limpid blue – something that had deceived many an innocent wench into thinking him the kinder of the two. 'By the manner of her father's dress, I imagine she is being taken to London for sale to the highest bidder.'

'I dare say he hopes to find husbands for

both sisters.' Gervase wondered at the slightly protective feeling towards the beauty that Jack's idle comment had aroused. For some reason he would not like to see the wench fall foul of his companion's amorous attentions. 'Which means that neither you nor I are likely to be interested, my friend...Unless you are in the petticoat market at last?'

'Not on your life,' Jack replied. 'That is the one redeeming feature of being a younger son. I do not have to marry to provide an heir for the family.'

'And as long as your luck lasts at the gaming tables you need not look for an heiress,' Gervase agreed with a mocking glance. 'Unless I decide to throw you to your creditors.'

Jack merely smiled at him. He was in debt once again, but Gervase had bailed him out as always. He would repay the loan when he was in funds again, because he did not like to be beholden to his friend, even if Gervase applied the reins only if Jack stepped too far out of line.

'You'd miss me if I was carried off to the debtors' prison,' Jack replied with his lazy smile. 'Who would amuse you when you're in one of your black moods?'

Gervase did not deign to answer, but merely settled back and closed his eyes as the carriage moved off. He was not sure why

11

he kept Jack around, for there were aspects of his character that did not sit well with him – and yet he was amusing, and of course there was the debt to be paid. Gervase would have died during the attack on Montcalm's stronghold had it not been for Jack, who had carried him to the surgeon as he lay wounded, and because of that much could be forgiven – *had* been forgiven in the past eight years of their friendship.

'Remind me why we are returning to London,' Gervase enquired, his eyes still closed. 'I know it was some damned dull thing...'

'The King has asked for you to attend him at court,' Jack replied, aware that Gervase knew exactly why they were returning. The air of boredom he affected was a mask that disguised a restless and clever mind. 'You were one of Wolfe's best aides, Gervase. You could have been honoured at court long since had you chosen to dance attendance on His Majesty.'

'I finished with all that after my father died,' Gervase said, his eyes now open and bleak. 'Had I not been with Wolfe at Québec...'

'It wasn't your fault that Helen died,' Jack said, sensing that his friend was haunted by the old nightmare.

'I am aware of where the blame lies,' Gervase replied. 'And believe me, one day

Sylvester will pay for what he did.'

Jack made no reply, for there was none that he could give to ease the other's abiding grief. Yet he would not stand in Harry Sylvester's shoes for any price.

Arabella felt a rising excitement as the carriage drew up outside the house in Hanover Square. For the past fifty years or more, building had been going apace in London, despite the laws and fines imposed to stop the sprawl of the city into open fields. Because of the restrictions of the past, some of the great houses of earlier times had been turned into stinking tenements that housed many poor families, but now there were fine squares and important houses to be found beyond the old city.

Passing through some of the poorer areas, Arabella had wondered what they might find at their journey's end. She was pleased to discover that her cousin, Lady Mary Randall, lived in some style, for she had not thought her rich. Indeed, in her letters she had complained of having to fend off her debtors since the death of her last husband. Lady Mary had been married first at the tender age of fifteen, and having now reached nine and twenty she had already buried three husbands.

'So we are here at last,' Arabella said to Nan as they were helped down from the carriage. 'I had begun to think that we should never arrive.'

Nan smiled at her impatience. 'We have been on the road some days,' she agreed. 'But the journey from Cambridgeshire is a long one, and we knew it would be tedious before we set out.'

'We might have accomplished it in half the time had Father hired a decent carriage,' Arabella said with a pout. 'That old thing rattles over every pothole and is vastly uncomfortable.'

'You know Father has no money for luxuries,' Nan replied. As the elder of the two by just ten months, she felt she had a duty to keep her sister in check, for Arabella was both wilful and impetuous. 'Come, dearest, stop sulking. Cousin Mary will be expecting us and we must make a good impression.'

'Yes, indeed,' Arabella agreed and laughed. 'Our fortunes depend upon her liking us, Nan. For if she will not keep us with her, we must return to the country and then we shall never find husbands!'

That was not quite true, for both might have been married when they had turned fifteen had they been inclined to take the offers of neighbouring squires. However, Lady Tucker had been alive then and had been more ambitious for her daughters than the ageing widowers who had wished to bury them in the countryside.

'I visited London when I was sixteen,' she had told Arabella just a few days before her sudden death from a virulent fever. 'I might have married a marquis – but he was fat, and Edmund was handsome then,' she had sighed. 'I chose love, but I have oft thought that the marquis's fortune would have suited me better. Lust fades swiftly, my love. Money is more enduring.'

Lady Tucker had, however, seemed content with her lot for many years, and although her husband's wealth had never matched that of the well remembered marquis, he had managed to keep his head above water until a recent series of losses – some from business ventures and others at the card table.

Sir Edmund's knock at the imposing front door of Lady Mary's house was answered by a footman dressed in colours of dark green and gold, who bowed low and ushered them inside before going out to direct the baggage to the back of the house.

'We had begun to wonder what had happened to you, sir.' A woman dressed in a neat grey gown came forward to welcome them into the front hall. She relieved Sir Edmund of his hat and turned her attention to his daughters, who had begun to take off their hats and gloves. 'I am Mrs Boswell, m'dears, and right pleased I am to see you. Milady awaits you in her private parlour, and I am to conduct you to her at once.'

'That is very kind of you, madam,' Nan replied. 'But ought we not to tidy ourselves first? We are stained from the journey.'

'Milady is impatient to see you,' Mrs Boswell replied. 'She won't care that your gown is creased, miss. And by the time you've taken tea with her, your trunks will have been unpacked for you.'

Nan frowned, for she would have preferred time to freshen up before meeting Lady Mary, but Arabella was as impatient to meet their cousin as she apparently was to meet them.

'That will be much better,' she declared. 'Come, Nan, we must not keep Lady Mary waiting.' She smiled at the buxom housekeeper. 'Pray take us up immediately, madam.'

'This way, m'dears,' Mrs Boswell said, and turned to precede them up the stairs and along the landing.

Arabella looked about her as she followed the housekeeper up a wide marble staircase and along a landing covered with rich carpets, noting the heavy mahogany chairs that stood against the walls at intervals and the fine paintings and mirrors. Her home was a crumbling manor house, filled with worm-ridden oak that was in danger of disintegrating and falling about their ears. Only a few threadbare rugs covered the worn boards of her father's house, any fine carpets having disappeared along with the silver and pictures to pay part of his debts.

She had half expected her cousin's home to be in the same order and was excited by this evidence of wealth. If Lady Mary was pleased with her cousins, she might take them into the society of rich men, and they would soon be able to find husbands. It was imperative that they did – and quickly for Sir Edmund's sake, as the burden of his debts was fast becoming insupportable.

As they entered Lady Mary's boudoir, Arabella caught the scent of a musky perfume more suited to a gentleman than a lady. If she was not much mistaken, her cousin had had a recent visitor!

It was a pretty room, in shades of cream and rose with painted furnishings and a tall dressing screen over which some of milady's petticoats had been flung. Arabella's eyes dwelt on the screen for a moment until her attention was drawn to the lady herself.

Lady Mary was clad in a wrapping gown of green-striped linen and wore her own dark hair loosely about her shoulders. She was an attractive woman, though past the first flush of her youth.

She got up from her dressing table, where she had been sitting contemplating a new head that had been delivered to her earlier, and came to greet her cousins with a smile.

17

'So, you are here at last,' she said and held out her hands to them. 'Welcome, my dears. Arabella and Nan. You must introduce yourselves so that I know who you are.'

'I am Arabella,' Miss Impatience said and laughed. 'But you will know that already, cousin, for I described us both in my letters.'

'And you are both just as you wrote, except that you were too modest concerning your looks, Arabella. You are beautiful, and we should have little trouble in finding you a husband. Nan is pretty too, but not quite as eye-catching.' She smiled to take the sting from her words. 'You must forgive my plain speaking, Nan. This business of getting husbands is a serious one, and not something to be approached lightly.'

'I was not offended,' Nan assured her. 'I know that Arabella is beautiful, ma'am. She might have married any of three gentlemen at home, but did not care for them.'

'Is this so?' Lady Mary's brows rose. 'Were they not gentlemen of sufficient fortune, Arabella? Did Sir Edmund not approve their suit?'

'Squire Rowley had deep pockets, so they say,' Arabella replied. She had taken off her hat now, allowing her hair to escape. It tumbled over her shoulders in a cascade of dark red curls that seemed almost to have a life of their own. 'But he was past forty and his

18

breath stank. I told Father I could not take him and he said I should not be forced to it.'

'Such considerations should not weigh too heavily if the gentleman has rank and fortune,' Lady Mary said with a slight frown. 'Beggars cannot always be choosers, Arabella. Neither of you has a fortune, which means that you must marry money. Remember that wealth and position remain long after lust has faded – and a wife may look elsewhere for a lover once she has provided her husband with his heir.'

'Mama always said the same,' Nan agreed. 'She would have brought us to London herself this summer, cousin, but as you know she died suddenly.'

'Yes, and I was sorry for it. I met your mother when I was a child about to be married to a man I hardly knew. I was but fifteen and frightened of all the duties I had been told I must perform for this man. Your mother took me aside and explained that there was nothing to fear; she showed me how to make things easier for myself, and I have always been grateful to her. It was for Beth's sake that I asked you both to come to me. We shall see what can be done to help you. Unfortunately, I am not a rich woman. I cannot provide a dowry for either of you, but I can help with clothes, and I can certainly introduce you to suitable gentlemen.'

'You are very kind,' said Nan as she

curtsied.

'This is such a lovely house,' Arabella said and looked about her once more. 'How can you live here if you have no money, cousin?' She thought she heard a muffled laugh from behind the painted screen, confirming her earlier suspicions, but although her eyes flicked to the screen she said nothing.

Lady Mary saw the glance and laughed huskily. 'The house is mine. I suppose I might sell it and live comfortably in obscurity, but I own that I detest the country. So I cling on here as best I can...' She gave a delightful little gurgle of mirth. 'There are ways if one has some beauty and a sprinkling of wit...'

Arabella smiled as she saw the naughty look in her cousin's eyes.

'I thought I detected a gentleman's perfume when we came in?'

'We are caught!' Lady Mary laughed again. 'You had better come out, Harry. My cousin is too clever for you.'

'Damn it, milady,' a very handsome dark-haired man said as he walked out from behind the screen. He was dressed in pale grey breeches and a white lawn shirt, but his waistcoat was undone and his neckcloth was awry. His blue eyes sparkled with mischief as he said, 'I vow I was vastly amused listening to the three of you. It was better than a play at the Haymarket.'

20

Arabella thought he had dressed hastily, and she realized that their arrival must have taken her cousin by surprise. They had obviously interrupted an intimate encounter of some kind.

'And learning more than was good for you, no doubt,' Lady Mary replied, but her manner belied her words. 'Cousins, may I introduce you to a rogue. This gentleman is Lord Sylvester, and not to be regarded as a suitable husband by either of you. He is usually in debt, must marry a fortune – and is a wicked fellow indeed.'

'But you adore me.' Harry Sylvester bowed over the hand she extended to him, then turned to let his gaze wander over the two sisters, quickly coming to rest on Arabella. 'Lady Mary's cousins ... Miss Tucker and Miss Arabella.' His burning look made no secret of which sister had aroused his interest. 'I am very pleased to make the acquaintance of two such lovely ladies.'

'None of that, Harry!' Lady Mary smacked his arm. 'I shall not allow you to seduce either of my cousins. It is my intention to make good marriages for them both.'

'And I am sure you will achieve your desires, ma'am. You usually manage to get your own way in most things, I have observed.'

'As do you,' she retorted, giving him an arch look. 'Pray leave us, sir. I vow we have had enough of your company for one day.'

'Alas, it is a sad thing to be dismissed from the company of beauty,' Harry murmured wickedly. His eyes roved over Arabella, lingering for a moment on the décolletage of her gown and the pearly sheen of her skin where her breasts were exposed. 'But I shall hope to see you at Vauxhall another night – and your delightful cousins with you.'

With that, he bowed to Nan and Arabella, a slight flourish in his manner as he retreated behind the screen to retrieve his coat before departing. A small silence followed before Arabella asked the question that was hovering on her lips. 'Is Lord Sylvester your lover, ma'am?'

'Arabella! You should not ask something so personal,' Nan scolded at once.

Lady Mary laughed and was not offended. 'Certainly Arabella may ask. Harry is my *indulgence*, cousin. He has scarcely a guinea to his name, and I sometimes indulge myself for an hour or so in his company. He is not my protector. Sir John Fortescue is neither as young nor as handsome as Harry, but he has a vast fortune. He says he feels comfortable with me, and is exceedingly generous. I dare say he would not be pleased if he knew of my little interludes with other gentlemen, but I shall never tell him, for I am fond of him and have no wish to offend his pride.'

Nan stared at her in silence, clearly

uncertain of how to respond to this information, but Arabella clapped her hands and laughed. 'How clever you are, cousin. I wondered how you could live in such a fine house, for its upkeep must be vastly expensive, but now I begin to see how it may be done.'

'Would you not prefer to marry Sir John?' Nan asked, frowning. 'If you suit one another so well...'

'Unfortunately, Sir John must get an heir fairly soon if he is to protect his name and fortune,' Lady Mary replied, a hint of sadness in her voice. 'I have had three husbands and no children. I believe that I am barren, and I would not rob my friend of the chance of an heir. I shall help him to find a suitable wife, and he will give me a handsome present when he marries.' She shrugged her shoulders. 'I can find another protector...'

'Does every lady conduct herself in this manner in London?' Arabella asked curiously. 'I have thought I should like to marry a man I could love.'

'Save your romantic ideals for your lover,' her cousin replied and looked at Nan. 'What are your thoughts on marriage, my dear?'

'I believe I shall marry for wealth and position,' Nan said, looking thoughtful. 'I have heard that the intimate side of marriage is almost always disappointing.'

'Where did you hear that?' Arabella was

surprised. Lady Mary's openness about such things was not a shock to her, for London manners were more sophisticated in these matters, but it surprised her that her sister should speak so boldly. 'You have never said a word of this to me.'

Nan flushed. 'It was just something I overheard Mistress Featherstone saying to Mama once – and Mama agreed.'

'It is not always so,' Lady Mary said, amused. 'But the pleasures of the bedchamber are more likely to be found with a lover than a husband.'

Arabella thought that it would depend on the husband, her mind picturing the handsome face of the man hiding behind the painted screen. The expression in Lord Sylvester's eyes as he looked at her had set up a tingling at the base of her neck. She believed that pleasure would be found in the bed of such a man, but was wise enough to keep her opinions to herself.

Lady Mary regarded her with speculation, almost as if she could read her mind. 'I dare say you are both weary from your journey,' she said. 'I shall let you retire to your chamber, where you may rest and refresh yourselves. We dine en famille this evening, for you must both have new gowns before you go into company. I have arranged for a seamstress to wait on us tomorrow.'

'You are generous, ma'am,' Arabella said,

and went impulsively to kiss her cheek. 'I am glad we came to you, and I hope we shall both be a credit to you.'

'La, child, that was a pretty speech,' Lady Mary said and flicked her cheek with her fingertips. She reached for a bell on the table beside her and rang it. Mrs Boswell appeared promptly. 'Be guided by me, my dears, and you will soon find yourselves being driven everywhere in your own carriages.'

The sisters thanked her again, and then followed Mrs Boswell from the room. 'Well, here we are, m'dears,' the housekeeper said, opening a door for them. 'Everything has been done for your comfort – but should you need anything, you have only to ring.'

'Oh, this is lovely,' Arabella cried, unable to contain herself as she saw the richness of the brocade furnishings. 'I am sure we shall be very comfortable here.'

'Then I shall leave you to rest.'

'How fortunate we are!' Arabella said to her sister as the door closed behind the buxom Mrs Boswell. 'I had hoped, but this house exceeds my expectations.'

'Yes, indeed it is a fine house,' Nan said, but seemed doubtful.

'What is worrying you, sister?'

'I had not thought our cousin would have quite such...loose morals,' Nan replied. 'I believed she was a lady of good character and received everywhere.'

'I am sure she is,' Arabella said. 'I dare say she is as proper and mealy-mouthed as any country goodwife in company. She wanted to be open with us for our own sakes, and I am glad that she was. You should not despise her for taking a protector after her last husband died, Nan. I dare say Lord Randall left her little but debts, for he was an unlucky gambler.'

'For that, no, I do not blame her. I think it necessary in her circumstances,' Nan said. 'But to risk everything with the other, when she admitted that he is an adventurer and a rogue.'

'Lord Sylvester...' Arabella dimpled as she gave her sister a sly look. 'But he is so very handsome, Nan. I understood why our cousin was tempted by him. Almost any woman would find him pleasing, do you not think so?'

'I did not trust him,' Nan retorted. 'And I would advise you to stay well clear of him.' Her eyes went over her sister. 'You have let your neckerchief slip again, Arabella. It is no wonder that men will stare at you so.'

'In London every lady of youth and beauty wears her dress so,' Arabella said and pouted at her reflection in the delicate little dressing mirror. 'I see no harm in it.'

'You did not care for the manners of the gentleman at that inn.'

'He was not a gentleman,' Arabella retorted. 'Had he any manners at all he would have stepped aside at once.'

'Had you covered yourself modestly he would not have insulted you by offering to buy your favours.'

'You are mistaken,' Arabella said. 'I have met others of his ilk, and it would not matter if I wore a nun's habit. He would ravish any woman he desired as soon as look at her!'

Arabella's eyes simmered with anger as she recalled the incident. It had remained with her for the rest of the journey, which had taken another two days because their carriage had suffered a broken pole. She had wanted to wipe the insolent sneer from the stranger's lips, but something had held her back. Had she slapped him, he would most likely have slapped her in return.

'Well, we must hope that we do not meet that particular gentleman again,' Nan said. 'I dare say we shall not, for he was an important man. I saw the crest on his coach and I enquired his name of the innkeeper. He told me he believed the gentleman was a marquis, though he did not know his title.'

'I do not care if he is a royal duke,' Arabella declared. 'I hate him and shall ignore him if we ever meet in company.'

'If you should meet him, you should greet him politely but distantly,' Nan advised.

'Since we shall both be dressed differently before we are taken into company, we must hope that he does not know us.'

'I shall know *him*!' Arabella muttered.

Despite knowing that she must try to catch a rich husband, Arabella's thoughts would not dismiss the face of the man she had met in Lady Mary's boudoir that evening. She continued to think of him throughout dinner, dreaming pleasantly of finding herself in his arms – though just before she woke the next day he was replaced in her mind by the arrogant gentleman they had met on the road.

She would think of him no more! And she would try not to think of Lord Sylvester either. Perhaps she would meet other attractive young men who would make her heart race with excitement soon.

Arabella was impatient for their visit to begin properly, but Lady Mary was determined that her cousins should be dressed fashionably before entering society as her protégées.

'You must make a good impression immediately,' she told them, and spent some time each morning instructing them how to behave. 'You are quality. Hold your heads high and behave as if you own the world. Your fortune is a private matter. You may leave the discussion of such trifles to me. As for you, Uncle, I should prefer it if you took yourself back to the country. Unless you mean to purchase new clothes?'

'I've no money to waste on fripperies,' Sir Edmund replied. 'It is my intention to trust my daughters to your care, ma'am. I shall depart as soon as the horses are rested.'

He took his leave of Arabella on the third day, a suspicion of tears in his eyes as he looked at her in the new striped green silk gown she was wearing. 'I vow it is painful to part from you, Bella. Were it not for my foolishness after your mother died...' He sighed deeply. 'Choose wisely, my daughter. I would wish you happy.'

'Of course,' she said, and kissed him. 'I am determined to marry a lord and pay all your debts.'

'And if Bella does not, I shall,' Nan told him as it was her turn to be kissed. 'Take care of yourself, Father.'

'I shall come to town for your weddings,' he promised them before going down the front steps to his waiting carriage.

'I doubt if he will,' Nan remarked to Arabella when they turned to go back into the house. 'Does it not seem to you that he grows thinner with every day? I believe he is ill.'

'Oh, do not say so!' Arabella cried. 'It is merely the worry of his debts.'

'Mayhap you are right. We must pay them for him, Sister. At least then he may end his days in peace.'

Arabella nodded, her throat tight. She had scarcely recovered from her grief over her mother's death. To lose her father would be almost unbearable. However, Nan seemed to have dismissed all thought of her father as soon as he had departed. She spent every moment she could with their cousin, practising her society manners.

'I am determined to find a suitable husband as quickly as I can,' she told Arabella when she complained that they never seemed to have a moment to spare. 'Lady Mary is generous, but I would prefer to be mistress of my own house.'

'Well, you will not have to wait long before you meet some gentlemen,' Arabella said. 'Cousin Mary is taking us to Vauxhall this evening.'

She wondered if they might perhaps see Lord Sylvester there. He had seemed to like her when she was dressed in her simple country gown. What would he think when she appeared in her fine new clothes?

Two

'I heard that Sylvester went down heavily at the tables again last night,' Jack Meadows remarked as he lounged in the wing chair opposite milord's impressive mahogany partner's desk. Roxbourne was writing a letter and appeared not to have heard him. 'They say his creditors are growing restless.'

'Yes, I had heard the rumour,' Gervase replied as he first sanded and then sealed his message. 'However, there is also a rumour that he has hopes of some wealthy cit's daughter. They will not move against him while there is a chance of payment.'

'If he marries money your chance will be gone,' Jack observed.

'I have waited this long, I can wait a little longer,' Gervase replied. 'If the coward would meet me I should kill him, but he refuses to be insulted. No matter what I say to him, he merely shrugs it off with a laugh.'

'Sylvester knows your reputation, Gervase. He is too careful to be caught in that trap – and he does not dream that you know he was responsible for what happened to

31

Helen. He thinks himself safe over that one.'

'I would call him out for it,' Gervase said. 'But the scandal was hushed up at the time and I shall not sully her memory now. Let her rest in peace. Sylvester will pay – if not with his life, then with the manner of its living. We shall see how he enjoys being in a debtors' prison. I have bought most of his debts.'

'Then why not have him arrested at once?'

'I prefer that he should stew in his own mess for a while longer,' Gervase replied, his eyes the colour of wet slate. 'As yet I have not been able to persuade him to sit down with me at the tables. I mean to humiliate him before I deliver the final blow.'

'It would be kinder to have a footpad cut his throat.'

'But far less satisfying – though I thank you for the suggestion, Jack. I may yet do so should I fail to exact full payment by other means.'

'God! You're a cold devil.' Jack shuddered. 'I shall know what to expect if I cross you.'

'Oh, I should challenge *you* to a duel and shoot you dead,' Gervase replied and grinned, the wintry expression disappearing. 'After all, I owe you my life. A trifling thing to be sure, but of some worth to me.'

Jack's gaze narrowed. 'I am never quite sure whether or not you are jesting, Gervase.'

'You should know that I never jest.' Gervase raised his brows. 'Out of funds again?'

'No – as a matter of fact I've hit a winning streak,' Jack said, and suppressed the shiver that ran through him. He believed Roxbourne might be capable of anything if pushed too far. 'I was wondering if you intended to visit Vauxhall this evening. Lady Eliza is back from the country. I believe it is her intention to be there with a party of friends.'

'Indeed?' Gervase yawned. '*That* was months ago, my dear fellow. I believe I shall seek fresh diversions this summer.'

'Then you will not mind if I take your place with her?'

'Do as you please. I am not sure she is worth the trouble – a cool beauty, Jack. I prefer a more passionate nature.'

'Like the wench you saw on the road?'

Gervase laughed. 'I must admit I have thought of her a few times. Do you imagine she has caught her rich merchant yet?'

'It is scarce a week! Give her time.'

'I dare say she will not need much time,' Gervase replied. 'Yes, Jack, I shall accompany you this evening, if only for want of more entertaining diversions. I vow I am bored. I need a challenge. Some new venture to occupy my mind.'

'You are a restless soul, Gervase. You should have stayed in the army.'

'I thought I might travel,' Gervase replied. 'Not the grand tour. I dare say that would be as tedious as London has become of late.'

'You do not think of the American colonies?'

'I have thought of trying my hand there,' Gervase admitted. 'As you said, I am a restless spirit. If it were not that I must settle with Sylvester, I think I should have gone before now. It is a country where a man can breathe, Jack. There is less corruption and hypocrisy, and the air is not fouled by filth and despair like the streets of London.'

'The colonists are a load of savages,' Jack declared, 'and I do not speak just of the native Indians. Look at the way they reacted to the Stamp Act. They just refuse to behave like civilized men. Think twice before you burn your boats, Gervase!'

'Perhaps they object to being taxed without seeing the benefit of their money. We have placed restrictions on the colonists for too long. It is little wonder that they resort to illicit trade with the French.'

'Now that might suit you,' Jack said. 'Smuggling to and from the West Indies. I could see you doing that, Gervase!'

'Yes, I imagine it might be diverting,' Gervase said, a glint of amusement in his eyes. 'And I could always return here if I wished. But do not worry, Jack. I have not yet made up my mind to leave England. And before I do anything I must finish this business with Sylvester.'

'You will not rest easy unless you do,' Jack agreed. 'And by then you will likely have found something to divert you here in London.'

'Would that I could,' Gervase said. 'But I grow tired of apparent virtue and hidden vices, Jack. Those in positions of power prate of the evils of gin and yet they do nothing to stop its sale, and the poor sink deeper into depravation. Talk is cheap, and the gentlemen who speak loudest of decency and the law then patronize the bawdy house on their way home to their wives.'

'As we all do on occasion,' Jack pointed out, but Gervase shook his head. 'Come, admit that this attack of conscience is merely because you are bored.'

'Yes, perhaps you are right,' Gervase agreed, smiling ruefully. 'And I must not bore you with my own preaching of virtue, must I? Come, let us take a stroll to St James's and see if we can find a game of chance to while away the afternoon.'

'We might obtain one of Harris's lists and see if there are any new nuns on the market,' Jack suggested, and laughed as milord pulled a face. 'I have always found his recommendations reliable for steering one clear of a dose of the clap.'

'I doubt they are as genuine as you might imagine,' Gervase remarked wryly. 'The man is no more than a pimp and as ruthless as any of his calling. A wench might be sold as virgin four times in a week and still be considered fresh in most bawdy houses.'

'You are too particular,' Jack said. 'Though I must admit I would prefer an assignation with Lady Eliza.'

'You would do far better to save your energies for this evening,' Gervase said with a wry smile. 'If cards do not appeal, shall we spend an hour or so with the foils? I believe you are getting fat, Jack. You need some exercise.'

Jack grinned at this obvious provocation, but decided to go along with his friend's suggestion. Gervase was right – London could prove vastly dull on a wet afternoon.

'There, my dears, I told you it would clear by the evening, did I not?' Lady Mary had entered the sisters' bedchamber to inspect their toilettes before they left for Vauxhall. 'The sun broke through the clouds half an hour ago, and though it is still a little cool, I am persuaded that it will stay fine for us.'

'How do we look, ma'am?' Arabella felt a thrill of excitement as she twirled in front of the dressing mirror, straining to see all of her gown. It was fashioned of a striped green silk over a petticoat of silver, the bodice fitted tightly to her shapely waist, with sleeves that ended at the elbow in a froth of lace. Around her throat she wore a black ribbon and a single fine pearl mounted in silver; it had belonged to her mother and was one of the few items of value that Sir Edmund had refused to sell. Her only other ornament was an ornate comb in her hair, which had been piled high on her head and allowed to fall in a simple ringlet on her shoulder.

'I think we shall not powder your hair this evening,' Lady Mary had decided earlier. 'You have exceptionally attractive hair, Arabella, and I think it should be worn *au naturel* for the time being.'

Lady Mary's own hair was hidden beneath an elaborate head that had been dressed for her by Monsieur Fouquet, a celebrated French coiffeure who attended only the favoured few.

'I refuse *absolument* to dress the heads of ugly women,' he had declared as he fussed over Lady Mary earlier. '*Moi*, I can only work with beauty.'

Monsieur Fouquet had cast a covetous eye at Arabella, but he had not been allowed to indulge his artistry beyond a few simple curls and a glossy ringlet. 'I could do such wonders with her,' he had sighed to Lady Mary, but she remained adamant.

'My cousin is a young girl and must

appear as such in company,' she insisted. 'I do not wish her to seem too sophisticated at first.' And now she nodded her approval as she saw Arabella dressed for the evening. 'Yes, it is as I thought. You look charming, my dear – and Nan, you are very pretty, too. That yellow becomes you well.'

'I think Nan looks beautiful,' Arabella said loyally as she saw a slight frown on her sister's face. 'Nan had just as many suitors as I at home, ma'am – but she would not marry because Mother wanted to bring us to London together.'

'Of course Nan looks well enough,' their cousin said. 'I have said I am sure we shall achieve something suitable for her.'

'Oh, I dare say I shall find someone,' Nan said. 'A comfortable home in the country will be all I shall require.'

'Oh, I want to live in town,' Arabella said, and then looked impatiently at her cousin. 'May we not leave now, ma'am?'

'We are waiting for—' Lady Mary smiled as she heard a knock at the door. 'That must be Sir John now. I asked him if he would be kind enough to escort us this evening. Come, my dears, we shall go down and greet him.'

As she left the room, Arabella touched her sister's arm. 'It is unfair of Cousin Mary to imply that you are not as attractive as I am, Nan. I think you are lovely, and that gown looks wonderful on you.'

'But she is right,' Nan assured her with a smile. 'I have always known you were the beauty of the family, Arabella – but I do not mind. I dare say some gentlemen might prefer my quieter manners.'

'Oh, indeed they would if they knew us both,' Arabella agreed, for she had sensed her sister's hurt and wanted to heal any breach before it became too wide. 'I talk far too much, and I haven't half your good sense.'

'Now that *is* the truth,' Nan laughed, her good humour restored. 'Come, we should not keep Sir John waiting. I am anxious to see what our cousin's friend looks like.'

Sir John Fortescue was a plump gentleman in his middle years, quite pleasant in looks – other than the extra flesh he carried, which Arabella thought unhealthy. To her he looked as though he might be carried off with a fit of apoplexy at any moment, for his face had a high colour and he wheezed a little as he walked. He also creaked when he got up or sat down, and since she was the one chosen to sit next to him in the coach, she found it a little cramped beside him and feared he might sit on her gown and crease it. However, his manners were impeccable and he took care not to disturb her toilette, smiling at her apologetically as she settled beside him.

'I fear my bulk leaves little room for you, Miss Arabella, but I shall be still and your pretty gown shall not suffer, m'dear.' He smiled at her, his eyes resting for a moment on the décolletage of her gown, which was even more revealing than the one Nan had complained of as immodest. 'May I be forgiven for saying that I think you quite the prettiest little thing I have seen in an age?'

Arabella dimpled and dipped her head, allowing him to think her shy, though she did not particularly care for his compliments. 'You are too kind, sir,' she replied. 'But do you not admire Nan's gown? I could never wear that shade, but it looks well on her, do you not agree?'

'Oh, certainly,' he said easily and nodded to Nan. 'You are as pretty as a picture, m'dear.'

'And shall we see some fine pictures this evening, sir?' Nan asked. 'I have heard much of the pleasure gardens, but do not really know what to expect.'

'Yes, indeed you may see several artists displaying their work in booths,' Sir John replied, preening a little under Nan's interest. 'There are pleasant walks to be had, besides music and dancing for those who incline to it ... though I do not dance myself these days. We shall have supper in one of the booths, of course, and listen to a concert. And perhaps later there will be a firework display.'

'Oh, I should like that of all things,' Nan said, and gave him a shy glance. 'Or do you think it will be frightening, Sir John?'

'No, no, m'dear, nothing in the world to be frightened of,' he said kindly. 'I dare say it may seem so to a young lady fresh from the country, but you will soon accustom yourself to such sights. And I shall be there, so you need not be afraid of anything.'

'No. If you are there I dare say I shall not,' Nan replied and looked down at her hands folded in her lap.

Arabella was surprised at her sister's manner. Was Nan setting her cap at Sir John? Surely not! He was kind enough, and very wealthy, but Nan could not want to be married to a man almost as old as her own father – and much fatter!

Arabella could not think of a worse fate. She had the picture of a face in her mind and was determined she would not settle for anyone who did not measure up to her ideal. There must be some handsome men in London who had no need to marry money! She did so want to be married to a man she could love.

The gardens at Vauxhall were everything she had hoped for and more. They were that night thronged with ladies and gentlemen parading in all their finery – and some of the clothes were so outrageous they had to be seen to be believed.

'Macaronis, m'dear,' Sir John remarked to Arabella in a low voice as he saw her astonished gaze following a gentleman dressed rather oddly. 'Italianate, I believe they call that style – but rather too elaborate for my taste and damned uncomfortable I should say.'

Arabella was hard pressed not to laugh as she imagined him wearing the short tight breeches of the Macaronis. 'They do look rather strange,' she replied, 'though I suppose it is the fashion?'

'For some,' he agreed. 'But I believe a man should retain some dignity.'

'Yes, I do agree,' Nan said. She was walking on his other side and laid a hand on his arm. 'Tell me, sir – is that one of the booths where we may see some drawings?'

'I should imagine that you might find something by Hogarth. There are any number of imitators since his death, of course, but I believe he is still the best. Or if his work is not to your taste, we may discover a new artist, then we may patronize him and set him on his way to riches...' Sir John smiled down at her. 'Shall we go and see?'

'I think I should enjoy that above all things.'

Nan *must* be setting her cap at him! Arabella glanced at Lady Mary to see how

42

she viewed Nan's behaviour but found that she was otherwise engaged. She had fallen behind them a little and was now talking to a young and handsome man that Arabella had not met before. She wished that she might fall behind too, but found that she was being gently but firmly steered towards the booths.

Arabella threw a glance of longing over her shoulder, but there was no help from her cousin. Lady Mary was laughing and fluttering her fan as she gazed up at the young man, clearly enjoying the encounter. It wasn't fair, thought Miss Impatience. She would far rather continue to stroll about the gardens than waste time looking at pictures.

However, when she saw that there was a set of Mr Hogarth's prints entitled *The Rake's Progress*, which was something she had wanted to see in its entirety, her attention was caught and she remained staring at them, smiling at their wicked humour after Nan and Sir John had moved on to look at another artist's work.

'Do they please you?' a man's voice said close at her ear. 'Shall I buy them for you? They are but a copy, but still amusing...'

Arabella jumped, for she had not noticed anyone come up to her, and her heart jerked with fright as she looked up into the man's dark face and knew him. By the expression of pure mischief lurking there, he had also

43

recognized her and her eyes glittered with sudden temper.

'No, sir, pray do not waste your money for I should not accept them from you. I want nothing from you at all!'

'Nothing?' Gervase's mouth quivered with suppressed amusement. 'What if I offered to cover that delectable body of yours in priceless jewels, my sweet? Would you not smile for me then?'

'You are impertinent, sir!' Arabella turned to follow Nan and Sir John, but he accompanied her. 'Pray go away, sir. I do not know you and I do not wish to know you.'

'The first may be remedied immediately,' Gervase said. 'I am Roxbourne, and I know your name, fair nymph. You are Lady Mary Randall's cousin and your name is Arabella Tucker.'

'Then I wish you would pay me the compliment of removing yourself from my company, sir. As you must now realize, I am not without friends – and I do not care to be insulted by your attentions.'

'Such fire in those eyes,' Gervase said and chuckled. 'I appreciate the little play, Miss Arabella, but there is no need for it with me, I assure you. I am not for marrying – but I would prove a most generous protector should you choose to go down that road. Marriage is a vastly dull and often dangerous enterprise for young women, so they say. For myself I would think it a pity if all that beauty should be wasted on some dolt without the wit to enjoy it to its full. And it would be a shame to see you made old before your time with constant child-bearing.'

'How dare you, sir!' Arabella glared at him and tossed her head. She itched to slap him, but that would cause a scandal and she dared not do it in public. If only she might be alone with him for two minutes – how he should suffer! 'I do not wish to hear such things from your lips.'

'Come, Arabella,' he murmured. 'Your eyes betray you. You are no modest society miss to faint at a little plain speaking. I can read your mind. You find so much of this boring, don't you, all the polite conversation that means nothing? You want some excitement in your life ... and I can give you all that you want, sweeting.'

'I have already told you that I require nothing of you, sir. Please leave me alone or I shall be forced to call for my friends.'

'Your sister seems to have captured Sir John's attention, but come – we shall join them.' He gripped Arabella's arm and steered her to where Sir John and Nan had turned to look for them. 'Good evening, Fortescue. Trust you to steal a march on the rest of us – two of the prettiest young women to come to town in an age and you

45

have them both to yourself. I ask you, is this fair?'

'Roxbourne...' Sir John was not sure whether to be flattered by this unusual attention from a man who would, as a rule, hardly deign to notice him, or jealous because he had commandeered the more beautiful of the two. 'May I introduce you to Miss Tucker and Miss Arabella – unless you have already met? I believed they knew no one in town.'

'We met briefly on the road,' Gervase replied easily. 'However, I do not believe I have been formally introduced to Miss Tucker. Your servant, mistress. I trust you are enjoying your first visit to London?'

'Yes, indeed, sir,' Nan said. 'Sir John has been most kind and instructive concerning some pictures I was anxious to see.'

'Ah yes,' Gervase said. 'I believe Miss Arabella was also interested in some pictures. We fell into a discussion of them and then realized we had met before – is that not so, Miss Arabella?'

'I believe *you* must be right, sir,' she replied. 'Nan, the marquis is very knowledgeable about paintings. Pray take my place and let me walk with Sir John for a little.'

Her request was accompanied by such a sweet smile that Sir John bowed and hastened to offer her his arm, forcing Gervase to

46

step back and permit the exchange. However, he gave no outward sign of disliking the arrangement and, when Lady Mary came up to them a few minutes later, offered them a place in his own supper booth.

'Sir John has already made arrangements, my lord,' Lady Mary said regretfully. 'We should have been glad to sit with you otherwise.'

'Then I must leave you,' he said, and kissed her hand gallantly. 'I see my friends and would not have them think I had deserted them – perhaps you would allow me to accompany you to Ranelagh another evening? Or the theatre and supper afterwards?'

'We should be delighted,' Lady Mary said. 'It is pleasant to see you returned to town, sir – please call on us. We are always at home on Thursdays and Sunday afternoons for tea.'

'I should be delighted, ma'am.' He threw a mocking glance at Arabella, bowed over Nan's hand, and left them.

'How fortunate that we should meet with Roxbourne this evening,' Lady Mary said, looking excited. 'He sometimes gives the most wonderful parties at his house. And he has asked me to be his hostess in the past, although Lady Eliza had that honour last year – but I am told on good authority that he is no longer interested there.'

'No, indeed,' Sir John agreed. 'I heard she was looking for a new protector – though I think she will find no better than Roxbourne. He is always generous with his friends – at least that is what they say.'

'Oh, indeed, yes, I know it to be true,' Lady Mary agreed. 'But as I heard it, Roxbourne told her that their arrangement was at an end.'

'You surprise me, ma'am. I had thought they were well suited.'

'They say she is cold,' Lady Mary whispered in his ear, and he gave a shout of delighted laughter, a roguish expression in his eyes. He offered his arm to her, releasing Arabella, who dropped behind to walk with her sister. Nan glanced at her.

'Roxbourne's manners are a little free,' she remarked, 'but he seems to have taken a liking to you, Arabella. He was asking all kinds of questions about you until our cousin joined us.'

'I hope you told him to mind his own business,' Arabella retorted. 'I cannot like him, Nan. Indeed, I hate him!'

'Surely not?' Nan's brows arched. 'I own he has a bold look, but I have noticed several men looking at you in just that way this evening. Before we came to London I expected we would find more refined manners here, but the gentlemen ogle one so, and even Sir John makes bawdy remarks –

though he is truly kind.'

'Yes, he is kind,' Arabella said. 'You seem to like him well, Nan.'

'I like him well enough,' Nan replied with a faint blush in her cheeks. 'He would be generous to his wife I dare say.'

'Nan?' Arabella stared. 'You would not think of it?'

'Why not, pray? He is wealthy and would be a comfortable companion. He has a house in the country that he visits a few times a year. I dare say he might do so more often if encouraged. Besides, once his wife is with child, he might think it best if she stayed there alone until after the birth...'

Arabella was horrified at her sister's suggestion. She could not think of anything worse than being forced to stay in the country while her husband returned to the pleasures of London, but she suspected that Nan was hoping for an arrangement of this kind. It was common enough, for men took mistresses all the time. Especially when their wives were breeding. It was a situation many women had to accept – but to actively encourage it! No, that would not do for Arabella. She was looking for a very different marriage, though she was not exactly sure what she expected of her husband.

'Well, if it is what you want, I wish you joy with him,' Arabella said. 'But I want something more...exciting.' For a moment she

49

recalled the marquis's offer and some part of her recognized a kindred spirit. Had he been less arrogant perhaps...But what was she thinking of? He had made it clear that he was not looking for a wife.

'Ladies, may I walk with you?' The sound of a merry voice made both sisters swing round. 'What – have you forgot me already?'

'Indeed we have not, my lord,' Arabella cried gladly. Her heart pumped with sudden excitement as she gazed into his mischievous blue eyes. 'We hoped we might see you here this evening – did we not, Nan?'

Nan merely nodded, declining to endorse her sister's welcome. She glanced towards Lady Mary, who seemed to be in earnest conversation with Sir John, wondering if this encounter might be embarrassing for her. However, Lady Mary turned at that moment and smiled at them.

'Ah, Lord Sylvester. How pleasant it is to see you. I collect you have introduced yourself to my cousins. I might have known you would not let such an opportunity pass.'

'Lady Mary, it is always delightful to see you,' he replied and bowed. 'Sir John, I bid you good evening. I was looking for a party of friends with whom I had engaged to spend the evening and saw you. What else could I do but throw myself on your mercy? It seems my friends have not come as they promised.'

'Then of course you must join us – you do agree, Sir John? We cannot allow Sylvester to spend the evening alone. He may dance with the girls after all, and we two shall sit and watch them.'

Sir John nodded approval of her plan. 'Yes, m'dear, that is fortunate, for as you know I am not the best of dancers – though I would have done my duty had it been required.'

'Well, now you may keep me company instead,' Lady Mary replied, giving him an intimate look that had the desired effect of settling feathers that had been ruffled by Lord Sylvester's appearance on the scene.

Arabella sensed that Sir John suspected he had a rival for his mistress's attentions, but for some reason of his own he appeared to turn a blind eye. She believed that he was genuinely fond of her cousin, and thought it a pity that he must marry for the sake of an heir. Despite what Nan described as her loose morals, Lady Mary was careful of her friend's feelings and seemed to care for him. They were, in Arabella's opinion, ideally suited, and would miss each other when he married – unless they intended to carry on their arrangement, perhaps a little more discreetly?

They were approaching the supper booths now. Arabella saw that some of the ladies were masked, and she suspected that they were probably married and keeping an assignation with a lover. Some of the ladies were openly caressing their companions, and allowing themselves to be fondled rather more intimately than seemed proper to Arabella's mind.

She was a romantic, of course, her mother had always said it. Love should be something that happened in private – perhaps in a wood on a bed of bluebells or primroses. And with a handsome lover, not a half-drunken lecher with foul breath.

'That was a deep thought,' Harry Sylvester murmured close to her ear. 'Share your thoughts with me, Arabella, for I have shared mine with you many times in my mind these past few days.'

The intimate, husky tones of his voice sent shivers through her. She looked at him, her eyes glowing as she met his burning gaze.

'You mean to tease me, sir.' He was looking at her much in the way Roxbourne had earlier, but she did not mind it in him. 'I dare say you have been too occupied elsewhere to give a thought to me.'

'Oh, I gave many more than one,' he assured her. 'You disturbed my sleep, sweet temptress. I closed my eyes and saw your face and sleep deserted me, for no dream could be sweeter to me.'

'I believe you are a wicked rogue, just as my cousin said!'

'Indeed I am,' he replied and laughed deep

in his throat. 'Your cousin did well to warn you of me – but I trust you will not heed her too closely.'

'A friend of my cousin's must also be mine.'

'Ah, what music that is to my ears.' His eyes quizzed her. 'Will you dance, Arabella?'

'If my cousin gives her permission...' Arabella glanced towards the covered area where some ladies and gentlemen were already indulging in a lively country dance. 'Of all things I love to dance – but you must ask Nan afterwards.'

'Of course. Come, let us waste no time.'

He requested permission from Lady Mary then, taking Arabella's hand, hurried her so that they were in time to join the next formation. Arabella laughed and looked up at him, her heart jumping with excitement. Oh, this was such heaven! She thrilled to the touch of his hand at her waist, feeling that the evening had suddenly become so much brighter. Harry was amused at her pleasure, insisting that they join the next set and then the next, persuading her each time that they would not be missed.

'Your sister will have found a partner long since.'

'No, she has not,' Arabella said, glancing guiltily towards the booth at the end of the cotillion. 'You must ask her now – please?'

'If you ask it of me,' he replied, 'then I must – for I can refuse you nothing.'

He took Arabella by the hand and began to lead her back towards the booth, but suddenly he pulled her sideways into the shadow of some flowering shrubs, catching her to him in a passionate embrace. His kiss took Arabella's breath away, and instead of holding him off as she ought, she clung to him, her body melting into his, her head spinning with this new sensation.

Now his mouth was at her breasts. He had pushed down the swathes of fine lace that had given her gown some modesty so that he could flick at her rosy nipples with his tongue. She gasped as she felt her senses swooning, shivering with delight. Oh, it felt so good! It made her want to be held close to him, to feel the burn of his flesh against hers. He was sucking at her, nibbling and teasing with his tongue, making her faint with pleasure.

'So beautiful,' Harry murmured huskily. 'And as fresh as country dew I'll warrant. You taste of peaches picked straight from the bough, Arabella. Are you virgin, sweet, lovely Arabella? I vow it would be a privilege to be the first to lie with you.'

His words shocked her so that she recovered her senses and she pulled away from him, fussing with her gown and rearranging the lace at her breasts. 'Of course

I am,' she said. 'How could you think otherwise?'

'I feared it was so,' Harry said and drew back reluctantly. 'You are a sore temptation to a man, Arabella, but Lady Mary would emasculate me if I deflowered you. And I owe her too many favours to displease her.'

Arabella's cheeks were heated as she heard the regret in his voice. What was she thinking of, allowing him such freedom as if she were a harlot? 'You were wrong to take advantage of me, my lord.'

'But your eyes begged me to make love to you,' Harry replied. 'How could I ignore your needs? You are an open book to me, Bella. You thirst for love and for life, and you cannot bear to wait for anything you want – is that not so?'

Arabella smiled reluctantly. 'Am I so easy to read, sir?'

'To me at least,' Harry said and grinned at her. 'If you had been born a man you would be just like me, Bella. Marry your rich cit quickly, my sweet – and then we may indulge ourselves as we please.'

'You insult me, sir!' Arabella's disappointment was so great that she was torn between anger and tears. He was as bad as Roxbourne! She turned away from him in some distress. How could he treat her so disrespectfully?

'Nay, do not be offended, sweet mistress,' Harry said, laying a persuasive hand on her arm. 'Forgive me if I made too free with you, but I have burned for you since we first met. You are the kind of woman that will not let a man rest easy in his bed, Bella. Yet I cannot marry you. You have no fortune, and I have little enough. I am extravagant and I need a wife who will keep me. Some grateful little mouse that I can pacify with a kiss and leave to tend the children while I go on my wicked way. As you see, I am a rogue.'

'But you do like me a little?' She gazed at him, a tearful appeal in her eyes. 'You do not think of me as some lightskirt you would bed for an hour?'

'I could never think of you in that way,' he declared instantly. 'I adore you, Arabella. You are beautiful and I would marry you if I had the means.'

'Oh!' She drew her breath in sharply. 'You do care for me.'

'As you care for me,' he said and frowned. 'Mayhap there is some way ... I have an uncle who might die and leave me his money. But I must not raise hopes that cannot be fulfilled.' He held out his hand to her. 'Forgive me. Come, sweet mistress. I swear I would give my life to please you, but I must return you to your friends before I lose all reason.'

Arabella smiled and took his hand. He

said that he could not marry her, but he loved her...He loved her. Her heart sang because of it and she knew that she would not give up the fight. She would find a way to make him change his mind.

Three

'So – what do you think of them?' Lady Mary asked as her companion heaved his bulk from her and lay back against the pillows, breathing deeply from his exertions. 'For myself I think you would be more comfortable with Nan. She seems a sensible gel and might suit you.'

Sir John rolled over on to his side, leaving the bed to retreat behind a dressing screen and relieve himself. He grunted and broke wind loudly, then went back to the bed before replying.

'She is a pretty little thing,' he said, and stood staring down at his mistress. Lady Mary might not be the beauty she had been when she was fresh on the town, but she had a generous nature and always gave of herself in their amorous encounters. Sir John was no fool and he understood his own short-comings, but he also knew that this woman accepted him as he was. She might enjoy an interlude with one of her young lovers, but she never made him feel that his touch was abhorrent to her. 'But she isn't you, Mary.

58

I'm not sure Mistress Tucker would welcome me to her bed.'

'Is that necessary in a wife?' she asked. 'Nan would do her duty by you, my friend – and if she is a little cold you would have no worry that your children were got on her by another man.' She leaned towards him, reaching out to caress him through the fine linen of his nightgown. 'And you can always come to me if you are lonely, my dear.'

Sir John felt his member respond to her caress. He was a man of healthy appetites, and had chosen his mistress only after careful consideration. It was her own idea that he should marry one of her cousins and continue their liaison in private – something he had thought an excellent suggestion at the time. However, that was before he'd cast eyes on Miss Arabella.

She was a prime piece if ever he'd seen one, and he had already made up his own mind which of the two sisters he would prefer to wed. However, he did not wish to lose what he already enjoyed, and had no intention of ending his relationship with Lady Mary until he had something better in view. Not wishing to betray his thoughts, he changed the subject to politics.

'For the life of me I do not know how His Majesty manages to put up with these damned Whigs. Since Bute was forced to resign they have become ever more arrogant.' He climbed into bed, the feather mattress sinking beneath his weight. 'We shall have more trouble with the American colonies before long, mark my words.'

Lady Mary was accustomed to his ways. Obviously he did not wish to discuss the subject of his marriage for the moment, and she acquiesced obligingly as she always did, falling in with his mood. 'I thought all that would be settled once Lord Rockingham succeeded Greville and repealed the Stamp Act.' she said.

'He has repealed it for the moment, but put the Declaratory Act in its place – which means that some damned idiot will take it into his head to tax them again. And that's when we shall have trouble.' He reached for her breasts, beginning to fondle them, but before he could press her back into the mattress she kneeled up in bed.

'You almost suffocated me the last time,' she said with a teasing laugh. 'Now – shall I straddle you or would you prefer me to kneel?'

He gave a shout of pleased laughter and showed her his preference by pulling her down on top of him. She was an exciting, sensuous woman and he would miss her if their relationship ended, but he would give her up willingly for the chance of bedding that wilful red-haired wench. Yes, he would have Miss Arabella if he could – even if it meant giving up his obliging mistress...

Arabella lay in bed, the events of the previous evening running through her mind. Beside her Nan was sleeping peacefully, apparently unmoved by the changes to their circumstances, whereas Arabella's mind was a hive of activity. She had loved their visit to Vauxhall, though her feelings were mixed concerning Lord Sylvester.

Did he truly care for her, or was he merely playing a game with her, hoping to seduce her? If she once allowed him to go too far her chance of making a good marriage would be over. Arabella might be reckless and impatient, but she knew that keeping her virtue intact was the only card she held. If she could make him so mad for her that he threw caution to the winds and...

Still half dreaming of the few heady moments she had spent in his arms, Arabella got up and dressed in a simple wrapping gown. At home she often walked in the gardens at this hour and saw no reason why she should not do so here. It was early; the servants would hardly be stirring as yet, and her cousin never left her apartments before noon unless they had an early engagement, which was not often. Like most fashionable ladies, Lady Mary liked to rest so as to be at her best in the evenings.

Arabella was not sure that the life would suit her, though she supposed she would settle in time. For the moment she had too much energy, and she needed some exercise to rid herself of this restlessness that had come over her.

Lady Mary's back garden was quite small and completely walled in, but there was a pretty paved courtyard with a fountain that cascaded into a pool of lilies and a rose arbour. She amused herself by picking a few scented buds with the dew still on them. What was it Lord Sylvester had called her? Something about being as fresh as country dew? He'd also said she tasted of peaches.

It was no use! She was as restless here as in her bed. Arabella sighed. She was foolish to let herself wish for something that might never be hers – yet how could she not? Even before he'd kissed her, Lord Sylvester had been often in her thoughts and now...

'Could you not rest, Miss Arabella?'

She turned with a start to see that Sir John had come into the courtyard. He was fully dressed and she was conscious that her gown was not the proper attire for walking, even in a private garden.

'It is my habit to walk early when I am at home,' she told him, a faint blush in her cheeks as she saw the way his eyes seemed to devour her figure beneath the thin gown. Arabella was well used to gentlemen staring at her in just that way, but she felt embarrassed at being caught dishabille. 'Excuse me, I must go. I ought not to have come down.'

'Nay, do not run off,' Sir John said. 'I am about to leave anyway. I chanced to see you from the landing window on my way downstairs and came to enquire if you were ill or troubled. But I shall not stay if my presence disturbs you.'

Arabella did not know how to answer him. She did not wish to offend Lady Mary's protector, but there was no mistaking the look in his eyes.

'That was kind of you, sir, but I should go.'

He caught at her sleeve as she would have passed him. 'You have no need to fear me, Miss Arabella. I have seldom met a lady I felt more tender towards. I would have us be friends if it would please you. Mayhap more than friends...'

Arabella avoided his gaze, not daring to let him look into her eyes lest she betray her dislike of his suggestion. 'As Lady Mary's... friend ... you must also be mine,' she replied in a subdued tone. 'How could it be otherwise, sir? I am very grateful to my cousin for all she is doing for us. I should never wish to offend her, sir.'

'Has your cousin told you that I am looking for a wife, Miss Arabella?'

Arabella held her breath. Oh, let him not

ask her! 'She mentioned something. I believe it is necessary for you to have an heir, sir.'

'Very necessary, for I am the last of my line. I have a great fortune and an old title, Miss Arabella. It would be a pity to forfeit either to the Crown – which would be the case if I died intestate or without issue.'

'Could you not bequeath your wealth to a friend, sir?'

'There is no one I care for sufficiently – at least, there was no one until now.' He cleared his throat. 'I would not embarrass you for the world, Miss Arabella – but will you think kindly of me? Remember what I have said, and in a little while I may ask something of you.'

Arabella made no reply – she could not! He studied her from beneath hooded lids, then released her arm, bowed his head and walked from the garden. She felt almost faint with relief as she watched him go. For a moment she had thought he meant to propose to her and she had dreaded giving him her answer.

She could never marry such a man! The very thought of being touched intimately by him filled her with disgust. If he asked she must refuse – but she prayed that he would not. He must surely have seen that she was reluctant. Perhaps if she kept her distance and was cool towards him, he would think better of his intention.

Arabella was thoughtful as she returned to the room she shared with Nan. From now on, she would encourage her sister's pursuit of Sir John. Perhaps he would decide that he preferred her to Arabella after all.

Gervase allowed his valet to finish shaving him, and then waved him away. 'You may leave me now, Fitzroy. I shall not need you until later.'

'As you wish, milord.'

Gervase sensed the disapproval in his man's voice but it did not weigh with him. He often chose to dress himself, except when he was going to a fashionable affair when it would have been insulting for him to appear less than impeccably dressed. However, it was early and he was restless. He needed some hard exercise. He pulled on his immaculate riding boots over silken hose, and tied a casual neckerchief, selecting a plain brown coat that fitted more easily than some of his society clothes.

'A country squire, that's what Fitzroy would think of you,' Gervase murmured, and grinned as he imagined his faithful servant's displeasure if he saw his master leave the house so carelessly attired. 'Damn it, I need a bruising ride to clear this head.'

He needed to get some air into his lungs after the excesses of the previous evening.

He and Jack had left Vauxhall at around ten o'clock, taking themselves off to what was rumoured to be an exciting new gaming club, but which had turned out to be a den of iniquity haunted by whores and sharpsters. Gervase had abandoned his friend, who refused to leave because he had hit a winning streak, and walked home alone in the early hours.

He was unafraid of the Mohocks who often ran wild through the streets at such an hour, for his skill with the sword was well known amongst the young bucks who loved to terrorize the citizens. Footpads stayed clear of him, looking for easier pickings, though when in one of the black moods that descended on him from time to time, Gervase would have relished a good fight.

He had no idea what had brought on his present mood – unless it was seeing *her* dancing and flirting with Sylvester. Knowing that particular gentleman for the careless rogue he was, Gervase had been filled with bitter anger at the sight of that lovely girl laughing up at her selfish companion.

Were all young girls so foolish that they could not see beyond a handsome face? He was beginning to think it must be the case. Helen was not the only innocent that Sylvester had ruined. Gervase would take heavy odds on there having been others since then –though he was fairly certain that

66

she had been the first. Sylvester had been twenty-two then. Eight years on, he was perhaps even more attractive to a young and naïve girl.

Damn the wench! Gervase made an effort to dismiss her from his thoughts. She was nothing to him, and she had made her indifference plain. Clearly she preferred the attentions of Sylvester. If she had not the wit to see beyond that charming smile, she was not worthy of his consideration.

But he had never ceased to blame himself for what had happened to his sweet sister. She had been no more than seventeen when Sylvester seduced her, and a few weeks from her eighteenth birthday when she died of her shame at giving birth to an illegitimate child – a child who had also died of neglect on Gervase's father's orders.

Helen had drowned herself in the river close to the house of the unkind guardian to whom she had been sent in order to conceal her shame from the world. And her child had been left to starve and die. Gervase would never forgive his father and great-aunt for the cruelty they had shown Helen and her child. And he could not forgive himself for not being there when his sister and nephew had needed him. The grief and pain their deaths had inflicted dwelled within him now and seldom let him rest.

Sometimes the hatred he felt for Harry

Sylvester burned in him so fiercely that he was tempted to take a horsewhip and thrash him – to see him bloodied and spent on the ground at his feet – and then kill him. It would be easy to pay someone to plunge a knife in Sylvester's back as Jack had suggested. Gervase had seen the rogue drinking too heavily night after night at the gaming tables. A simple matter then to have him followed and...But that would bring Gervase down to Sylvester's level.

Devil take his conscience! He would do better to be more like Jack, who was seldom troubled by the right or wrongs of his actions.

A smile touched his lips as he thought of his friend's frustration the previous evening. Jack had made no headway with his pursuit of Lady Eliza. She had made it clear that she was more than willing to renew her relationship with Gervase – but that was out of the question! At the beginning of their liaison, he had made it clear that he would not tolerate betrayal of any kind. Lady Eliza had taken Sylvester into her circle, and therefore Gervase had broken with her. He suspected that she might have invited his enemy into her confidence as well as her boudoir, if not her bed. As far as he was concerned, that was the finish of their relationship, though he continued to acknowledge her whenever they met.

She had never been a passionate lover, but she was intelligent and he had enjoyed her company. It was inconvenient more than anything else, Gervase thought as he made his way to the mews where his horses were stabled. He must either look for another mistress or remain celibate, for his taste did not run to whores.

On occasion he was persuaded to accompany a party of friends to one of the high-class brothels that flourished in St James's and the fringes of Mayfair. Madame Elizabeth le Prince had run her Maison de Tolerance in Great Marlborough Street until a year or so earlier, when she had moved to South Molton Street.

Her house was particularly elegant, styled in the French manner and intended to pander to the more discerning. She was patronized by nobility, though even the wealthy winced at the extortionate prices she charged for her girls. However, since sometimes she numbered well-born ladies amongst them she was entitled to charge for their services.

Gervase preferred a private arrangement. He would in time seek out a lady who would accept his protection, though for the moment he had seen no one who appealed. Except that wilful red-haired wench from the country...

It was a pity she must marry a wealthy cit

before she indulged herself in an affair, he mused as a groom led out his horse and helped him to mount. The first man to bed her would be a fortunate fellow. He was almost tempted...But no, that was going too far. Gervase had no desire for marriage. One cause of the friction between him and his father had been Gervase's refusal to do his duty by the family.

'I have cousins, Father,' Gervase had replied. 'If I am killed in action, Matthew will be only too delighted to step into my shoes.'

'You are an unnatural son!' the then Lord Roxbourne had raged. 'Have you no pride in your name and family?'

'Pride – for what? We came to the title through a king's whore!' Gervase replied. 'We have done nothing to earn our fortune – except grow rich on the labours of others. I see no reason for excessive pride, sir.'

'Insolent dog!' Lord Roxbourne had struck out with his riding whip. Gervase still bore a small scar at his temple from that particular blow, though there were others received as a child that did not show on the outside.

He was not sure why he had provoked his father that time, for it was before he had left to join the army, before his sister's death. He had disliked his father and all he stood for for many years, but the hatred did not come until after he discovered what had been done to Helen. Gervase's father had been a hard, cold man. A man who had enclosed land and seen his villagers starve for want of a bit of common land to graze their cow or pig. Gervase had righted that wrong as well as others when he became Lord Roxbourne, but he had not been able to bring Helen back to life – or her son.

He was scowling as he urged his horse to a canter through the silent streets. Sylvester must be brought to pay for his crime. Gervase had let things drift these past years, but that could not continue.

His thoughts returned to the red-haired wench. He smiled as he wondered when their next encounter would be.

Her first ball! Arabella glanced about her with interest, entranced by the glittering scene that met her gaze. She had attended several small private affairs over the past two weeks, but nothing as elegant or wonderful as this. Such clothes! Such jewels! She felt a flutter of excitement as she realized she was being scrutinized by ladies and gentlemen alike.

One of the first gentlemen to approach them was Lord Sylvester. She had known he would be here, and had promised to save two dances for him. He wrote his name down for a cotillion and the supper dance.

'That is to make certain I escort you into supper,' he told her with a look that made her heart race. 'You are more beautiful than ever this evening, Arabella. That colour green becomes you well. But then, anything you wear would become perfect. You are perfect and I have scarce slept for thinking of you.'

'You are a flirt, sir!' Her eyes challenged him. 'You have sweet words for all the ladies.'

'Ah yes,' he acknowledged. 'But I mean them only when I say them to you.'

Arabella laughed, pretending not to be taken in by his flattery, but her heart sang because of it. Surely he did care for her. He had become a frequent visitor to the house, and though he had not tried to kiss her again, he lost no opportunity to touch her. Just a brush against her arm, or the lightest caress of a finger on her naked shoulder.

Arabella knew that he did these things deliberately, that he was trying to seduce her with his eyes, but she also knew that she must resist or she was lost. It would be heaven to lie in his arms, to feel his lips on hers – but if she gave into him she would be ruined.

However, Lord Sylvester was not the only gentleman to be intrigued by Arabella, and within a very short time her card was full. Sir John had of course asked to be excused almost as soon as they arrived, taking himself off to the card room where he stayed until supper.

Lady Mary did not dance that evening. She sat gossiping with her friends, watching with approval as both her cousins took the floor with their partners.

'You must be proud of your charming cousins,' Lady Eliza said to her. 'The red-haired gel is a beauty.'

'Yes, I believe she is generally held to be so.' Lady Mary smiled, though she found this woman cold and proud. 'I have hopes for both of them.'

'I dare say you will get plenty of offers for Miss Arabella, but you will do well to marry the other one off to the first bidder. She is pretty enough – but I think her sly.'

'Do you?' Lady Mary was surprised. 'I had not particularly noticed it.'

'I observed her the other evening at Vauxhall. She was making up to Sir John. You will lose him if you do not take care.'

'Ah yes.' Lady Mary smiled once more. 'I believe she likes him.'

Her smile vanished as the other woman moved away, but was untouched by what she believed was merely spite. Lady Eliza was still suffering from being given her congé by Roxbourne. Yet it would not suit her to lose Sir John altogether. She had thought to choose his bride in order to retain his friendship, but perhaps she ought to steer him away from Nan. Arabella would certainly not be a compliant wife! She would not welcome his advances, and soon send him running to his mistress.

Her eyes sought out the younger of her two cousins, who was dancing with Harry Sylvester. It was clear that Arabella was fascinated by him, but there was no fear of an involvement there. Harry could not afford to marry the girl, and he would not seduce her. He owed Lady Mary money. She had helped him pay his debts on more than one occasion. She was sure he would do nothing to disoblige her.

Her gaze moved round the crowded ballroom, lighting consideringly on various gentlemen. If her arrangement with Sir John were to end it could make her life uncomfortable. She would need to find another protector. Unfortunately, there was no one she felt as comfortable with as Sir John. Lord Martlesham was reputed to have finished with his mistress recently, but he had a reputation for meanness. Her eyes travelled on, coming to rest at last on Roxbourne.

She had always admired Roxbourne from a distance, and had willingly hosted a ball for him. She had been married to her third husband then, and Randall had been a close friend of the marquis. There had been no question of anything between them at the time, but the case was different now. Yes, she believed she might be content to replace Sir John with Roxbourne – if he were interested, of course.

She saw that he was frowning, his intent gaze following someone – Arabella! Yes, she was almost certain of it. He was so caught up in his own thoughts that he had not answered when the Earl of Whytton spoke to him, and they were firm friends!

It would be wonderful if Roxbourne could be brought to offer for Arabella! Her thoughts of beginning a relationship with him herself were soon brushed aside in her excitement. It would be such a coup if Roxbourne married her cousin. It was surely time he married. After all, he must be past thirty by a year or so. He must be thinking of getting himself an heir, though he was at least ten years younger than Sir John, of course.

He wanted Arabella. She could see that by the way his eyes constantly followed the chit. Yes, he was on fire for her – but could his lust be exploited? A good many hopeful mamas had cast covetous eyes on Roxbourne these past years, but all in vain. He showed no sign of wanting to take a bride.

Some ladies said that he had no heart. Others, who had had personal experience and knew better, said that he preferred to keep his freedom. Yet a clever woman might be able to snare him. Had Arabella the wit for it? She was certainly beautiful enough, Lady Mary decided generously. And there was no reason why she should not succeed, if she would be guided in this by her cousin. It would not be easy, but there were ways of ensnaring a gentleman, and Roxbourne was certainly that – of the highest order. He was said to be hard and ruthless in business, and had certainly increased his fortune since coming into his estate, but he was also said to be scrupulous in matters of honour.

Yes, it would suit very well. Lady Mary smiled as she made her way unhurriedly across the room towards her quarry. She was giving a dinner party the following week, and she would take this opportunity to invite him – which meant that she would not invite Lord Sylvester. However, that might be just as well, in view of Arabella's partiality for the younger man.

Unaware of her cousin's plans for her, Arabella went happily into supper with Lord Sylvester. As he went off to procure food for her she was disturbed to discover Lord Roxbourne at her side.

'You would do well to avoid the company of a rogue like Harry Sylvester,' Gervase said. 'Be careful, mistress. He will never marry you. He has other plans.'

Arabella flushed. Her eyes snapped with

temper as she looked up at him standing there. He was like a dog quarrelling over a bone, she thought resentfully, jealous because she had shown her preference for another.

'I find you insulting, sir. You would not speak so to Lord Sylvester's face, I dare say.'

'You think me afraid of him?' Gervase's upper lip curled back in a snarl. 'I would have killed the swine long ago if he would meet me. It is he who is the coward, Mistress Arabella. I give you this warning for your own sake. There are half a dozen gentlemen present this evening who would fall over themselves to wed you given a chance – open your eyes and look elsewhere or you will live to regret it.'

'Please leave me, sir. I have nothing to say to you. I detest you!'

His dark eyes met hers in a long, cool stare, and it was Arabella who looked away first.

'I have given you my warning. You will have only yourself to blame if he ruins you.' With that, Gervase bowed his head and walked away, leaving her to stare after him.

Oh, he was the most arrogant, despicable man! She wished that she might take a horsewhip to him. She would like to tear his heart out and feed it to the stray dogs that haunted the alleys of the city.

'Have I kept you waiting, Arabella? You

77

frown so I fear I have displeased you.'

Arabella glanced up as Harry set a plateful of delicious morsels on the table before her. Her hands had been curled tightly, her nails digging into the soft flesh of her palms. She forced a little laugh and shook her head. 'Indeed no, sir. I had not noticed the time. It was someone else...'

'Someone else displeased you? Tell me his name and I shall make him apologize to you.'

'He called you a coward,' Arabella said. 'He warned me not to trust you.'

'Clearly I have a jealous rival,' Harry said easily. 'Who was this fool?'

'No fool,' she replied and shivered. 'It was the Marquis of Roxbourne. I think he...I think he hates you.'

Glancing up, she saw that his face had gone white. There was a look in his eyes that made her think he had reason to fear the other man.

'What is it, my lord? Why do you look so?'

'Roxbourne is my enemy. He has tried to force a duel on me, but I refuse to rise to his lure. He is an expert with both the sword and the pistols. If I accepted his challenge, he would kill me.'

'Why?' Arabella sensed more than he had told her. 'What have you done that he should hate you so?'

'I have done nothing,' Harry replied. 'The

man is moody – a cold, ruthless devil. I suppose that I must have upset him in some way. Perhaps I won a lady he desires for himself – who knows? I swear that I do not.'

'I sensed that he was ruthless,' Arabella agreed. 'I confess I do not like him – and I would trust nothing that he said to me.'

'I am glad his spite has not turned you against me, Arabella.'

'Oh no,' she replied, smiling at him. 'Nothing that man could say or do would make me dislike you, my lord.'

'Then he may go to the Devil for all I care!' Harry lifted his wineglass to her. 'I salute you, Arabella. Your beauty will attract many suitors – but I pray you, do not let Roxbourne be one of them.'

'I would rather become a nun!' Arabella cried and wondered why his eyes gleamed with amusement. She was not yet familiar enough with London ways to know that the term was often applied to young, fresh whores. 'Why are you laughing?'

Harry recollected himself. 'I do not see you spending your life in prayer, mistress. It would be such a waste. You were meant for earthly pleasures.'

Arabella dimpled at his words. She suspected him of some wickedness but let it pass. She was enjoying herself in his company far too much to quarrel with him. 'Well, I told Lord Roxbourne that I did not wish to speak to him, and I hope that he has finally accepted it,' she said. 'Now, tell me, sir – when shall I see you again? Do you dine with us next week?'

'Alas, I have not been invited,' Harry replied. 'But I shall certainly call on you very soon.'

'Then I shall look forward to your visit.'

Arabella glanced around the supper room as she nibbled the dainty trifles on her plate. She could not see Lord Roxbourne anywhere, so she concluded that he had taken himself off. She hoped that he would keep his distance in future. Surely she had made her dislike of him plain enough now!

'Roxbourne!' Arabella stared at her cousin in dismay. 'Why have you invited him to dine, ma'am? He is the most arrogant, conceited devil – and I dislike him above any other I have met since coming to town.'

'He does not dislike you,' Lady Mary said, frowning at her. 'I saw him watching you dancing last evening. And I must take this opportunity to remind you that Harry Sylvester must marry money. You would be foolish to hope for anything from him, Arabella. Besides, he cannot pay his own debts, let alone your father's.'

'I–I like him, cousin, that is all. He is amusing.'

'I am well aware of that. I too enjoy

Harry's company – but I can afford to amuse myself, you cannot. You are here to find yourself a wealthy husband. Must I remind you of your duty?'

'No, ma'am.' Arabella blushed, realizing that she had annoyed her cousin. 'But may I not have a little pleasure?'

'I know Sylvester is charming, but he cannot marry you, Arabella. Nor would your family permit it. You waste your time with him. Roxbourne would be a far better catch. Indeed, if you could pull it off it would be the match of the season.'

'I have no desire to marry Roxbourne!'

'You are too particular, Arabella. Had you a fortune of your own you might choose whoever you liked, but that is not the case. You must marry, and Roxbourne is extremely wealthy. One of the richest men in England I dare swear.'

'Is money everything then?'

'Do not be wilful, Arabella. I was given no choice in the matter of my first husband. I was but fifteen – and he was nearly fifty. You have no idea how terrifying that is for an innocent child. You I think are not so innocent. Oh, I do not say you have lain with a man. I believe you to have too much sense for that, but your wedding night will not come as such a shock to you as it does to many young gels.'

Arabella blushed at her cousin's plain

speaking. 'It is true that I know...I have seen lovers in the hayloft at the farm on my father's estate. A young labourer and his lover.' A smile hovered on her lips. 'She was smiling when she left him, and I asked her if...if doing that had made her happy.'

'And what did she tell you?' Lady Mary was amused despite Arabella's wilfulness.

'She told me that it was the best thing that had ever happened to her and that she was in love.' Arabella looked wistful. 'Is it so much to ask that I should be allowed to love my husband?'

'I am afraid that is a secondary consideration for a young woman in your situation. Love is something you may look for when your husband has his heir.'

'But supposing I refuse to marry a man I cannot like?'

'Then I should wash my hands of you,' her cousin replied. 'Believe me, Arabella, there would be no sympathy for you here if you disregarded all that I have tried to do for you. I do not say that you must take Roxbourne if you dislike him so much – but you must take someone like him. Why not think of Sir John? I promise you that he would leave you alone once you were with child. He is very malleable and I would do my best to keep him with me – though you would have to give him at least two sons before he could be certain the succession was safe.'

A shudder ran through Arabella, though she did her best to suppress it. 'I think I would rather take Roxbourne, ma'am.'

'Well, that is your choice,' her cousin said calmly, though there was a glint of displeasure in her eyes. 'If you have the wit to catch him – it will not be easy. Why not think of it as a challenge, Arabella? And one that will pay handsome dividends I'll swear. I think you would find Roxbourne the equal and more of your young labourer in the art of love.'

'I dare say he will not ask me,' Arabella said. 'There are other gentlemen who seem to like me, cousin.'

'To whom are you referring?' Lady Mary's eyes held a look of steel. 'Wellingborough is on the catch for an heiress – though he is not in such a sad case as Sylvester. Borrowdale is eligible but as old as Sir John, and Fairhaven is ruled by his mother. If she takes to you, you might stand a chance, but I know for a fact that she has her eye on a duke's daughter for her son.'

Arabella bit her lip. Put like that, she saw that her choice was not as wide as she had imagined. At least three of the gentlemen who had paid particular attention to her were older than Sir John, and just as distasteful to her. She had quite liked Lord Fairhaven, but if his mama wanted a titled lady for him...'Perhaps someone else will take a liking to me.'

'I dare say a good many will find you attractive,' Lady Mary replied. 'But the young ones are either not looking for a wife, or tied by the apron strings until they come into their fortunes. Roxbourne has been hunted unsuccessfully for years, but I think you might manage it if you are willing to be guided by me.'

Arabella hesitated. She had no intention of being coerced into a marriage she disliked, but it would not do to fall out with her cousin or she might be sent home before she'd had a chance to make Harry Sylvester mad with love for her.

'I–I do not know, ma'am,' she said in a subdued tone. 'I am of course willing to be guided – but may I not have a little time? We do not know if Roxbourne will offer yet... and there may be someone else I could like of whom you also approve.'

'Well, it is not beyond the bounds of possibility that Fairhaven will shake off his mother's rule once he inherits the money, which is quite soon I believe. There is no hurry after all. I ask only that you should be polite to Roxbourne. Do not seem to encourage him for he may take fright and bolt. Be polite but distant and it should intrigue him.'

'Yes, cousin. I shall do exactly as you wish.'

Arabella hid her smile, for it was exactly what she had intended all along. Only Roxbourne and she would know the true situation...

Four

'You look flushed, Miss Arabella. Would you care to take a turn on the balcony? I am sure the air would refresh you...' Harry Sylvester laid his hand on her bare arm.

She had been longing to leave the over-crowded rooms, and the chance to be alone with him even for a few minutes was not to be resisted. 'Why not, my lord?' she asked. 'I vow this heat has given me a headache.'

It was not her head that was suffering so much as the rest of her, Arabella thought wryly as she laid her hand on his arm. They made a leisurely progress through the throng of chattering guests, going out on to the balcony, where they remained in full view of anyone who chanced to glance their way.

Harry ran a finger down her arm, making a little shiver of pleasure dance along her spine. 'Could we not walk to the far end? I believe the view is superior from there...'

Arabella glanced back towards the lights of the ballroom. Her cousin would be annoyed if she saw them, but she was nowhere in sight. It was a risk, for being out here alone could cause gossip – but she had almost reached the stage where she no longer cared. She wanted so much to be held by this man, to be kissed and caressed...to melt into his arms and feel the heat of his body burn into her.

'We must not stay long. My cousin...'

'I would do nothing to harm you. You must know that, Bella.' His voice was low and urgent, filled with suppressed longing, and she was not proof against him.

When they were out of sight of the French windows, he drew her against him, kissing her hungrily. She had known he would and, as she felt the deliciously heady sensation begin to sweep over her, she clung to him, her body melding with his, wanting him to go on and on.

'Oh, Bella, Bella,' he moaned, his mouth searching greedily for the soft mounds of her delectable breasts. 'What am I to do about you? I swear you are driving me mad with desire. I cannot sleep for thinking of you.'

His words were as sweet music to her ears. She could hardly check her eager response, for his mouth and tongue were making it impossible for her to think beyond the delight they gave her. All she wanted was to lie with him, to know the glories of making love. Every part of her body burned to know his touch and she could scarce breathe for the frantic beating of her heart. Oh, what did it matter that they could never marry? To know the sweet pleasure of...

'Miss Arabella, are you out here? Lady Mary was looking for you.'

At the sound of Sir John's voice, the lovers sprang apart. Arabella turned away to hastily rearrange her gown, while Harry strolled to meet him.

'We were admiring the view,' Harry said in a cool, bored tone. 'Miss Arabella felt a little faint from the heat, but I believe she is better now. Excuse me, I have a partner for the next dance.'

He sauntered back into the lighted ballroom, leaving Arabella to follow. She took a moment to compose herself before going to join Sir John. His eyes went over her, noting the flush in her cheeks.

'Has that fellow been upsetting you, m'dear?'

'No, not at all,' Arabella said. She smiled at him. Her senses were clearing now and she realized that she ought to feel grateful to this man. Had he not come...She had been close to surrendering her all for the pleasure of the moment. 'It was kind of you to come in search of me, sir. Lord Sylvester brought me out here because I was not feeling well.'

'It is a very humid evening,' he said, not quite believing her. He had seen the shape of their bodies standing very close together in the shadows at the far end of the balcony and could guess what Sylvester had been about. He could not blame the fellow for attempting to seduce Arabella – she was enough to drive any man out of his senses! Had he thought he stood a chance, he might have attempted it himself. However, he disliked making a fool of himself, and he knew that his only chance with her was to offer her a good marriage. 'Do you feel like returning to the ballroom now?'

'Yes, of course,' Arabella said. 'I simply needed a little air.'

He offered her his arm, and she laid her hand lightly upon it, allowing him to lead her back into the ballroom. As her eyes moved round the assembled company, she saw that Harry was talking to a rather plain plump girl. The girl was simpering up at him foolishly, Arabella thought, then realized she must appear almost as foolish herself.

'That was a deep sigh, Miss Arabella,' Sir John said. 'Does your head still ache?'

'A little,' she lied. 'But do not concern yourself, sir. I shall be better presently.'

'You do look unwell,' he said, clearly concerned now. 'Would you like to be taken home? I would be happy to escort you.'

'Oh, how kind of you,' Arabella replied. 'But I could not take my sister away from the ball...'

'She may remain here with Lady Mary. You will be quite safe with me, m'dear. I would never presume on a lady's vulnerability – especially when she is unwell.'

Arabella was reluctant to be taken home, and yet the encounter on the balcony had left her shaken. Her plan had been to drive Harry Sylvester mad with love for her so that he was forced to marry her. Instead, she had been on the verge of allowing him to seduce her – and it was no more than two weeks since their first visit to Vauxhall! No doubt he imagined that he had only to keep pressing her and she would fall into his honeyed trap. And the terrible truth was that he was right.

She must do something to shock him out of his complacency. She must make Harry jealous. If he saw her leaving with Sir John it might make him fear losing her to another man.

She smiled up at her companion. 'Are you sure you do not mind leaving early, sir? I am afraid my head *is* painful.'

'Then we shall go as soon as I have spoken to your cousin. Sit here quietly by the window and I shall return immediately.'

'So kind...' She sighed and sat down, her eyes straying back to Harry Sylvester, who was now dancing with the young woman he had been talking to earlier.

'Her name is Miss Jane Archer,' a voice said and she looked round to see Lord Roxbourne standing close by. 'Her father is a wealthy merchant, I believe. She is here with an aunt who is married to a bishop, and a friend of our host's. I dare say she is a good catch for someone of Sylvester's ilk.'

Arabella's eyes flashed fire at him, but she answered mildly enough. 'Do you say so, sir? I am sure I do not know.'

'Why are you sitting here alone? Have you no partner for this dance?'

'I–I am feeling a little unwell,' she lied. 'Sir John has kindly offered to take me home.'

'You will be safe enough with Fortescue. He is a decent enough fellow,' Gervase said, his gaze narrowed. 'I could not say the same for Sylvester. You should not trust him too far, mistress.'

'What has he done to you that you hate him so?'

'Perhaps I shall tell you one day.' He inclined his head to her as Sir John approached. 'I hope you are soon recovered from whatever ails you, mistress.' He waited until Sir John came up to them. 'Good evening, sir. I understand Mistress Arabella is feeling unwell. I pray you, take good care of her.'

'Yes, of course...' Sir John stared after him as he walked away. Damn Roxbourne for his interference! His words had made it a matter of honour that Arabella should reach home unmolested. It had not been in Sir John's mind to press his advantage, but he resented the marquis's manner. 'Come, m'dear. Lady Mary was most anxious that you should leave if you wished to.'

'You are thoughtful, sir.'

Arabella's mind was wrestling with the doubts Lord Roxbourne had brought into being. Why would he not leave her alone? He could not be ignorant of her dislike, but he would insist on warning her against Harry Sylvester. She needed no warnings! She was well aware that Harry would steal what he wanted from her if he could. It was a game they played – a dangerous one for her! She had escaped with her virtue intact this time, but for how long?

Allowing Sir John to escort her out to the carriage, Arabella was very subdued. For once she had no answers and closed her eyes as soon as she was settled, giving the impression that she really was unwell. She sighed deeply. She did not know what to do, but instinct told her that she must not be alone with Harry again until she had extracted a promise of marriage from him.

'Does your head hurt very badly?' Sir John's hand found hers in the shadows of the carriage. He patted her kindly. 'You must not let that rogue Sylvester upset you, m'dear.'

'No, no, he did not...'

'If you are ever in trouble you can always turn to me...But I shall say no more this evening. Rest and we shall soon be home.'

Arabella felt the sting of tears. For a moment his tone had made her think of her father. She missed him, and she wished that he had remained in London. She could have confided in him, but there was no one else. Her cousin was a little annoyed with her, and Nan had become withdrawn, no longer wishing to confide in Arabella.

'I–I shall remember, sir.'

Arabella was confused and annoyed with herself. He would propose to her, she was sure of it – if not this evening, then soon. And by allowing him to take her home she had encouraged it. She gave a faltering sigh and pressed a hand to her head.

Please, let him not ask her this evening!

Sir John was kindness itself as he delivered Arabella to her door, kissing her hand solicitously and telling Mrs Boswell to take good care of her before departing.

'I shall call tomorrow to see how you go on, Miss Arabella.'

She thanked him and walked up the stairs, retiring immediately to her own room. The housekeeper followed in concern, fussing over her and promising to bring a restorative tisane.

Arabella did not refuse it. Her mind was

occupied elsewhere as she allowed the maid to undress her and loosen her hair from the elaborate style she had worn that evening. She dismissed the girl and brushed her own hair, feeling too restless to go to bed and half regretting her early departure from the ball. When Mrs Boswell brought her the refreshing hot drink, she took a few sips then left it to go cold as she began to pace the floor of the bedchamber.

What was she to do? If Sir John offered for her she would refuse him, but that would make her cousin angry. Arabella sensed that Lady Mary was already annoyed because Harry Sylvester had transferred his attentions to her. If she sent Arabella back to the country, she might never see him again.

It would break her heart if she never saw Harry again! Arabella knew that she was in love with him, had fallen for him that very first moment their eyes had met. Yet she also knew he was a rogue. Charming and handsome, but a rogue. She almost despaired of ever achieving her heart's desire.

Arabella turned from the window she had been staring out of as the door of the bedchamber was flung open. Her thoughts had been so caught up with Harry Sylvester that his name was on her lips, but she gasped as she saw her sister standing in the doorway. Nan was looking at her with anger and dislike.

'It is as I thought!' Nan cried, clearly in a temper. 'You are not ill at all. I told Cousin Mary it was merely a ruse to make Sir John bring you home alone.'

'Why should I want to do that?' Arabella was surprised by the vehemence of her sister's attack.

'You want him for yourself, of course!' Nan accused. 'You knew I had made up my mind to take him and you deliberately set your cap at him. It is always the same with you. You must be the one to have every man's attention!'

'Oh, Nan,' Arabella said, feeling shocked and hurt by her spiteful words. 'How could you think I would do such a thing? Sir John insisted.'

'Only because you smiled at him so sweetly.' Nan's mouth drooped sullenly at the corners. 'I saw you coming from the balcony with him. I think you are selfish and—'

'I did not go out there with Sir John. I merely wanted some air.' Arabella felt a pang of guilt, remembering that she had encouraged Sir John a little, but only to make Harry jealous. 'You know I do not want to marry him.'

Nan's expression of spite and meanness had robbed her face of its prettiness. Arabella saw her as she might be in a few years – a plain, bitter woman.

'I would not take him from you if he is the one you want,' she said and approached her sister with her hand outstretched. 'I care for you, Nan. You must know that?'

'Well, you have a strange way of showing it,' Nan replied and moved away from her, not willing to accept her apology. 'Why can you not be content to have half the gentlemen in town after you?'

'There is only one I want,' Arabella said softly. 'I am in love, Nan, with Lord Sylvester.'

'You cannot be so foolish,' Nan answered waspishly. 'I heard only this evening that he is after some wealthy cit's daughter.'

'No, no, that is not true,' Arabella said, hurt by her sister's unkindness. 'He loves me. I know he does.'

'He will never marry you,' Nan said. 'You would do better to save your smiles for Lord Roxbourne, Arabella. He likes you very well.'

'You are mistaken. He likes only to mock and lecture me. I wish he would keep his advice and his opinions to himself.'

'You are a foolish child,' Nan replied, her mouth hard. 'You will find that no gentleman will marry you if it is believed you have become too intimate with Lord Sylvester. You throw away your chances at your peril, Sister. You should try to find yourself a compliant husband before it is too late.'

'Go to bed, Nan,' she said. 'I am going down to the library. I need to be alone.'

'I will have Sir John,' Nan said as she reached the door. 'You shall not have your own way this time.'

Arabella closed the door behind her, feeling a little sad. She was hurt by Nan's accusations. It was as though her sister hated her, as if she had been jealous of her for a long time.

'Sir John wishes to speak to you, Arabella.' Lady Mary had been reading a letter when the girl entered her boudoir two days after the ball. 'I imagine you can guess what he wishes to say to you. He is calling here at two this afternoon. You will receive him downstairs in the visitors' parlour.'

'Must I see him, ma'am? Could you not make some excuse?'

'Certainly not!' Lady Mary frowned at her. 'I imagined you had made up your mind to take him when you permitted him to bring you home alone the other evening.'

'It was a mistake,' Arabella admitted. 'I did not realize quite how it would seem until too late. Besides, Nan wants him – and I would not stand in her way for the world.'

'I thought Nan would do for him at the start,' Lady Mary said. 'However, I have since revised my opinion. I think she is too sour to make him happy, despite her sweet smiles. Your sister is sly and unkind, Arabella. I shall not encourage a match between her and my friend. No, you would suit him much better. Do not be fooled by his appearance. I dare say he is a little fatter than is good for him, but he is an insatiable lover. He would keep you bedded for a month I expect, but by then you may be with child and can send him back to me. You may rely on me to keep him with me until long after your child is weaned. If you are lucky and give him a strong son, he will leave you in peace much of the time.'

'I do not care for such a marriage, ma'am.'

'Then bring Roxbourne up to scratch,' Lady Mary said, her eyes glinting. 'If you defy me I shall finish with you, Arabella. If you take neither Roxbourne nor Sir John, you may go and visit your great-aunt Rosalind, for I shall not keep you here.'

'Please do not be angry with me,' Arabella said, her head downcast. 'I must refuse Sir John for Nan's sake – but I shall do what I can to encourage Roxbourne.'

'You give me your word?'

'Yes, cousin.'

Arabella's fingers were crossed behind her back, and she kept her gaze fixed on a fine French gilt clock on the mantelpiece. She had no intention of giving Lord Roxbourne so much as the time of day unless she was forced – but she needed more time.

'Very well.' Lady Mary reached for a sweetmeat from a small silver dish at her side and popped it in her mouth. 'We shall have no more of this nonsense with Harry Sylvester. I have told him he is not welcome here until you have left my house – and that will be either as a bride or to stay with Rosalind Hathaway in the country.'

Arabella made no reply. Nothing on this earth would make her marry either Sir John or that detestable man Roxbourne. If that meant she was destined to be banished to the country in disgrace then so be it. She would send a message to Harry somehow and hope that he would follow her – unless he proposed marriage to her in the meantime...

Arabella was trembling inside as she faced her suitor that afternoon. She had dreaded this interview, but she knew there was no escape.

'Miss Arabella...' Sir John began, but she spoke immediately to forestall him.

'Pray do not say anything just yet, sir,' she said holding up her hand as if to ward him off. 'I would share a secret with you.'

'A secret...' His eyes narrowed, gleaming intently. 'Pray continue.'

'I believe Nan is in love with you,' she said. 'And I would be glad to have you as my sister's husband, sir. I know you to be a good and generous man, and I would see my sister happy.'

'Mistress Tucker is a delightful lady, of course, but...' He paused to clear his throat and Arabella began again before he could speak those fateful words.

'I–I am expecting a proposal from a man I care for at any moment,' she lied. 'He...he is a man of fortune and distinction, though I am not at liberty to mention his name for the moment.'

Sir John's expression hardened to anger. 'Lady Mary said nothing of this to me when I asked for permission to address you.'

'She...she may not yet be aware, but I have expectations, sir.' She knew it was a bold lie and could turn back on her, but met his furious gaze bravely. 'Now, sir – was there something more you wished to say to me?'

'Is that your final answer? I suppose I should thank you for speaking so plainly.' He did not look at all grateful. 'I shall waste no more time on you, mistress. You have misled me...'

'I think not, sir. I think you have misled yourself.'

'You are a wilful wench and will no doubt come to a sorry end.' He glared at her as she raised her head proudly. 'If you have hopes of Roxbourne you should stay clear of Sylvester. The marquis would not touch that rogue's leavings, believe me!'

Arabella remained silent, though her cheeks were tinged with pink. She fought her temper, not moving a finger as he took a hesitant step towards her, then stopped and turned on his heel, clearly deciding to take refuge in dignity.

'I bid you good day, mistress.'

Arabella sagged with relief as he went out. Thank goodness she had spoken out! It had been unpleasant enough as it was, but could have been so much worse if he had attempted to make love to her. He was angry, of course, and would be even more so as time passed and there was no announcement of her forthcoming marriage. She could only hope that her hints about Nan would take root and ease the blow to his pride.

'I heard an interesting rumour this afternoon...' Jack Meadows grinned at milord. 'You might have told me first, Gervase.'

'What rumour is this?' Gervase looked up from the letter he had been reading. 'You intrigue me. Pray do not keep me in the dark.'

'It is all over town...' Jack had come hotfoot to communicate the story. 'They tell me you are thinking of taking a bride.'

'Indeed?' Gervase's brows arched. 'And who have the gossips chosen this time?'

'You do not know?' Jack slapped his own thigh and gave a bellow of laughter. 'I knew it was nonsense. Everyone is talking of it, though. You are supposed to be on the verge of proposing to Lady Mary Randall's cousin, Arabella Tucker.' He ended on an air of mischief, waiting for the twist of disgust on milord's lips.

'Ah...' Gervase regarded him in silence for a moment. 'And who imparted this information to you?'

'It was Lady Eliza who mentioned it first, but there have been others since,' Jack replied. 'She wanted to know if it was true. I told her I doubted it. The wench may be a beauty, but I cannot see you being caught in that particular trap, Gervase.'

'Did she happen to say where she heard this rumour?'

'I believe Sir John Fortescue told her it in confidence. I told you everyone is whispering of it. You will have to snub the girl in public to scotch it.'

'They may whisper to their hearts' content,' Gervase said and yawned. 'If you hear any more such tales, ignore them, there's a good fellow. These rumours grow tedious.'

Jack stared at him feeling puzzled. Gervase was a close one! He had neither admitted nor denied the rumour – but surely it could not be true? Mistress Arabella Tucker was beautiful, but she was far from rivalling the sophisticated ladies that Gervase usually favoured with his attentions.

Jack decided that he would pay more attention to Miss Arabella Tucker next time he chanced to be in company with her.

Gervase frowned over his wine when his friend had at last departed, leaving him alone with his thoughts. Where had the rumour come from? Had Sir John read more into his causal remark that evening? Or had Lady Mary begun it herself?

He would not put such a thing beyond her. She had already hinted more than once that Arabella would make a delightful wife for any gentleman. Several times she had assured him that Arabella's mother came from good stock.

'She was Mountbank's youngest,' she had told him. 'We were friends. A delightful lady. Her family hoped for great things from her when she was first out, but she chose Sir Edmund. He was far from a good catch for her, but she loved him. Arabella takes after her mother. If she once gave you her heart she would be a loyal and faithful wife.'

'Ah – but would her husband be as faithful?' Gervase had replied, a smile of derision on his lips.

Lady Mary had merely tapped him on the arm with her delicate painted fan and said nothing, but there had been a determined gleam in her eyes that left Gervase in no doubt of her hopes. She would see him wed to her cousin if she could manage it.

Gervase wondered at himself that he had not given her a severe setdown. Neither had he done anything to scotch the rumour, of which he had been aware even before Jack had come to tell him the tale. He was not sure why he had allowed it to continue when a lift of his brows would have been sufficient to kill it.

He could not be thinking of making Arabella an offer? No! it was out of the question. He had no desire to marry anyone...A picture of her face came to him then. He could see her lying in his bed, her hair spread on the pillows, her mouth slightly parted in anticipation of his kiss.

'Damn the wench!' he muttered aloud and flung the slender flute into the grate, watching with pleasure as its fragile air-twist stem disintegrated into a thousand pieces. 'She is nothing – forget her!'

He wondered what was wrong with him. He had never allowed a woman to get so deeply beneath his defences before, and he did not enjoy the feeling it gave him now. He would be a fool to let himself care. Women were best kept at a distance. They could give pleasure, but the pain inflicted by betrayal was sharp.

Was he really thinking of making her an offer? He would offer her his protection if he believed for one moment that she would accept, but marriage...that was another question.

'Sir John asked me whether your engagement to Lord Roxbourne was soon to be announced,' Nan said when she returned from driving out with him that afternoon. 'I told him I was not sure, but I imagined it would be soon.'

Arabella was horrified as she watched Nan take off her chip-straw bonnet and lay it on the bed. Her sister was looking pretty in a green silk carriage gown and also rather pleased with herself, but she wasn't sure why.

'You should not have told him that,' she said. 'It isn't true, Nan.'

'Cousin Mary says she is sure he is on the verge of proposing,' Nan said. 'And I have observed the way he looks at you. It will be your own fault if you do not catch him, Bella.'

Nan had not called her that for a while. Her eyes narrowed as she saw her sister's look of satisfaction. 'Why are you looking so very pleased with yourself?'

'Sir John asked me to marry him and I said yes,' Nan said triumphantly. She did not know that he had first asked Arabella, for neither she nor Lady Mary had told her. 'He will settle the most pressing of Father's debts and another ten thousand pounds on me. I am to have the income and also a clothes allowance – though the capital is secured to my first child. Do you not think that generous, Arabella?'

'Yes, indeed. Very generous,' Arabella replied. Nan was gloating over her success, clearly relishing the opportunity to shine above her sister. 'I know it is what you wanted and I am very happy for you.'

'Father will be surprised,' Nan said and there was a vicious pleasure in her words. 'You were always his favourite, and he thought you would be the first to catch a husband.'

'I am sure he thought no such thing,' Arabella replied. She could see that Nan was still not prepared to forgive all the slights she imagined she had suffered because of her sister. 'As for me, I always thought he liked you best.'

Nan smiled smugly. 'He told me he much admires your beauty, but thinks you rather too free in your manners. He said that a man could not be sure you would not cuckold him, and that he had decided I would make a far better wife.'

'I have always thought it,' Arabella said. Nan's spite was wounding, but she was determined that they should part friends if holding her tongue would manage it. 'I am glad you are to marry, Nan – but I shall miss you.'

'Well, you may come and stay with me sometimes,' Nan said, deciding to be generous. 'And if Roxbourne does not come up to scratch, you may be my companion.'

Oh yes! Nan would like that, Arabella thought. It would just suit her to have her sister in the position of a poor relative.

'Perhaps I shall marry someone else...'

Nan gave her a pitying look. 'You are a fool if you imagine Lord Sylvester will wed you. Be guided by my example, Sister. Marry the first man to ask you.'

Arabella made no reply. She would rather stay at home and keep house for her father. It occurred to her that she might be able to do just that, at least for a while. If Sir John was prepared to pay Sir Edmund's most pressing debts, there was no need for her to marry immediately.

'Your father has declined to come up for Nan's wedding,' Lady Mary told Arabella a few days later. 'He says he has a slight chill but that I should send word as soon as I have news of you.' She looked at her expectantly. 'You danced with Roxbourne at Vauxhall last night. Did he say nothing to you?'

'He said I looked more beautiful than ever, and sent his congratulations to my sister,' Arabella remembered and fumed inwardly. She had felt that he was mocking her because she had not yet secured an offer of marriage. She was still hoping, but her plan to keep Harry at bay was not working. Each time he stole a kiss from her she came one step closer to surrender.

'Roxbourne really is the most infuriating man!' Lady Mary pulled a face. 'I knew it would not be easy to snare him, but I swear he wants you!'

'As his mistress perhaps,' Arabella replied and pouted. 'Everyone says the same of him – he will never marry.'

'Why do you think that is?' Lady Mary wondered aloud. 'Has he been crossed in love – or does his aversion go deeper? I must see what I can discover. I do not despair of him yet. Perhaps you should give him a little more encouragement?'

'Should I take him to the rose arbour and seduce him?'

'Do not be impertinent!' Lady Mary snapped. Her hand clenched at her side as if she were tempted to slap her. 'You are too wilful, Arabella. If you are not careful you will lose him – and no one else has looked like offering for you.'

That was because society as a whole was too busy laying odds on whether or not Roxbourne would come up to scratch. One or two gentlemen who had considered the possibility of offering for Mistress Arabella had retreated. No one wanted to offend

Roxbourne, who was known to have an uncertain temper and a certain skill with the rapier. Besides, it was a delicious scandal. Especially as she was thought to have a partiality for Sylvester, and everyone knew how the case stood between Roxbourne and that particular gentleman, though only a discreet few knew why.

'Then it will have to be Roxbourne or no one,' Arabella said. 'Unfortunately, he does not seem to want to ask me.'

'Well, he has asked us all to a small supper dance he is giving next week,' Lady Mary informed her with a severe look. 'It is two days before Nan's wedding and will be our last outing before then. Use your opportunity well, Arabella. It may be your last.'

Arabella retired to her bedchamber with her cousin's threat ringing in her ears. She was aware that Lady Mary was out of temper with both her and Nan. She could not be sure, of course, but she believed that Sir John might have told his mistress that their affair was over. Nan confirmed Arabella's suspicions on the evening they were to attend Lord Roxbourne's supper dance.

'I made it clear that I should not tolerate a mistress – at least until we have our sons,' she told Arabella with a sour smile. 'If we want the succession to be safe, Sir John must give all his efforts in that direction to me.'

'I thought you wanted him to return to London and leave you alone in the country?'

'I have decided that will not satisfy me after all,' Nan replied with a twist of her mouth. 'A wife must have influence over her husband if she wants him to respect her – and a mistress may interfere with things that do not properly concern her. Especially if the relationship is a long-standing one.'

There was something in her manner at that moment that made Arabella feel sympathy for Sir John. He was decent enough in his own way, even though his manner towards Arabella had been much colder since her rejection of his offer. She wondered what kind of a life he would have when married to her sister, but it was after all his own choice.

'Well you must do as you wish, Nan.'

'I intend to, Sister.'

Nan's mouth looked thin and mean. Arabella realized that she did not like the woman her sister had become of late. Or perhaps this side of Nan had always been there without her knowing it.

Arabella dismissed the thought, wanting to think well of her sister. Perhaps Nan would be more like her old self when she was wed. Besides, there were only two more days before the wedding, and Arabella did not wish to fall out with her.

However, there was the supper dance at Lord Roxbourne's house to come first. Lady Mary would be expecting him to propose to her and when he did not, she was going to be very angry. Arabella thought it quite possible that she would be packed off to stay with her great-aunt before many days had passed.

Arabella must see Lord Sylvester! She must speak to him before she was banished to the country. There was no likelihood of his being at Lord Roxbourne's house, of course, but perhaps she could send him a letter. Yes, she would write to him and ask if they could meet...

Five

Lady Montrose was the hostess for Roxbourne's dance that evening. A lady of mature years and impeccable virtue, her acceptance of his offer had for once not given rise to speculation about their relationship. Besides, the betting on whether or not he would offer for Arabella had spiralled to fever pitch in the coffee houses and clubs frequented by the racier element of London society.

Unaware of all the interest, Arabella continued to show a cool politeness to Roxbourne, which was taken as a clever ploy on her part. Opinion was divided over the eventual outcome, for the more astute had noticed something in Roxbourne's manner towards the young girl that had not previously been there.

'I'll wager she'll get him yet,' one young buck remarked to his friend as they watched Arabella dancing with her host that evening. 'She must either be an extremely fine actress or very cunning to maintain that air of indifference. One would almost think she genuinely did not care whether he offers for her or not.'

'Completely false,' his companion tittered maliciously. 'Any woman in her position would die for the chance. He's as rich as Croesus, don't you know.'

'And wouldn't I like to know where he gets his money,' the first man replied. 'I lost a fortune at the tables last night.'

Their conversation took a more personal turn, but the earlier part of it had not been lost on a lady standing just behind them. Lady Eliza was consumed with jealousy. If she had been honest, she would have admitted that her affair with Roxbourne had ended months before Mistress Arabella had come on the scene, but she had hoped to win him back before she realized that he was in hot pursuit of the girl.

Lady Eliza knew Roxbourne as well as most, and she was certain that the young country girl had appealed to something inside him that few knew existed. She also knew to her cost that he hated Harry Sylvester, though not why.

Perhaps it was jealousy that prompted her to whisper to a friend that Roxbourne might not be so eager to pursue Mistress Arabella if he knew of the latest rumour concerning her and Lord Sylvester.

'And what is that, pray?' the lady asked, intrigued.

Lady Eliza merely arched her brows and then laughed mysteriously. 'Now that would be very wrong of me. I shall not spread gossip – nor speak one word that might ruin a young woman's good name.'

It was nothing and yet it was enough. The rumour spread through the assembled company like wildfire, and had become something much more malicious by the time it was repeated to Jack Meadows.

'I do not believe it,' Jack said. 'The girl is an innocent – anyone can see that.' He frowned as he watched her dancing with a gentleman he knew to be one of the most salacious rogues in London. 'Depend upon it, some malicious tongue has started this tale.'

He noticed at once that Arabella was looking uncomfortable. What was that old goat saying to her? Earl Maxwell was sixty if he was a day, and riddled with disease. No sensible woman would have anything to do with him. Jack looked for Gervase, expecting that he might do something to rescue the girl, but he was dancing with his cousin Matthew's wife. It was clearly up to Jack to rescue her himself – especially if she was destined to be his friend's bride. He must do his best to be on good terms with her.

He went up to her as the dance ended, skilfully extricating her from the grasp of the old lecher with a smile and a touch on her

114

arm and steering her across the room to stand near the open windows that led out to a terrace and a garden.

'There – is that not better, Mistress Arabella?'

'Thank you, sir,' Arabella said and fanned herself. 'I was a trifle warm.'

'And so I should imagine,' Jack replied. 'You were ill advised to dance with Maxwell, mistress. Has no one told you of his reputation?'

'I have danced with him before but he seemed different this evening...more offensive.'

As well he might with that malicious rumour circulating, Jack thought. No doubt the old goat had thought he might secure himself a pretty young mistress. 'Let me warn you to be careful of men like that,' he said. 'Forgive me if I presume, sweet lady, but I believe you may not yet have been in town long enough to realize what evil is abroad.'

'Thank you, sir. I know you are Lord Roxbourne's friend. We have met but briefly – but you were indeed kind to rescue me. I was desperate to escape but could not do so without giving offence.'

She glanced round the room, fanning her cheeks to cool them. The things that evil old man had said to her! She had been shocked by the lewd suggestions he had made to her.

How could he be so disrespectful to a young woman? Surely she had done nothing to make him imagine she might be open to an invitation of that sort?

'Ah, here is Roxbourne,' Jack said as the marquis came up to them. 'Gervase – a word with you in private if I may?'

'Later, Jack. I believe I know what you would tell me.' Gervase was frowning. He had noticed Arabella's discomfort while dancing and was relieved that Jack had rescued her, but having caught a whisper of the latest rumour he was angry – angry for Arabella's sake and angry with her. 'Mistress Arabella, I believe you need some air. Allow me to take you outside for a moment.'

Arabella was tempted to refuse, but she was still feeling bothered by the hot, damp touch of the earl's hands and assented to Roxbourne's offer. They walked to the end of the well-lit terrace but he did not suggest moving into the seclusion of the shrubbery, standing far enough away from her to observe the proprieties.

'You should refuse to dance with Maxwell and others of his ilk. Your reputation is in danger, Mistress Arabella. Have a care for it while there is yet time.'

'I shall never dance with that man again!' Arabella replied, but without her usual spirit. She was feeling sickened and humiliated and wished that she might be alone for a moment to recover. 'He – he asked, and I had no partner, but I did not expect...His behaviour was not what I might have expected...' She faltered and bit her lip as a wave of hot shame rushed over her.

'I shall make sure that Maxwell does not offend you again,' Gervase promised, a grim slant to his mouth. 'But you brought this upon yourself, Arabella. You have been too free with Sylvester and it has been noticed. I warned you what would happen. People are whispering and it gives scum like that a licence to behave as they will towards you.'

'I have done nothing wrong...' she began, but blushed and looked down as his eyes accused her. 'A kiss or two...But I have hopes that he will marry me.'

'Then you deceive yourself.' Gervase's voice was harsh, perhaps more so than he intended. 'I shall speak to Lady Mary. We must do what we can to scotch this tale or you may be ruined.'

'Surely not?' Her startled gaze flew to his. 'But I have truly not...I am innocent!'

'Society believes what it wishes to believe,' Gervase replied. 'It may be for the best if you leave town for a while.'

'But my sister's wedding...' She was close to tears. She had been more distressed by the filth that had been whispered to her by the lecherous earl than she cared to admit.

'After the wedding, of course.' Gervase's

expression softened slightly. 'Come, Mistress Arabella, have courage. Perhaps you will marry and return to town in triumph. As the wife of a country squire you may please yourself who you choose as a lover.'

'I have no wish to be the wife of a country squire,' Arabella snapped, her spirit returning as he provoked her. 'Nor do I intend to cuckold my husband as soon as I am wed. I know you think ill of me, sir, but...' She broke off as he laughed, delighted with his success at restoring her temper. 'Oh, I hate you. You love nothing better than to see me humbled.'

'You wrong me, mistress. I like not to see your spirit so worn down. And my opinion of you may not be what you imagine.'

'You speak in riddles to confuse me!'

'Do I, Arabella?' Gervase smiled oddly. 'Mayhap I shall speak in a manner more pleasing another time – but you are not yet ready to listen. My advice is that you should go away and reflect on what you truly want of life. You may see things differently then.'

Arabella stared after him as he bowed his head and left her. Her feelings were bruised, her thoughts in confusion. Was she really in danger of losing her reputation? Behind her she could hear music and laughter. Were they laughing at her? She believed some of them might be. Perhaps it was in part her own fault...but she loved Harry Sylvester.

She had done nothing that was so very wicked.

'Arabella!' She turned with a little start as she heard her cousin's sharp tones. 'What are you doing out here alone? I saw Roxbourne return...what did he say to you?'

Arabella walked slowly towards her. 'He said nothing that would please you, ma'am.'

'Can you wonder at it?' Lady Mary replied sourly. 'It is all over town, Arabella. Everyone believes you have lost your innocence to Sylvester.'

'No! It is a lie,' Arabella defended hotly. 'You cannot believe that, ma'am?'

'It is a matter of what society believes,' Lady Mary said. 'You are a foolish girl. Well, you have had your chance. I can do nothing more for you. You will leave town the day after your sister's wedding.'

Arabella watched as her sister was married to Sir John Fortescue. Nan seemed serene as she walked down the aisle to stand by his side, and when the ceremony was over she left the church to pealing bells with her hand proudly on his arm.

Arabella envied her a little as she was congratulated by the wedding guests and made much of by their friends. She wished that she might have married a man she could love and respect, but her letter to Harry Sylvester had brought no response.

He was not present at the wedding, and she heard someone say that he had left town in a hurry.

'His debts have caught up with him after last night,' one lady confided to a friend with a significant look in Arabella's direction. 'They say he is completely ruined.'

Arabella could not ask her cousin about the rumour, for Lady Mary had scarcely spoken to her since the night of Roxbourne's dance, but when she chanced to find Jack Meadows standing alone she plucked up the courage to ask him if the rumour was true.

'May I say you look beautiful,' Jack said and kissed her hand. 'You outshine the bride, mistress – but as for the question you ask, I know only that Lord Sylvester lost a great deal of money at the tables last evening. I can tell you no more than that. It would not surprise me if he had fled town, but I cannot say for sure that it is true.'

Arabella was certain that he knew more than he was prepared to say, but she dared not ask. Roxbourne was coming towards them with a determined gleam in his eyes, and she made her escape before he could join them, leaving the room with Nan as she went up to change into her travelling gown.

'You were a lovely bride,' Arabella said generously and kissed her sister. 'I wish you happiness and everything you wish for yourself, dearest.'

'Happiness...' Nan gave her a wintry look. 'You expect too much of life, Arabella. Until you learn that you cannot have all you want, you will make trouble for yourself. It is your own fault that you are to be banished to stay with our aunt. You will see no one there, for she is old and does not entertain, but in a few months I may send for you to join me.'

'I may ask Father if I can go home,' Arabella said. She might have said more but did not wish to quarrel with her sister. 'Come – may we not part as friends?'

'We have never been friends,' Nan said coldly. 'You were always the favourite and you did not notice. Oh, you smiled and called me sweet names when you chose, but you always had your own way. Well, now I have my way, and you will learn what it is to be humiliated.'

Arabella stared at her but remained silent as her sister swept from the room. She waited for a moment before following to join the other guests in throwing rose petals over the bride and groom, but she did not smile as she watched the carriage drive away. It was only as she turned to go back into the house that she noticed she herself was being watched.

'Lord Roxbourne,' she said. 'Have you come to say goodbye? I doubt we shall meet again. I am to leave for the country in the morning.'

'So I understand,' he said and smiled. 'Do not despair, Mistress Arabella. I dare say we shall meet again one day.'

'I am not in despair,' she replied, lifting her chin. 'I like the country. Perhaps I shall go home to my father.'

'Oh, I think not,' he replied softly, a gleam in his eyes. 'I believe Lady Mary has other plans for you.'

'She is not my guardian. My father will let me go home if I write to him.'

'Perhaps,' Gervase said. 'You must not be impatient, Arabella. All may not yet be lost...' He bowed his head and walked away, leaving her to stare after him as she had on the evening of his dance. Now, what did he mean by that? The provoking man! If he imagined it would please her to have the prospect of seeing him again he was mistaken. If she never saw him again it would be too soon! She tossed her head and walked into the house to be greeted by a smiling Lady Mary.

'Ah, there you are, Bella. Did you happen to see Lord Roxbourne before he left?'

'He said goodbye,' Arabella replied crossly. 'He is an impossible man. He said nothing that would please you, cousin.'

'Did he not?' Lady Mary's expression did not alter. 'Well, I dare say it does not matter. I have some news for you, Bella. Instead of

122

sending you to your great-aunt Rosalind, I have decided to send you to a friend of mine. She lives a few miles outside Bristol and goes into company more than your aunt. You have been a foolish girl, but there is no need to punish you too harshly – and it may be that you will find a husband there. They will not have heard that spiteful rumour, which I have done my best to scotch, and who knows? You may yet return to town as a bride.' She surprised Arabella by kissing her cheek. 'So do not despair, child. The blackest hour comes always before the dawn.'

Arabella stared at her. Now *she* was talking in riddles! It was too much. First Roxbourne and now her cousin...Alarm bells rang.

'And who is this lady I am to stay with, ma'am?'

'Oh, you would not have heard of her,' Lady Mary said airily. 'She does not come to London much these days, but we used to be close. Her name is Lady Margaret Spencer, and I think you will like her. She is not so very much older than you are yourself.'

Arabella was suspicious. 'Why, pray, should this lady be interested in me?'

'She is a friend, I told you,' Lady Mary replied. 'Pray do not ask so many questions, Arabella. Be thankful I have relented, and do not make me cross or I may change my mind again!'

Arabella opened her eyes as the carriage jerked to a halt. Because of various delays, due to changing the horses and some damage to a wheel, their journey had taken a day longer than expected. It seemed that they had arrived at last, however, for when the door was opened and the steps let down, she could see that they were outside a large country house. It was pretty rather than imposing, with a thatched roof and tiny leaded windows, but rambled over a considerable area in a haphazard way as though it had been added to as the family grew in importance.

'I vow I ache all over!' Arabella remarked to the woman who had been hired to accompany her on her journey.

Mrs Dunmore was a person of strict morals. 'Respectable and trustworthy', as Lady Mary had described her. 'Her duty is to escort you safely to Lady Spencer's house – so do not get any foolish ideas into your head.'

Arabella was not sure what she meant. Since she'd heard nothing from Harry Sylvester she thought it unnecessary for her cousin to warn her against doing anything foolish.

At times during the journey, Arabella had

felt close to weeping. She did not know Lady Spencer and would have preferred to go home to her father. Indeed, she had written asking his permission, but so far there had been no reply. She would write again once she was settled. However, she gave no sign of distress as she was helped from the carriage.

There were lights shining from all the windows in the house, and as a footman opened the door to admit Arabella and her companion, she could hear laughter and music. Her hostess was obviously holding a large party that evening.

'Ah yes, madam,' the footman replied as Mrs Dunmore announced them. 'Her ladyship expected you yesterday. She gave instructions that your rooms should be ready whenever you arrived. The housekeeper, Mrs Winterbottom, is busy with other guests at the moment, but if you will allow me to show you upstairs...'

'Well, really!' Mrs Dunmore pulled a face at Arabella. 'This is not what I would have expected.'

Arabella scarcely heard her. She had noticed that a young man who had just come into the hall was staring at her, and the wicked gleam in his eyes as they went over her made her first blush and then smile.

'Who have we here?' he asked, coming

towards them. 'Lady Maggie didn't tell me she was expecting a beautiful stranger in our midst.'

'Excuse me, sir,' Mrs Dunmore bristled at him. 'We have but this moment arrived after some days on the road and must change. Come along, Arabella!' She gave her a little push towards the stairs, obliging her to go ahead.

'Arabella...' the young man said and grinned. 'I shall remember you, fair goddess.'

Her spirits lifted. He was not Harry Sylvester, but he was young and handsome – perhaps her stay here would not be so very unpleasant after all.

She was smiling to herself as she was shown upstairs to a suite of very pretty rooms, which comprised bedchambers for her and Mrs Dunmore, a sitting room and a dressing room for Arabella.

'Now this is more like it,' Mrs Dunmore observed with satisfaction. 'Yes, this will do very nicely, Arabella.'

'Do you think Lady Spencer expects us to join her this evening?' Arabella asked, listening to the sounds of music and laughter that floated up to her.

'I intend to retire as soon as I have had my supper,' her companion replied. 'A tray is to be brought up for both of us, and I advise you to eat something and then go to bed. You may greet your hostess in the morning when she has more time to see to you.'

Arabella made no reply. She was curious about their hostess and would have preferred to join the company downstairs, but dared not do so without an invitation.

She contented herself with looking round her own room after taking off her travelling cloak, and was about to ring for a maid to help her undress when the door of her bedchamber opened. A young woman came in. She was a little plumper than Arabella, but very attractive with blond curls and blue eyes that sparkled with good humour.

'Oh, how lovely you are,' she said, coming to greet Arabella with hands outstretched. 'Welcome, my dear. I am delighted to have you here as my guest.'

'Lady Spencer?' Arabella's spirits took a flying leap. She was immediately drawn to her hostess and felt much better than she had in an age. 'It was good of you to have me.'

'Not at all. We do not often go to town, for my husband is not a well man.' She looked sad for a moment. 'But William loves company and he will adore you, Arabella.' She gave a delighted laugh. 'This party was to celebrate your arrival, for we expected you yesterday – will you not come down and join us?'

'I should love to, ma'am,' Arabella replied instantly. 'But I fear I am not dressed for the evening – my gown has become sadly crushed during the journey.'

'Oh, no one will mind that,' Lady Spencer replied. 'My friends all want to meet you.'

'Mrs Dunmore has retired...'

'You do not need her now that you have me,' Lady Spencer declared. 'Come, my dear. I shall take you down to meet everyone.'

Arabella made no further protest for she had longed to meet everyone and did not feel in the least like sleeping. Any guilt she might have felt at abandoning Mrs Dunmore to a lonely supper was banished by memories of her prim manner and fault-finding during the journey.

Her heart skipped a beat as she was taken into the large drawing room and introduced to the assembled company. The laughter and chatter died away as everyone turned curious eyes on her, bringing a faint blush to her cheeks, but then Lady Spencer began introducing her to a bevy of ladies and gentlemen. They all greeted her kindly, but she saw no sign of the young man who had cast such warm looks at her as she arrived.

It was only after several minutes that four young men came from the direction of what Arabella gathered was the games room, where they had been indulging in some sport. They all looked warm, as if they had been exerting themselves physically, and were greeted with teasing cries.

'Pray, tell us who won?' someone called out. 'Tell us the truth, Carstairs.'

As the men came further into the room, Arabella's heart jerked to a sudden stop and then raced on, beating so fast that she found it difficult to breathe.

'Why, Sylvester won, of course,' the young man who had stared at Arabella so earnestly earlier replied. 'Who else? He always beats us all at tennis.'

Across the room Arabella's eyes met those of Harry Sylvester. For a moment she thought she must be dreaming. Surely it could not be true? Harry, here this evening! When she had been thinking they might never meet again...

'There she is, the beauty I told you of...' Harry's friend was staring at her again in open admiration. 'What the Devil!' He had become aware of something in Harry's manner. 'Never say you know her! Damn my eyes, Sylvester! You have the Devil's own luck.'

Arabella caught her bottom lip with her teeth. Harry was coming towards her, a gleam of something between amusement and triumph in his eyes. 'Mistress Arabella,' he said. 'I am surprised and delighted to find you here this evening.'

'You know each other?' Lady Spencer

looked amazed, then gave a gurgle of laughter. 'How delightful. Arabella has come to stay with me for some weeks – and how long do you intend to stay with Mr Carstairs, sir?'

'Oh, some weeks,' Harry said vaguely and shrugged his shoulders eloquently. 'Until Carstairs throws me out, I dare say.'

'Which will be instantly if you claim a prior interest in Mistress Tucker,' John Carstairs quipped, coming to stand by Harry's side. 'This fellow has just beaten my friends at tennis, mistress, but I see no reason why he should have you all to himself.'

Arabella laughed. The way Harry was looking at her made her feel excited. Fate must be on her side to give her this unexpected opportunity. She had been sent here as a punishment, but now all kinds of possibilities had suddenly opened up. It would be far easier to meet Harry here than it had been in town!

'Oh, I think you should rather ask whether I have an interest in Lord Sylvester,' Arabella said, giving John Carstairs a flirtatious look. 'I choose my own companions, sir.'

'That's done for you, Sylvester!' Carstairs chortled, delighted by the reply. 'In that case, will you ride with me tomorrow, Mistress Tucker?'

'If Lady Spencer permits,' Arabella replied, glancing at her hostess, who seemed to be amused by the young men's rivalry.

'We shall all ride together,' she replied, 'but not tomorrow, gentlemen – the following day at eight. Tomorrow I want Arabella all to myself.'

Carstairs acknowledged her superior claim, but the teasing rivalry went on between Harry and his friend all evening as they competed to bring her wine and to engage her in conversation.

There was a far more intimate atmosphere here than there had been in the social gatherings in town, and Arabella found herself enjoying the affair so much that she was sorry when her hostess announced that she and Arabella were about to retire.

'No visitors tomorrow,' she decreed. 'But the day after we shall hold open house for anyone who cares to visit...'

She linked her arm with Arabella's as they walked up the wide staircase together, smiling at her with good nature.

'We shall have time to get to know one another tomorrow,' she said. 'I dare say you are tired now, and my dear husband will be exhausted, much as he loves to entertain.'

Having met Lord Spencer only briefly, Arabella had gained an impression of a gentle, rather frail man who adored his young wife and indulged her every whim. She had no doubt that it was Lady Spencer who loved to entertain her friends, and her husband who remained quietly in the background, watching and allowing her to do just as she wished.

'Is Lord Spencer really ill?' she asked now.

'Oh, it is nothing that causes him pain,' Lady Spencer replied. 'Merely a weak constitution. He must be careful not to take a chill, for his chest will not stand it, but otherwise...' She shrugged. 'But he makes nothing of it and so we all do our best to forget it.'

Arabella nodded, sensing that Lady Spencer had a true fondness for her husband despite the difference in their ages. She kissed her hostess goodnight, thanked her for a pleasant evening and went into her own chamber.

Later, when she was lying somewhere between sleep and wakefulness, she wondered what her cousin would say if she knew that Lady Spencer was entertaining the man she had been forbidden to see. It was odd that she had sent Arabella here rather than to her mother's elderly cousin.

Still pondering the reason for Lady Mary's change of heart, she fell asleep to dream of a man who told her that she was his heart's desire.

'And when do you expect to leave for the country?' Jack Meadows asked as he yawned over his wine. 'Forgive me...dashed tired.

Late night, don't you know? Or early morning...' He grinned at Gervase. 'Don't want me to come with you I suppose, keep you company?'

'It is merely business,' Gervase replied. 'You would be bored, my friend. Besides, I do not intend to remain long from town.'

Jack nodded, his eyes intent beneath the lazy lids that implied disinterest. It had not been lost on him that Gervase had been restless of late – ever since Mistress Tucker left town, which was over a week now.

'Only business?' he asked. 'I thought you visited your estates a couple of months ago?'

Gervase frowned, slightly annoyed by his friend's intrusion into his private affairs. He was not yet ready to speak of his plans – even to Jack, who had been privy to most of his thoughts for some years now.

'My cousin Maggie wants some advice,' he said, not quite truthfully. 'As you know, Spencer could die at any moment, and with no heir the estate will pass to a distant cousin. Maggie wants to be sure that she will be well provided for – without asking her husband.'

'Surely that was all sorted in the marriage contract?' Jack sensed that Gervase was being evasive and pressed the thorn deeper into his side. 'Where was it you said Mistress Tucker had disappeared to?'

'To stay with a friend of her cousin's, I

believe,' Gervase replied with a harsh look for the other. 'Sometimes you presume too much, Jack – and this is one of those times. Mind your own damned business!'

Jack laughed good-naturedly, for he had gained the information he needed without it actually being spoken of. 'Delighted, Gervase,' he murmured wickedly. 'I don't blame you one little bit – the beauty is well worth a little trouble. Besides, I didn't believe all that nonsense about her and Sylvester anyway.'

'I believe I know who started the rumour,' Gervase replied, a grim line to his mouth. 'If I knew for sure...But there is no point in making more trouble. Should I decide to ask Arabella, and should she accept, the rumours will cease at once – or I will want to know the reason why they continue.'

'No one would believe them if you married her,' Jack said. 'Your feelings for Sylvester are well known – though not your reasons for hating the man. They are a mystery to most...'

'And must remain so,' Gervase said, frowning once more. 'Sylvester has fifty creditors after him and will not dare to show his face in London for months, if not years. If he does he will be arrested and thrown into prison.'

'So you finally ruined him,' Jack said, a shiver running down his spine. 'There were times when I thought you had almost decided to let him go...that you had lost your taste for revenge.'

'Did you?' Gervase's eyes were cold as ice. 'Then you were mistaken. I have made an end to it.'

'Yes,' Jack agreed. But was it because of the old tragedy – or because Sylvester had come close to ruining another innocent girl? Jack had his own opinion on the matter, which he was wise enough to keep to himself. 'Then I shall bid you adieu,' Jack said, heaving himself from his chair. 'I look forward to hearing of you soon, Gervase. Good news I hope.'

Gervase lifted his brows but made no reply. He had not been certain before Arabella left town, but her going had left a surprising hole in his life and he had realized that the wench had come to mean more than he had ever thought possible. It seemed that the only way to have her was to marry her, and he had reluctantly decided that he must follow her sooner than he had planned.

He had thought a month or so in the country would give her time to reflect on her life as it was and as it might be with him, and yet he had still hesitated over asking her to wed him – still hoped he might gain her as a mistress. She was not his equal in birth, for he might have looked as high as he

135

pleased, but he had never intended to marry at all and thought himself a fool for contemplating it now.

Arabella was not in love with him. If she consented to take him it would be for the advantages such a marriage might bring her. Was he truly content to take her under those terms? His pride pricked and he had wrestled with himself for several sleepless nights, but she would not leave him be. His thoughts were constantly of Arabella, and he knew he would never rest until he had bedded her – but what then?

Gervase knew that there was every possibility that she would betray him with another man – perhaps even Sylvester. No, he would put a stop to that, even if it meant getting rid of that rogue. But if not Sylvester, then another...A woman who married without love could not be relied on to be faithful. He would be a fool to marry her...

And yet he could not put a very different picture of her from his mind. Sometimes in his dreams she came to him with love in her eyes, but she was not the Arabella he had tormented and teased in London. It was as if he were seeing her some years ahead, seeing a woman who had learned to regret.

Gervase gave himself a little shake. He had been disturbed by feelings he did not understand of late, and snatches of dreams haunted him...dreams that concerned Jack.

No, that was stupid! He put the foolish thoughts from his mind; there was no danger for his friend or for Arabella and these premonitions that came to him in the dark hours were merely a part of the black moods that had always descended on him from time to time.

It was his fault for dithering! He ought to have spoken to Arabella when she was in London. If he wanted her then he must marry – otherwise he must forget her now, but he knew that he could not forget her.

Gervase laughed ruefully as he came to this decision. He had taken so much time to make up his mind to ask her, and when he did so she would very likely refuse him. He was a fool and no doubt he would regret this decision one day, but now that it was made there was no point in delaying. He would go down to Bristol in the morning.

Six

'How long do you mean to torture me this way?' Harry demanded as he pressed Arabella against the trunk of an ancient oak. 'You know that I adore you, Bella. You must know that you haunt my dreams. I cannot sleep for wanting you.'

Arabella laughed up at him. She had enjoyed herself hugely this past ten days or more, setting Harry and John Carstairs against each other, for she knew that Harry was jealous.

'You torment yourself, my lord,' she murmured wickedly. 'You know that I love only you.'

'Then why will you grant me no more than a few kisses? I burn for you, Bella. I cannot think of anything but lying with you.'

'Oh, Harry...Do you truly love me so much?'

'You know I do.' He sighed and pulled a face at her. 'Damn it! I will marry you if I must.'

'You *will* marry me?' She felt her resolve melting as he pushed the bodice of her gown lower, his mouth seeking and finding her nipples, which were peaked with desire. 'You swear it, Harry – on your honour?'

He sensed that she was near to capitulation. 'I swear...I swear...' he muttered, pushing her back against the tree. His hand moved down her skirt, bunching it up, reaching beneath it, his hands searching for and finding that moist centre of her femininity. 'So hot...so wet,' he muttered greedily against her breasts. 'I knew you were ready for me. You want it as much as I do...'

Arabella was vaguely unhappy with this speech, but she was too far gone to resist him now, and she made no further protest as he bore her to the ground. Then he was parting her legs, probing with his fingers before mounting her. She felt the warmth and hardness of his member pressing against her inner thigh before he suddenly thrust into her, and she gave a little cry.

Her cry was muffled by his mouth on hers, his tongue inside her mouth, exploring hers, his possession of her greedy and urgent. Yet she was as eager for his loving, responding freely, giving herself to him, holding him to her as he spilled himself inside her.

For a few moments he lay heavy upon her, then he rolled on to his side and drew her with him in a comforting embrace, whispering words of love into her hair as he kissed her.

'I was too hasty,' he murmured, a note of apology in his voice. 'I have wanted you too long, my sweet. Will you forgive me? I promise to be more considerate next time.'

Arabella would have forgiven him anything at that moment. She *had* felt a sharp, tearing pain for a moment, but the pleasure of loving was all that mattered to her. She wished only that it might have gone on for much longer – and told him so, which made Harry give a shout of laughter and begin to caress her breasts once more.

This time he was more considerate, lingering over each stage of his lovemaking, and when he entered her again she gasped with pleasure. His thrusts were measured, slow and deep, making her writhe beneath him, the exquisite sensation mounting until she felt tears of joy on her cheeks. She had never known she could feel this way. If she died now it would not matter, for she had experienced paradise on earth.

It was a long time later that Harry helped her brush the debris from her gown and tidy herself.

'Oh, what do I care if anyone guesses,' Arabella cried, her eyes like stars as she laughed up at him in her new confidence. 'I belong to you now, Harry. No one can part us. We shall marry soon, shan't we?'

'As soon as I can find sufficient funds to provide for you,' he promised. At that moment he was reckless enough to promise her anything. 'I adore you, my sweet. We shall be married, but you must be patient for a while – and this must be our secret.'

'Why, Harry? I am sure my father would offer us a home with him. Nan paid his most pressing debts, and with you to manage the estate for him we would get by.'

The last thing Harry wanted was to be buried in the country with a wife and father-in-law to support, but he was wise enough not to tell her that for the moment.

'It was Roxbourne's fault that I had to leave town in a hurry,' he said bitterly. 'The man hates me, though I swear I do not know why. I must find a way to settle some of my debts before I can return – but my uncle may help me if he thinks I am ready to do my duty and settle at last.'

'Will you write and tell him that we are to be married?'

'Of course, Bella,' he replied, smiling as he lied. He had no intention of telling his uncle about her, though he might write some other news to his wealthy relative. However, he was not about to let this prize slip through his fingers too soon. When he'd had his fill of her he would put his plans into action, but for the moment he intended to enjoy her as often as he could. 'Trust me, my sweet. You know I adore you. Keep our secret until I have my uncle's blessing, that is all I ask.'

She could deny him nothing. Although she longed to shout her happiness to the world, Arabella managed to behave naturally as she went back to the house. Fortunately, she was able to go up and change for the evening without anyone seeing her, which was as well since she found a damp stain on her gown and blood on her linen.

She had just finished dressing when Lady Spencer tapped the door and came in. Arabella dismissed the maid, who took away her soiled gown to sponge and press it.

'Did you enjoy your walk this afternoon, my dear?'

'Yes, very much, thank you. It was such a lovely day. I walked as far as the lake and the wood beyond.'

'Goodness! No wonder you did not return to take tea with us. I was a little anxious, but my dear William thought you could come to no harm on the estate.'

'Oh, I was quite safe,' Arabella replied, feeling a little guilty at this evidence of her host's kindness. 'I met Lord Sylvester on my return. We stopped to exchange a few words.'

'Ah...' Lady Spencer laughed. 'That explains it.' She hesitated, then said, 'I have heard that my cousin plans to visit us. We may expect him next week. He would have been here sooner but has been delayed on

142

business.'

'Your cousin, ma'am?'

'Yes...' Lady Spencer seemed puzzled. 'I thought you knew Lord Roxbourne. Gervase is my cousin. It was his suggestion that you should come to stay with me.'

Arabella felt the shock run through her. How could she have been so stupid as not to have realized the significance of Lady Mary's change of heart? She ought to have known that there was some reason for it. She bit back the hasty words that rose to her lips. The situation was awkward and needed some careful thought. She must speak to Harry before she said or did anything rash.

'That will be pleasant, ma'am,' she said carefully. 'I knew you were a friend of my cousin's, but not of the connection to Lord Roxbourne.'

'Oh yes.' Lady Spencer smiled at her. 'I am very fond of Gervase. It was through him that I met my dear William. When he asked me to invite a young lady he admires and wishes to know better I was delighted to oblige. I have oft hoped that Gervase would find a woman he could be happy with for we feared that he might never marry.'

How could Lady Spencer be so misguided? There was no possibility of Lord Roxbourne offering for her, and if by some chance he did, she must refuse him. She was committed to Harry Sylvester now. In her own mind Harry was already her husband. She could never think of marrying anyone else.

'I am sure Lord Roxbourne will marry when he chooses,' she replied, a faint blush in her cheeks. 'You must realize that we are only a little acquainted.'

'Yes, of course – but that will not always be the case.' Lady Spencer smiled. 'You look lovely this evening, Arabella. Shall we go down and join the others?'

'What are we to do?' Arabella asked, looking at Harry anxiously the next afternoon. She had slipped away once more to meet him in the woods, blessing the fine weather that continued to make their affair possible. 'If Roxbourne comes...'

'I shall not be able to visit the house while he is there,' Harry said. 'Damn the fellow! Why must he come here now?'

Arabella did not tell him that she feared it might be on her account. 'I wish he would not come,' she cried. 'But it will not stop us meeting here like this. Oh, pray say it will not, Harry!'

'No – why should it?' he asked and pushed down the bodice of her gown to kiss and fondle her breasts. 'We can still meet here like this – as long as he knows nothing. If he discovers I am here I may have to leave in a hurry.'

'Oh, please do not say so!'

'He could have me arrested for fraud. I wagered money and property I do not own against him.'

'Oh, Harry...how could you?' She stared at him in dismay.

'He trapped me into it,' Harry said resentfully. 'Made it impossible for me to refuse to play against him. And then I lost so heavily that I was forced to pledge him money I did not have and a house that I had already sold.'

'You could go to prison for a long time.' Arabella was horrified, but more at the prospect of losing him than at what he had done. 'If you leave, will you take me with you?'

'I am not sure,' Harry began doubtfully. 'I have so little money, Bella. It would not be fair to you.'

'But I love you. I would rather be your wife in poverty than another man's in silk sheets.'

'My sweet Bella...how could I deny you anything?'

Harry took her down, making love to her hungrily and yet with sweetness. He cared for her as much as he had ever cared for any woman. She was beautiful, warm and generous in her loving. He would be loath to part from her too soon. At the back of his mind lingered yet another reason to take her with him...

Roxbourne wanted Arabella. London had been rife with rumours that he meant to marry her. Harry had taken a bet of five hundred guineas that he would not come up to scratch. He could never pay the debt if he lost, but Roxbourne would never offer if he knew she had been Harry's mistress. He was far too proud to marry a woman who had been used by a man he despised.

Yes, it might be worth his while to take her with him. She would be ruined, of course, but he eased his conscience with the thought that she had never been meant for marriage to some country squire. If she used her wits, she would find a wealthy protector when he left her. Yes, it would be much better for her than a life of obscurity in the country. One day she would thank him for it.

'Oh, Harry...' Arabella lay quivering in his arms, unaware of his thoughts as he rolled from her and gathered her against him. 'I am so happy...so very happy to be with you like this.'

'You were made for loving,' he murmured against her throat. 'You were born for this, Bella. I am privileged to have been your first lover.'

Arabella stiffened. What did he mean – her first? He had promised to wed her as soon as he could. She wanted to remind him of his promise but held her tongue, merely burrowing against him with a little mew of pleasure as his hand idly caressed her. If she nagged him too much he might go away without her.

'I love you,' she whispered. 'You will take me with you if you go?'

'Yes, of course, Bella. You know I adore you.'

A little doubt nagged at the back of her mind, but she refused to let it spoil her pleasure in the afternoon. Here in this place of dappled shade and sunlight, she had found true happiness. She had dreamed of being with him like this for so long, and she could not give him up now.

'Make love to me again, Harry,' she whispered.

'You are insatiable,' he murmured and laughed as he reached for her once more. 'That is why I cannot refuse you...'

Giving herself up to his loving, Arabella shut out her doubts. Harry loved her. He would take her away with him. He would marry her. He must! He must...

Gervase watched as Arabella walked across the lawns towards the house. She was carrying her chip-straw hat by its ribbons, and her glorious hair was hanging loose about her shoulders, glinting with red fire in the sunshine. His stomach clenched with desire

at the sight of her. She looked so beautiful...different somehow...that smile on her
lips...

She looked like a woman who had been
making love! Surely he was mistaken. She
had been here a little over two weeks. It was
not possible that she had found a lover in so
short a time.

'Ah, here she comes,' Lady Spencer said,
coming to stand at his shoulder in front of
the window. 'Arabella loves to walk. She
goes for long walks every afternoon, but I
think the exercise suits her. She has blos-
somed since she came here – do you not
think so?'

Perhaps it was merely the fresh air that
had brought that glow to Arabella's eyes,
but Gervase was suspicious. His gaze narrowed as she came in through the French
windows, giving a little start of surprise as
she saw him.

'Oh...I did not know that you had arrived,
sir.'

'You look very well, Arabella.'

'Thank you.' She blushed and glanced
down at the floor. 'I dare say the air suits me
here – and the weather has been wonderful
since I arrived.'

Was that a look of guilt he'd seen in her
eyes before she'd dropped her gaze – or
was he a jealous fool? Was he so besotted
with her that he must imagine she gave

148

her favours to others? He was worse than Shakespeare's Moor!

'So you have not been miserable here?'

'No, indeed, sir. Lady Spencer has made me very welcome, and her friends have all been kind to me.'

'Arabella has half the young men in the country running after her,' Lady Spencer trilled. She had immediately sensed Gervase's hunger and was determined that he should come to the point at last. 'I believe John Carstairs is in love with her and she is generally admired.'

'Oh no! You make too much of mere kindness,' Arabella disclaimed. Lady Spencer had not yet mentioned Harry Sylvester but she might at any moment. 'Mr Carstairs is a flirt, ma'am. You must know he does not mean the things he says.'

'You are too modest, Arabella,' Lady Spencer said with a naughty glance at Gervase. 'But I shall not make you blush, my dear. Indeed, I shall leave you to talk with my cousin for I have something I must say to my housekeeper.' She gave a gurgle of laughter and took herself off, leaving them to stare at one another in silence.

'I had no idea my cousin could be so rattle-headed,' Gervase remarked. 'Do not look so apprehensive, Arabella. No one expects you to live like a nun. You are young and beautiful and men will always admire you...' He was a fool to be jealous! He would conquer his feelings. 'Tell me, have you heard from your father?'

'No. No, I have not.' Arabella frowned. She had been too deep in her affair with Harry to think that strange until he asked, but now she wondered at it. 'I had expected him to write before this.'

'As I understand it he has been unwell,' Gervase told her. 'I was near your home a few days ago and called on him. He bid me tell you there is no cause for concern. It was merely a chill that went to his chest. He is feeling much better and sends you his constant love.'

'Thank you.' Arabella's eyes were unexpectedly moist. 'It was kind of you to call on my father, and to bring me news of him.'

'I can be kind sometimes,' Gervase said and smiled at her in a way that was oddly unsettling. 'It is just that I have a perverse sense of humour – and a wicked tongue. I fear that my teasing has given you a dislike of my company, mistress.'

'Oh...no, of course not,' she said, feeling flustered. He had never spoken to her so gently before and she did not know how to respond to a man she had never glimpsed or suspected existed. 'That is...you have made me angry several times, sir.'

'I know it and must beg your pardon for it,' Gervase admitted wryly. 'Come, Arabella

– may we not be friends? I would be a kind friend to you if you would let me.'

She felt shy as she looked at him, wondering whether to believe in this man or not. Surely this could not be the same man she had cursed a hundred times? She had always been sensible of his charm, though it had not often been turned on her, but this soft note to his voice was almost mesmerizing. She seemed drawn to him against her will.

'I–I don't know. Perhaps,' she said hesitantly.

'You do not trust me,' Gervase said. 'I cannot blame you, for I have behaved ill towards you, but I shall make amends. Lady Spencer tells me you like to walk. Perhaps you will allow me to walk with you tomorrow?'

It was the last thing she wanted! Arabella's mind broke free of the spell he had seemed to cast over her. She remembered that he was Harry Sylvester's enemy and therefore hers.

'I prefer to walk alone,' she said. 'But we shall be friends if you wish it, sir. Perhaps you would like to ride with us in the morning? Your cousin and I usually ride with a few friends most days.'

Gervase had sensed her withdrawal. Despite his determination not to judge her, he was suspicious. Why did she want to walk alone – was it because she was meeting a lover?

This man, John Carstairs, had he taken Harry Sylvester's place in her affections? If she was so shallow she was not worth his attention. He would do better to ride away now and never see or think of her again.

Damn the wench! He was caught like a rabbit in a trap. She held him whether he liked it or not.

'You are late,' Harry accused, giving her a sullen look the next afternoon. 'I have been waiting half an hour – and there was a shower of rain. I was forced to shelter in a woodsman's hut.' He sounded indignant.

'I could not come while it rained,' Arabella said. 'It would have looked so odd if I had insisted – and Lord Roxbourne is suspicious. He says nothing but I feel him watching me.'

'So he is here then?' Harry was annoyed. 'I had hoped he would change his mind.'

'Yes, he was there when I got back yesterday.' She glanced over her shoulder, half expecting to find that he had followed her. 'I cannot stay long. Lady Spencer was not pleased that I came out at all.'

'What does it matter?' Harry demanded, reaching for her. He pushed her against the tree. She could feel the wet bark making her gown damp and tried to pull away, but Harry held her there. He pulled her skirt up, thrusting his knee between her legs almost viciously. She made a slight protest, but his mouth was on hers and in a moment she felt the pulsating heat of his manhood probing at her. He lifted her, holding her as he thrust himself into her, taking her angrily, more roughly than he had since that first time.

Arabella felt anger at being so roughly used, but then the excitement of what he was doing to her overcame her scruples and she moaned as her knees trembled. She was faint with pleasure. His roughness was exciting her even as it angered her, though at the back of her mind a nagging worm reminded her that he had not troubled to ask if she were willing.

As he slumped against her, spent and moaning softly, she sank her teeth into the lobe of his ear. He gave a yelp that was as much surprise as pain and clapped a hand to his ear.

'Why did you do that?'

'To remind you that I am not a thing to be used without so much as a by your leave!'

Harry saw the glint in her eye, not sure whether to react in kind or be amused by her flash of spirit. He gave a rueful smile as he saw blood on his fingers. Her teeth had broken the skin. 'Vixen,' he muttered. 'I should teach you some manners.'

'Mayhap you should learn some!'

'You can be a bitch, Bella.' Harry laughed. 'But I deserved it.'

'Yes, you did.' She was not to be won so easily.

'It was your speaking of that devil Roxbourne,' he grunted. 'He has destroyed me, Bella. I have nothing but a few coins I won from Carstairs last night.'

'Why does he hate you, Harry?'

'I think he hates anyone who might be a rival to him,' Harry replied. 'I don't think I can stay here more than a few more days. Carstairs was talking of moving on...going to see a bare-knuckle fight.'

'You won't go with him?'

'If I can win a few guineas I'll go back to London,' Harry said. 'I could stay at an inn outside of town – try to find a few games. If I can win several hundred guineas I might settle my most pressing debts.'

'You have heard nothing from your uncle?'

He had not written, but he shook his head and pulled a wry face of regret. 'The old skinflint would probably do nothing for us, Bella. I fear we must live on our wits, my sweet.'

'But you will let me come with you?'

'Yes – have I not given my word?'

Roxbourne had come here for a reason, and now that he'd had time to reflect on it, Harry knew what it must be. He wanted

Arabella, Harry was certain of it. He would snatch her from beneath Roxbourne's nose. It made him laugh inside to think of the marquis's fury when he realized that he had lost the woman he wanted to make his wife.

'When shall we go?' Arabella asked. 'I am frightened Lord Roxbourne might discover that I am meeting you. If he follows me and sees you he could cause trouble for you.'

'Tomorrow. We'll go tomorrow,' Harry promised, suddenly reckless. He would make sure he won heavily that evening. Carstairs was a careless player. Harry could easily have taken more from him before this, but had been careful not to anger his host. He had served his purpose and could be discarded once his guineas were in Harry's pocket. 'Yes, we'll go tomorrow. Make some excuse when the others go riding. Slip away and meet me here – I'll have a carriage waiting.'

'Oh, Harry!' Arabella flung her arms about him. 'I do love you. We'll run away together and then we'll be married. It will be wonderful.'

Harry kissed her. He was tempted to make love to her again, but there would be plenty of time for that now. He had not yet tired of her, which was surprising, for he usually lost interest after a woman gave herself to him. He would never marry her of course, but he might keep her with him for a few weeks – just until he was ready to move on.

'Arabella...' Gervase smiled as he saw her walking through the wood towards him. She was alone. He had thought she might have come here to meet a lover, but he had misjudged her. 'You look like a wood nymph.'

'And what does a wood nymph look like, sir?' Arabella laughed. She was too happy to be sulky even with him. In the morning she was going away with Harry! They would be married and then she would send word to her father. She had a small dowry left her by her mother, and that would help them survive until Harry was on his feet again.

'Beautiful, wild and free,' Gervase said, describing Arabella as she seemed to him at that moment. 'Arabella, I know you do not yet trust me, but I must tell you that I have come to admire you...'

She stared at him, shocked. What was he saying? He could not mean it? Was he about to make her an offer?

'I pray you...' She stopped, catching her breath as he moved closer. He was going to kiss her! She could see his purpose in his eyes and knew she must prevent it. This must not happen – it was too late. What did she mean, *too late*? Her thoughts whirled in confusion. It was not right. She was suddenly terrified of being kissed by him. 'No! No, you must not!' She dodged past him and started running. She knew that he must not kiss her, that it would be a terrible mistake if she allowed it, though she did not know why.

'Arabella! Come back! There's no need to be frightened. I did not mean to startle you.'

She heard Gervase calling to her but sped on regardless. She must not listen to him, must not be persuaded by that look in his eyes – a look that had frightened her. Why should she be afraid of that look? It touched something buried deep within her – and she must not allow it to do so. She belonged to Harry! She was going away with him. She would be his wife and it was what she wanted with all her heart.

Arabella was panting by the time she reached her bedchamber. She stood with her back against the door, trembling all over. How foolish! How stupid of her to bolt like a frightened filly. Lord Roxbourne had meant her no harm. He would not have raped her. She was almost certain that he had been on the verge of proposing marriage to her.

He must not! It was impossible. Too late. She did not want him to speak. She was not sure why, but she knew she would do all she could to prevent him from speaking.

★ ★ ★

Arabella was reluctant to go down to dinner that evening, yet knew she must face Roxbourne. Somehow she must keep a distance between them this last evening.

To her relief there was no sign of him in the drawing room. Lady Spencer's guests were gathering for the card party she was giving that night, but Roxbourne was not amongst them.

'Gervase had some business in Bristol,' she told Arabella. 'A nuisance, but necessary I gather. He asked me to give you his apologies – and this.' She handed Arabella a small package. 'I have no idea what it contains. Do open it, my dear.'

Arabella did so reluctantly. She stared at the magnificent jewel lying on a bed of black silk. It was a huge emerald set in a square of diamonds and pearls.

'I cannot accept this,' she breathed. 'It is too valuable.'

'A mere bauble to a man of Roxbourne's wealth,' Lady Spencer said. She took the brooch and pinned it to Arabella's gown. 'There, my dear. It looks well on you. Gervase said he had upset you. He wished to make amends. Accept it, to please me if nothing more.'

'What can I say – it is too precious but I must take it if you wish it.'

'You must not misjudge my cousin,' Lady Spencer said gently. 'I know he can sometimes seem harsh – and he does tease one so – but he has a good heart. I believe he would be a devoted husband to the woman he loved. Gervase is a man of strong passions, my dear, but he is generous to a fault. You could do worse...'

Arabella turned away with a blush. She felt terrible. Lady Spencer had been kindness itself. She would be hurt and angry when she discovered that Arabella had abused her hospitality.

She had made several friends here, Arabella realized as the evening progressed. These people were warmer and kinder than many she had met in London. She might have been happy living amongst them had things been otherwise.

She must not allow herself to have such thoughts! It was too late for regrets now – she had no regrets! Of course she didn't! She had gained her heart's desire. She was going away with Harry in the morning and they would be married...

Arabella gathered together the things she could carry with her. Just a few undergarments and an extra dress. She looked ruefully at some of the pretty gowns she would be forced to leave behind, but of course they could be sent on later.

She packed a few of her personal treasures – a silver-backed hairbrush given to her by her father, her mother's pendant, and the brooch Lord Roxbourne had sent her the previous evening. She hesitated over this last, twice laying it on the dressing chest before picking it up again. She ought not to take it with her. It was not morally hers, even though Lady Spencer had insisted that she take it.

Her hostess was resting in her room, complaining of a headache. Arabella had sent word that she was too tired to go riding that morning. She must use this opportunity to slip away.

She walked down the stairs clutching her bundle, her heart racing. Supposing someone saw her? Supposing they tried to stop her?

She reached the back parlour unchallenged, leaving through the French windows and running across the expanse of smooth lawn as fast as she could. She felt sick and guilty somehow, and close to tears. Everyone would think she was wicked to behave so badly. Her hostess would be angry that she had sneaked off without a word. She had considered leaving a letter but decided against it. Better to say nothing until she could tell her father she was married to the man she loved.

She did love Harry. She did! This guilty, anxious feeling, this sense of loss would go when she was with him. It was foolish to feel so low when she was gaining everything she had longed for.

Reaching the woods, Arabella caught a glimpse of an elegant carriage beginning to sweep through the grounds of the Spencers' house. She thought it was probably Lord Roxbourne returning from his business in Bristol, and the thought made her increase her pace. She must reach Harry before Lord Roxbourne discovered that she was missing! Something told her that he would come after her if he guessed that she was running off with Lord Sylvester.

He must not find her! She did not know why the thought of Lord Roxbourne's anger should disturb her so, but it did. She must not allow him to take her back...

Arabella walked quickly through the trees until she saw the carriage drawn up at the edge of the wood where it joined the high road. Harry was pacing up and down, look-ing anxious. Her heart lifted as she saw him.

'Harry...'

'You came.' He smiled and moved to take her bundle from her. 'I thought you might change your mind. You are a brave girl, Bella.' For a moment he genuinely admired her courage and felt the nearest thing to love he had ever experienced.

'I love you, Harry.'

'I know you do.' He kissed her briefly on the mouth, then opened the carriage door for her to get in. 'Quickly, Bella! I do not want to be stopped now.'

Arabella obeyed. She was trembling as she sank back against the squabs. There was no going back now. She was a fallen woman and soon everyone would know of her shame. She thought of her father's disappointment and it was like a thorn pricking her heart. He would understand. He must understand! She would write and beg him to forgive her as soon as she and Harry were married.

She turned to smile at Harry as he climbed into the carriage with her after giving the driver the order to move off.

'Where are we going?'

'To London,' he said and grinned at her. 'We're rich, Bella. I won five hundred guineas last night from Carstairs. He was none too pleased this morning, but he paid up. We have money to keep me going at the tables. My luck has turned. You'll see, we'll be rolling in it before long.'

Arabella wasn't certain she shared his optimism. Five hundred guineas was indeed a fair sum – they might have lived comfortably on it for a year or more in the country – but money was as easily lost as won at the tables. How long would it be before Harry was in debt again?

Once they were married she would try to make him see sense. They could go home to her father and live quite comfortably on what Harry could earn by managing the estate with economy. Yes, she would wait until they were wed and then she would persuade him that they should make their home with Sir Edward.

Her sense of panic was beginning to fade. There was no need to feel guilty. She was doing nothing so very wrong. And Lord Roxbourne would soon forget all about her...

'Gone! What do you mean, gone?' Gervase stared at his cousin in growing frustration. 'How can she have simply disappeared? Has she taken her clothes?'

'I think one or two things are missing...I cannot be sure.' Lady Spencer sighed. 'I had a headache and stayed in bed. I thought Arabella meant to ride with friends, but apparently she sent word that she was tired.'

'Have you made a search for her?'

'Yes. At least I have sent a servant to look for her. I did not wish to make a fuss. She may have gone home or something. She seemed a little odd last evening. I thought perhaps you had quarrelled with her?'

'We did not quarrel.' Gervase scowled. 'I went to the receiving office on my way back here. There was a letter from her home, which I have taken the liberty of opening.'

'Gervase! You had no right.' Lady Spencer

was shocked.

'I had news myself – her father is desperately ill. She is requested to return at once.'

'Perhaps she has gone home,' Lady Spencer suggested, looking relieved. 'She may have got word...'

'How? Has any other letter come for her?'

'Not to my knowledge. Perhaps her friend told her – he may have heard.'

'What friend?'

'Oh – I forgot. He has not been to the house since you arrived. A young man, a friend of Mr Carstairs – Lord Harry Sylvester. They know each other – a family friend I imagine.'

'Sylvester has been here in this house?'

Lady Spencer gasped as she saw the fury in his eyes. 'Yes – is something wrong with that, Gervase? He appeared to be a pleasant enough man. Always respectful. Arabella seemed to like...' She clapped a hand to her mouth. 'You do not think...? No, surely not! She would never do something so wicked – would she?'

'I do not know, but Sylvester is a careless rogue. She would not be the first innocent he has duped and ruined.'

'Oh, Gervase! I did not know. Truly I did not.'

'Mine is the fault,' he said grimly. 'I have kept silent too long. I should have spoken out long ago. Sylvester ruined my sister and abandoned her. She died of shame after giving birth to his child, who later died of neglect. And that was my father's shame.'

'My dear...forgive me. I would never have had that evil man in my house...'

'You could not know.' Gervase's eyes were bleak. 'We do not yet know that she has gone with him. I beg you, Margaret, be discreet. I must go to her home and do what I can for her father.'

'She may be there,' Lady Spencer said. 'Yes, yes, she may be there.'

'I pray God she is,' Gervase replied. 'But I fear she has gone with Sylvester.'

'Then she is ruined.'

'Yes.'

He turned and strode from the house without another word.

Seven

Gervase's mood had not improved since his return from the country some six months earlier. Jack had been told little of what had transpired there, but he had deduced that Arabella had disappeared, seemingly without trace.

'Damn the wench,' he said now and received a scowl for his pains. 'She isn't worth it, Gervase. No woman is.'

'I promised her father on his deathbed that I would find her,' Gervase replied, his tone cold, emotionless, hiding the tumult of anger and fear raging inside him. 'It is for no other reason that I have spent so much time trying to find her.'

'She might be anywhere,' Jack pointed out reasonably. 'If she went with him—'

'We do not yet know for certain that she did,' Gervase snapped, angry despite knowing that his friend was probably speaking the truth. 'I have found no evidence, though my agents have made countless inquiries.'

'Did not one of them say a young woman resembling Mistress Tucker had been seen in a coach with a man on the London road?'

'There was one sighting, but Sylvester is so damned devious it might easily have been a ploy to deceive. As yet, I've had no reports of his being seen in his old haunts.'

'Surely he would not dare to show his face in town?' Jack said, and raised his brows. 'He must know he would be arrested.'

'Sylvester must live on what he wins at the tables,' Gervase replied. 'If he found somewhere on the road where he could use his talents to his advantage, he might linger there. Indeed, it might serve his purpose better than being in town.' His eyes were bleak as he looked at Jack, betraying more than he knew. 'Where is she, Jack? What has he done to her?'

'You fear she may be dead, that she may have perhaps killed herself in a fit of despair?' Jack guessed at his private nightmare. 'Nay, my friend, you let your memories mislead you. Mistress Tucker is not your sister. Helen was gentle and timid, easily brought to tears and shamed. Arabella Tucker is a survivor. She would not take her own life – even if he abandoned her as he did Helen.'

'You are a good friend.' Gervase smiled. 'I must believe you, for otherwise I am damned. I should have told her what kind of a man he was.'

'The blame was not yours.'

Jack privately thought the wench had always been ripe for seduction, and wondered at Gervase's interest in her. She was beautiful, but there were other women as lovely. What was it about her that tormented Gervase?

Gervase could not have answered him had he asked. In the night when he woke from a nightmare, sweating and tormented, he told himself angrily to forget her. She was just another woman – and she had chosen to run away with the man he hated above all others.

He should forget her – and yet the thought that she might be alone and in trouble would not let him rest, haunting his dreams until he cried out and woke in fear. He must find her and make certain she was not harmed, if only to fulfil the promise he had given to her father as he lay dying.

Where had Sylvester hidden her? Were they still together? Knowing what a careless rogue Sylvester was, Gervase thought he might have abandoned her long since.

He must and would find her – somehow!

'Why must we move again?' Arabella asked. She was feeling tired, even though she carried her pregnancy well and still looked beautiful at nearly six months gone. 'You said we were going to London. You promised we would marry once we got settled there.'

'And we shall,' Harry said and stooped to drop a kiss on top of her head. She still smelled as good as ever, though her life had not been easy these past months as they travelled from inn to inn, never staying in one town for more than a few days at a time. He wondered at himself that he had not left her behind in one of those towns. Once he had left their bed meaning to sneak off before she woke, but she had called out to him softly in the darkness and he had gone back to her. Besides, he had been lucky at the tables and he half believed she had brought him the luck – and he still wanted her. 'You shall have your way, Bella,' he said now and grinned at her. 'We're going to London this afternoon.'

'Truly?' She had been resting on the oak settle in their bedchamber with her back against a cushion, but now she jumped up and hugged him. 'And we shall be wed?'

'Don't nag me, Bella,' Harry said. 'I'm taking you to London. I'm sick of moving from town to town in the hope of finding a young fool I can fleece. Last night I won a paltry five guineas. It's not enough. I need a rich pigeon for plucking and I'll find him in London.'

Arabella looked at him doubtfully. Once she would have asked him if he cheated the young men he played with night after night.

It was not often that he lost these days, and she could not help wondering if there was more than luck and skill on his side. However, they had argued fiercely on three occasions when she had pushed him too far, and she was afraid to do it again.

A part of her still believed that he loved her, that he would eventually marry her, but the doubts were more prevalent these days. Harry was capable of wild mood swings – one moment charming and loving, the next sullen and withdrawn. She had learned that the only way to tease him out of his moods was to coax him to bed. Sometimes she wondered what would happen in the last months of her childbearing. Would Harry grow tired of seeing her body heavy and swollen? Would he leave her when he did?

No! She denied the traitorous thought as unworthy. Harry loved her. He must. He must...She felt the sob rise in her throat as a wave of unbearable misery swept over her, but she held it back. She must never let Harry see her when she was less than her best.

Arabella's worst moments were when she thought of her father. She had almost written to him several times, but shame had made her hold back. If Harry married her she could beg her father to forgive her, but until then she was afraid of what he might say or do.

She knew that in the eyes of the world she was ruined. No decent woman would acknowledge her now, let alone invite her into her home. Lady Mary would think her a fool and Nan...Arabella did not wish to imagine what her sister might say.

Arabella did not think about the Marquis of Roxbourne. Whenever her thoughts strayed that way, she cut them off sharply. He would have forgotten her by now. He had warned her that she would be ruined, and no doubt he was congratulating himself on having had a lucky escape.

No, she would not think about him.

'A penny for your thoughts, Bella?'

She smiled up at Harry. 'I was thinking I might buy a new gown when we go to London – my old ones are becoming rather tight.'

'You should have said.' He took ten guineas from his pocket and gave them to her. 'That should buy you something pretty.'

Arabella smiled and thanked him. Used wisely, the money would enable her to buy several things she needed for herself and her child, for she would visit one of the establishments in London where it was possible to purchase good quality second-hand clothes. She would hoard her small store of money carefully. Harry was generous when he had money in his pocket, but his luck would surely not last for ever.

She must have something by her in case he needed it.

'Oh, Harry – this is wonderful!' Arabella cried as she looked round the tiny house he had taken for them. It was situated in the quiet area of Hampstead not far from the heath. 'So much nicer than the inns we've been staying in.'

'I thought it would be better for you,' Harry said, his eyes moving over her reflectively. She was seven and a half months gone now and beginning to look awkward, her skin a little blotchy and pale. Until this last week he had still wanted to make love to her, but his interest had waned. 'You will have Betsy to look after you – and you will need her soon.'

Betsy was the maid he had engaged to look after her and the house. A nice, pleasant girl who seemed to find nothing odd in the situation between her mistress and master.

'You are so good to me,' Arabella said and kissed him on the lips. 'It is a lovely little home for us.'

'Well...I may not be here often,' he told her, his gaze sliding away from her bright eyes. 'My work is in the gaming clubs and I must stay late to be sure of winning. I cannot come all the way out here afterwards. And you will be comfortable here with your maid to care for you.'

'Not here...' She swallowed the cry of protest that rose to her lips. She knew that he was beginning to find her unattractive, that he thought her body ugly and ungainly. 'You will visit sometimes?'

'Of course. I shan't abandon you, Bella. I want to see my son sometimes, and I'll look after you.' He smiled at her, feeling a return of the affection he had had for her. 'But I must win money for all of us.'

Arabella's spirits lifted as he kissed her. She would not look ugly and awkward for ever. Harry would love her again after the child was born, and if she gave him the son he insisted she was carrying, he might marry her.

She had ceased to ask when they were to be married now; it merely served to make him look sullen and she knew that if she pushed him too far he might walk away. Her illusions had faded, and she knew him for the selfish, careless man he was – but she still loved him. And sometimes they were happy together.

'This is for you and the baby,' Harry said, giving her a little pouch of soft leather. 'Fifty guineas. Take care of it, Bella. I was lucky last night, but you know that I may lose one day.'

Was that guilt or fear in his eyes? Arabella wasn't sure, but she sensed he was uneasy.

'Is something wrong, Harry?'

'No, of course not – why should anything be wrong?' He avoided her gaze. He had met some men he knew the previous evening, and it could only be a matter of time before Roxbourne learned he was in town. He drew Arabella towards him, kissing her on the lips. At least he had taken her from the marquis – nothing and no one could deny that. 'I have to go now. I'm not sure when I'll be back. Take care of yourself and my son.'

Arabella clung to him as he kissed her, her throat tight, stomach churning with emotion, but she did not weep or beg him to stay. It would only annoy him. She must pray that he came back to her when he was ready.

'I shall be thinking of you.'

'I'll be back.' Harry grinned at her in his old, confident way. 'You can't lose a bad penny, Bella. You haven't seen the last of me yet.'

She nodded but could not speak, letting him go as he pulled away from her. Something inside was telling her that her dream was over, but she would not listen to the devil that tormented her when Harry was away from her. He would come back – he had promised.

But he had promised to marry her...

★ ★ ★

'You say Sylvester was gaming at the Black Hood two nights ago?' Gervase looked hard at the man who had brought him the information he had sought so long. 'That is one of the worst gaming hells in London – only fools and knaves play there.'

'Yet it attracts foolish young gentlemen who think it is clever to go somewhere their friends dare not,' the agent replied. 'It is known that more than one gentleman has lost his fortune at the tables there – and his life in one case we both know of.'

'Yes, you are right.' Gervase nodded, a grim smile on his mouth. 'So he has been forced to come back and show himself at last. You have been keeping a watch there for him?'

'Yes, of course, my lord. He was followed last night to an inn nearby.'

'And the lady?'

'Not there, sir.' Agent Rossiter shook his head. 'Lord Sylvester was alone at the inn. The lady you seek has not been seen there.'

'Keep watching and following him,' Gervase instructed. 'The moment anyone thinks they have found her I am to be informed.'

'Yes, of course, sir. My men all have their instructions.'

'You have done well to find him,' Gervase said. 'Thank you.' He handed the agent a purse of gold. 'Five hundred guineas to the man who finds her, on top of your fee.'

'That is generous, my lord. We'll scour every inn in London. She will be found. I give you my word.'

Gervase nodded, dismissing him. He had hoped that when they found Sylvester they would also find Arabella, but his worst nightmare was that she was lost – either ill or dead.

By God, Sylvester would pay if she had suffered because of his carelessness. He would give him a week or two, allow him to lead them to Arabella if he would, and then...

Harry looked uneasily over his shoulder. He had felt that he was being followed these past few days, but he wasn't sure who was behind it. He had fleeced more than one foolish young man at the tables and there was always the possibility that one of them might try to take his revenge in a dark alley.

It might be that his creditors had got wind of his being in town. Harry knew that he had been recognized by men who would once have invited him to their homes. Which meant that he might have to leave town in a hurry.

He would not be taking Arabella with him. She was well into her eight month of pregnancy now. He had not been to visit her since he'd given her the fifty guineas. A part of him felt guilty, but there was no point in dwelling on it. She had come with him of her own free will, and he was not prepared to drag a woman who might give birth at any moment all over the country. She would slow him down, hamper his decisions.

He had only two choices, he realized. Go abroad or...He glanced over his shoulder once more as two large men came towards him out of the gloom. Fear clutched at his guts and he started to run.

'Come back, sir!' one of the men shouted. 'You can't get away. I have a warrant for your arrest...'

He had delayed his departure too long! He should have left town the instant he saw those friends of Roxbourne at the hell.

He turned and fled down the nearest alley, hoping to reach the river and perhaps evade his pursuers, but even as he thought he might be getting away from them, two more burly figures stepped out to confront him. Harry put up a fight, punching and struggling as they grabbed him, trying his best to get away again, but the others had caught up with them and he was surrounded, outnumbered.

'Come along, sir. There's no point in resisting and causing more trouble for yourself. Debts are one thing – don't make it a hanging matter.'

Harry gave up. In the Fleet he would live

as well as he could afford to. If he could get food and wine sent in he would be able to survive until he could find a way of settling his debts.

Roxbourne could whistle for his money. It was the money he owed to various tradesmen that must be found. Roxbourne would never press for payment of a gambling debt – it wasn't the done thing, and the marquis was too proud to soil his hands with such a sordid matter.

No, if he could but find a way of paying his other creditors he would be in the clear, though he might still not be able to retake his place in society. For a moment he regretted the fifty guineas he had given Arabella, but it was a mere drop in the ocean. He would send word, for she might help him with money for food, but if he hoped for release he must look elsewhere...

Harry had been arrested for debt and was in prison. The pain of it swept over her, making her feel dizzy and ill. It had been two weeks before the news of his imprisonment finally reached her, and she had been at her wits' end, wondering if she would ever see him again.

Arabella read the letter through again before laying it on the table beside her. Harry had written in terms of endearment, apologizing for what he had brought her to and telling her that he had been afraid of ending like this, and for this reason alone had decided to cut the ties with her.

For if my creditors knew of your existence, they might try to obtain payment of debts from you, Bella. You must not trouble yourself over me, for I know your time is near. Think only of yourself and the child, and forget me. Your loving Harry...whom you should never have loved.

Arabella wept bitter tears over his letter. Her poor, dear Harry was in prison for debt and the last thing he had done was to take a house for her and give her fifty guineas. His letter convinced her that he loved her and that she had been both wicked and cruel to doubt him. Loneliness had made her almost regret ever having loved him, but now her faith was renewed and all she could think of was his suffering, her own misery of the past few weeks forgotten.

She regretted now that she had spent most of the money on things for the child. Harry needed help. She must find money for him somehow. He loved her and she must go to him as soon as she could.

Twenty guineas were all she had left of the money he had given her. He was welcome to that, of course, but it would not last long in prison, for everything he wanted would be charged at double the cost. The wardens made money from buying food for the inmates, and everyone knew they cheated the poor souls who could not get out to purchase their own food, and had no relatives to do it for them.

What could she sell to help him? If she could find enough money he might be able to pay the most pressing of his debts and then they might release him. She fingered her mother's pearl pendant, thinking with reluctance that it was the only thing she had of value, and then she remembered the brooch Lord Roxbourne had given her.

It was not hers to sell, not truly. She ought not to sell it. She ought not to have taken it in the first place, but she had and it was too late for regrets.

He would be angry if he knew his gift had been sold to help a man he hated, but he need never know. If Arabella could raise sufficient money to settle some of Harry's debts, they could leave London and go back to the country. He might even be grateful enough to marry her, and then she could go home and beg her father to take them in.

The goldsmith looked long and hard at the woman who had brought him the costly jewel. It was always difficult to know how to handle the purchase of something like this. The emerald was fine and rare in that it had few flaws. Greed tempted him to offer her a few guineas for it, but she looked as though she were gently born and might have influential friends, and it would do his business no good to have it said that he had cheated her. The brooch had probably cost the purchaser at least five hundred pounds in his estimation, though because of its rarity it might be more. He must think of his profit, but he would offer a fair price.

'I'll give you two hundred and fifty pounds for it,' he said and held his breath.

Arabella held back her gasp of dismay. She had expected to be offered no more than a hundred guineas at most, and she hesitated for a moment. If the brooch was so valuable, perhaps she ought to find a way of returning it to the marquis.

The goldsmith mistook the reason for her hesitation. Having offered for the brooch he did not now want to lose it. 'Very well, three hundred pounds – and that's my last offer. You won't get more, mistress.'

Three hundred pounds! It seemed a small fortune to her. She squashed her scruples. She must not allow her doubts to stop her helping Harry as much as she could.

'I will take it,' she said before he could change his mind.

She tucked the money into a small pouch and placed it inside the bodice of her gown, pulling her cloak tightly about her. Knowing she was carrying such a large sum of money made Arabella nervous as she summoned the driver of a rather shabby coach, which was waiting for hire at the side of the road.

She asked to be driven to the Fleet debtors' prison. He looked her over, taking in the shabby condition of her clothes, and demanded payment of two shillings in advance. Arabella paid him from a purse at her waist, which contained only a few shillings and coppers.

The Fleet ditch had once been notorious for its stench, which came from all the filth that had been thrown into its murky waters. The criminals who lived in the narrow courts and alleys of this district often disposed of dead bodies there. After the Great Fire of London, the ditch had been converted into Bridewell Dock, extending from Fleet Street to the river. It had been arched over in 1765, giving place to New Bridge Street, but many of the wretched hovels still remained and it was a far from wholesome place to visit.

The prison itself stood on the east side of Farringdon Street. The main building was four stories high, and in these miserable galleries, as they were called, whole families sometimes existed on what they could beg from friends. Family of the person imprisoned was free to come and go as they pleased, and for the payment of 1s 3d a week easement would be granted. The common room was free but unpleasant, the food scarcely eatable, and the privacy of a better apartment in one of the upper galleries could be bought for the sum of 4s 6d a week. Those who could not raise these pitiful amounts were forced to rely on the charity of people who placed coins in a box outside the prison, and the prisoners often begged for succour from passers-by through a grill.

And it was to this terrible place that Harry had been brought! Arabella felt pity for the other poor wretches confined here as she was conducted through the exercise yard to one of the upper galleries. She was surprised but delighted to discover that Harry had the apartment to himself.

'I was fortunate enough to have a few coins in my pocket when I was arrested,' Harry said when she kissed him and told him she was happy he had not been forced to endure the indignity of the common room. 'But I have scarcely enough left to pay for food this week.'

Arabella had brought a basket containing bread, cheese and a bottle of wine. She gave it to him and then took the pouch of money from her bodice, offering it to him anxiously.

'This is all I could manage,' she said. 'Three hundred pounds – is it enough to settle your debts?'

'Three hundred...' He took it from her eagerly. 'It would settle one or two, but it will keep me in comfort here for some time.' He smiled at her. 'I suppose you have sold something, Bella. You should have kept the money for yourself, but I am grateful for what you have done.'

'Then it will not secure your release?' she asked, disappointed.

'I fear that ten times as much would not do that,' Harry said. 'I owe four thousand pounds to tradesmen and more than ten to Roxbourne.'

'But surely he would not press for payment of a gambling debt? It is a debt of honour, but you cannot be held here for that.'

'If I could pay the tradesmen I could secure my release.' He looked at her, suddenly alert. 'Do you have anything else you could sell?'

She shook her head, barely holding her tears in check. 'No, I am sorry. I could never raise that sum.'

'Then I must stay here until I can find some way of paying,' he said, and looked at her. The strange expression in his eyes chilled her. 'You should go away and forget me, Arabella. You must find your own way now.'

'No, Harry!' she cried and felt the misery

rise up inside her, catching at her like a physical pain in her belly. 'I cannot just leave you here. I shall visit from time to time with food and a little money, if I can earn it somehow.'

'No!' His tone shocked her because it was so harsh, so final. 'I do not want you to come here again. Please give me your word that you will not.'

'Harry...' She bit her lip, because she could see that he meant it. 'What am I to do?'

'I cannot help you,' he replied coldly. 'You must make your own life now. After the child is born you should visit your cousin and ask her if she could introduce you to one of her friends. You should find yourself a wealthy protector, Arabella.'

'No!' she cried, the tightness in her chest making it difficult to breathe. Her head was beginning to spin and she felt ill. 'You cannot mean that? You cannot mean that you want me to become the mistress of another man?'

'Unless you can find a wealthy cit to marry you,' Harry replied in a dismissive tone. 'You have no other choice, Bella. It is either a protector or the streets for you. No gentleman would take you now. Surely you know that?'

How could he say something like that to her so coldly? It was cruel and it hurt her more than she had thought possible. She stared at him, but he was not looking at her, and she sensed his own misery. He was being cruel to be kind, she realized. He did not believe that he would ever be released from prison and wanted her to make a new life for herself – which must mean that he did still care for her a little.

Blinking back her tears, she went to kiss his cheek. 'I shall come back when I have money for you,' she promised softly. 'Do not give up hope, my dearest. Perhaps there may yet be a way to get you out of here.'

Harry did not reply. He had walked away from her and was looking for a place to hide the money she had given him. Arabella turned away sadly. She was so close to tears and she did not want to weep in front of him; it was obvious to her that he was suffering terribly and she could not bear to see him so low.

Arabella was thoughtful as she left the prison and began to walk along the street, hardly knowing or caring where she was going. She was conscious of a pain beginning in her back, but gave no thought to what might be the cause. Her heart felt as if it was breaking, but she did not know what she could do about her situation.

Harry had told her to find herself a rich protector, but no one would want her as she was now. She could do nothing until her child was born, but afterwards...Was she prepared to sell herself? The idea horrified her, and yet she knew that Harry had spoken only the truth. No gentleman would marry her if he knew her situation...

Arabella's thoughts were abruptly brought back to the present as pain ripped through her. Was her child about to be born? She had not thought it would happen for another week or more, but she could feel something damp between her legs and she believed her waters might have broken.

She clutched at herself as the pain made her bend over double. What was she going to do? She couldn't give birth here in the street, but her house was too far away for her to walk in this condition. She must look for a carriage to take her home to Betsy – if one could be found to take a woman who was about to give birth.

Seeing a driver standing by the roadside talking to a man unloading a wagon, she went over to him, trying to keep herself from crying out with the pain. If the driver guessed what was happening he might refuse to have her in his carriage, shabby as it was.

'Would you please take me to Hampstead?' she asked, and then a loud cry was forced from her as the pain struck again. The baby was coming! She was sure she could feel it pressing down on her. 'Help me...help me please!'

'She's 'avin' a kid,' the wagon driver said. 'Gawd luv us! She's gonna 'ave it 'ere in the road if yer don't 'elp the poor bitch.'

'Not flamin' likely,' the carriage driver said. 'It were bad enough when my missus 'ad 'er last. I ain't 'avin' no woman in me carriage screamin' 'er 'ead orf.'

Arabella grabbed his arm, but he pushed her away and she staggered, falling to the ground, where she lay writhing in agony and begging for help.

'Please, please help me...' she wept, but the men walked away. People were crossing the street to avoid her. She was going to die...She would die because she could not bear this terrible pain that ripped through her every few seconds.

'What is going on here?' She heard a woman's voice dimly through the mist of pain that had rendered her almost unconscious. 'Oh, you poor soul. Is there no one who will help you? May I send to your home?'

'I live in Hampstead,' Arabella whispered. 'Please help me. My child is coming early...'

'Yes, of course I will help,' the woman said. 'Here! You over there. Help get this woman into my carriage and I shall pay you a shilling each.'

Arabella closed her eyes as three men bent over her. She moaned in protest as they lifted her none too gently, carrying her to a carriage that had stopped in the middle of the road and was now blocking the way for wagons and other carriages.

'Careful you dolt!' the woman said sharply. 'I do not want her harmed or you will find yourself in prison for murdering a poor woman. Treat her kindly. She needs your consideration.'

'Thank you...so kind,' Arabella murmured through dry lips. She moaned as she felt the pressure of a head pressing against her; the child was trying to push its way into the world. 'I–I think it's coming.'

'Hold on a little,' the woman comforted, climbing into the carriage beside her and taking her hand. 'I live just around the corner and we shall be there in no time. Soon you will be lying in a comfortable bed, and I myself will assist your child into the world.'

'Oh...' Arabella gasped. 'What is your name, mistress? How can I ever thank you for saving my life?'

'Names and payment are not important now,' the woman replied, crooning over her as she stroked the damp hair from her forehead. 'Just try to relax, my dear, and breathe slowly. You will soon be much better.'

'Thank you...' Arabella gasped and tried to breathe slowly as she had been told.

'What will your family think when you do

not come home?' the woman asked. 'May I send word to them?'

'I have no family,' Arabella said, biting at her bottom lip. 'My...my friend is in the Fleet for debt. I have only my maid Betsy and she is in Hampstead. She may worry, but perhaps...'

'Yes, yes, do not worry over a maid,' the woman said, a little smile of satisfaction on her lips. 'We shall send word and then you can ask her to bring your clothes to you when you are over the birth.' She stroked Arabella's forehead as she writhed with agony. 'It will not be long, my dear, and you have me to look after you now. I shall do everything possible for both you and the baby.'

Arabella clung to the woman's hand as the pain struck again. 'Are we nearly there?' she whispered. 'Only I do not think...'

'Here we are,' the woman said. 'Just lie there and close your eyes, and I shall bring help. Trust me, my dear. You are quite safe now, I give you my word.'

Eight

Arabella opened her eyes as someone bent over her, laying a cool hand on her brow. She looked into the smiling face of a woman, feeling tired and uneasy. She was not in her house at Hampstead. Where was she? And how had she come to be here? Her mind was confused and for a moment she could not remember anything. Instinctively her hands went to her stomach and she suddenly knew why she felt so ill, so drained of life. She had been through so much pain that she had thought she would die.

'My baby...He took so long to come,' she said fretfully. 'There was so much pain. Where is my child?'

'The pain of childbearing is always terrible, but it is over now, my dear. All you have to do is rest and heal.'

'Where is my child?' Arabella repeated. 'Please, you must tell me! I had a son. Someone said it was a boy. I remember...'

It was like a nightmare, a strange dream peopled by faceless creatures and flickering candlelight. Yet somewhere amidst the pain,

the terrible, destroying pain that had wrack-
ed her for endless hours, she could recall
hearing a woman speak of the child and the
thin wail of a newborn babe.

'I'm sorry, my dear.' Elizabeth George
looked at her sadly. 'The child was a boy as
you say, but he died only minutes after he
was born. He took such a long time to
come. We all feared for your life but I'm
afraid it was your child that died.'

'Dead? My baby dead?' Tears welled up
in Arabella's eyes and trickled down her
cheeks. 'God forgive me. I sinned and He
has punished me by taking my son.' She was
filled with a terrible sense of loss and grief.

'Do not fret so, mistress,' Elizabeth said.
''Tis often the way with a first child, especially when the mother is young. You will have
others.'

Arabella shook her head, turning her face
to the pillow. She did not want other children, for they would not be Harry's. He did
not love her. He had told her to find herself
a rich protector and in doing so had broken
her heart. The shock had brought on the
birth of her son in the street and now the
babe was dead. She had nothing left to live
for, nothing to give her hope for the future.
Why had she not died too? She plucked
fretfully at the bedcovers.

'Better I had died and my child lived.'

'Nonsense! You shall not talk like that, you

foolish girl. You are amongst friends now and we shall look after you and make you well again.'

'You are very kind but I do not wish to live.'

'Not wish to live? You are a wicked girl to blaspheme so! Life and death is in God's hands. If He chose to let you live you should give thanks, not lie there and feel sorry for yourself. Otherwise He might change His mind.'

'Do you believe in God?'

'Lord have mercy!' Elizabeth cried and crossed herself. 'Think yourself fortunate that there is only me to hear you, child, or you might find yourself being whipped for your wickedness. Women have been stoned in the streets for less.'

'I'm sorry,' Arabella said and sighed. 'You've been so good to me, ma'am. I do not think I am worth your trouble.'

'No more of this foolishness,' Elizabeth said and smiled at her warmly. 'What you need is some of my nourishing broth inside you and then you shall soon feel better.'

'Yes, perhaps I am a little hungry.'

'There, you look brighter already. You shall lie still and rest and I shall bring you the broth in a few minutes.'

Arabella closed her eyes as the good woman went out. She felt empty and un-happy, her grief washing over her in a great wave. If only she had died before her visit to the prison! She need never have known that Harry did not love her. She need never have known that her son was dead.

For a moment she felt the unbearable sorrow of her double loss and truly wished that she might die, but then her natural spirit began to assert itself. Perhaps Harry had been thinking of her. Perhaps he had thought that she would have no means of supporting her child without him? It hurt her that Harry's son was dead, and she knew the grief would remain with her for a long time, but without a child to support she would be able to work. If she could somehow earn enough money to pay for Harry's release he would surely come back to her.

How could she find the money Harry needed? There must be some way. Perhaps her father or sister might help her. She was not sure how she would get it, but somehow she would be with Harry again. With that thought in her mind she drifted into a peaceful sleep.

Arabella woke as she heard the sound of laughter close by. It was not the first time she'd heard it and it intrigued her. Mistress Elizabeth, as she'd been told to call her benefactress, seemed to have a lot of company in her house. Gentlemen as well as ladies, for she had heard their voices passing her door.

She was aware of feeling much better that morning. A week had passed since the birth and death of her son. The grief was still sharp when she thought about it, but she did not let herself think of it very often. She had to get well and then she could leave this house and start collecting money for Harry.

The laughter was outside her door now. It sounded pleasant and made Arabella curious. 'Who is there?'

Silence followed and then the door opened cautiously and a pretty girl peeped round. She did not look more than sixteen and her eyes were bright with mischief.

'Mistress Elizabeth will have my guts for garters for disturbing you,' she said and crept into the room. 'Are you feeling better, Mistress Arabella? Mistress Elizabeth told us we were not to disturb you at any cost. You have been very ill and we were all so sad to learn that your child had died.'

Arabella blinked back her tears and looked at her curiously. 'Who are you – and what is your name, please?'

The girl seemed to hesitate for a moment, then came to perch on the edge of the bed. 'I am called Thea by my friends and I am... Mistress Elizabeth's niece by marriage.'

'I am so pleased to make your acquaintance, Mistress Thea.'

'Please, call me Thea,' she said, a dimple in both cheeks. 'Are you going to live with us, Mistress Arabella?'

'No, I don't think so,' Arabella said with a slight frown. 'Mistress Elizabeth has been good to me, but she cannot want the burden of my presence in her house.'

'Oh, I do not think she would find you a burden for long. You are much too pretty,' Thea said, and started to giggle. She was little more than a child and perhaps not even as old as Arabella had first thought.

'I do not believe I shall find a husband that easily,' Arabella said and was surprised when the other girl giggled even more. She was about to ask her to explain when Elizabeth came bustling into the room.

'Thea, you naughty girl,' she said in a mock scolding tone. 'Did I not tell you Arabella was to be allowed to rest for a few more days? She has been too ill to want to hear your foolish talk, my dear.'

'I am sorry,' Thea said and shot a look at Arabella. 'I haven't said anything to upset you – have I Arabella?'

'No, of course not,' Arabella replied. 'Besides, I am feeling so much better now that I shall be glad of company. I think I ought to be getting up soon, Mistress Elizabeth. I already owe you more than I can pay. I must go home and sell something, and then I can pay you.'

'No talk of payment,' the older woman said, holding up her hands in protest. 'You are like another niece to me, Arabella. I like my girls to be happy, and they like to make me happy – don't you, Thea?'

'Yes, of course we do,' Thea said and smiled oddly. For a moment there was something in her eyes that told another story, but then in an instant it had gone. 'You take care of us, Mistress Elizabeth, and we should not fare so well without you.'

'As long as you remember that,' Elizabeth said, smiling benignly on the girl as she went out. Watching her, Arabella was aware of something hidden, something not quite right, but the older woman was looking well pleased as she turned to her again. 'I am glad you are feeling so much better, Arabella. I am holding a little dinner tomorrow evening, and if you are feeling up to it I should like you to help me entertain my guests.'

'But...' Arabella stopped as she saw the hardness in the depths of the other woman's eyes. Some inner instinct warned her that the older woman might not be all that she appeared to be. 'Of course, if you wish for my company. How could I refuse after you have done so much for me?'

'I did not think you were so ungrateful,' Elizabeth said, all warmth and charm now. 'It is just a little entertainment for some friends, and they like to see new faces. Yours is such a pretty face, Arabella my dear. All I require of you is that you smile and talk to my guests for a few hours. That is not so very much to ask – is it?'

'No, ma'am, it is very little.'

'Then we shall not fall out over it,' Elizabeth said. 'I shall have someone bring you some food – and a pretty dress to try on, my dear. We must have you looking your best for the dinner tomorrow, must we not?'

'Thank you, ma'am. You are very kind.'

Arabella frowned as the door closed behind her hostess, her suspicions confirmed. She had been uneasy almost from the start, and the visit from Thea explained some of the noises she had faintly heard coming from other rooms. Mistress Elizabeth was running a bawdy house! It was clearly an establishment of the highest order, where gentlemen came to play games of chance and end the evening in the arms of one of Mistress Elizabeth's *nieces*!

Arabella was sure she was not mistaken. Had she been an innocent she might have been deceived for longer, but Harry had spoken of such places many times, and her aunt had mentioned an unfortunate country girl who had fallen into the clutches of such a woman.

After all, why should Mistress Elizabeth have taken her into the house and cared for her unless she had some reason for doing so? Such kindness was seldom found in strangers. Yet had she not come along when she did, Arabella would likely have given birth where she lay in the street, and probably would have died. Naturally Mistress Elizabeth would expect payment. But what kind of payment would be asked of her?

Arabella knew what danger she was in, but what was she to do about it? She was not so naïve as to imagine that she could simply walk out of the house. For one thing, she had nothing to wear but the nightgowns Mistress Elizabeth had provided for her. Her own dress had been discarded because it was stained with blood and filth from the street. For another, there must somewhere be a manservant who guarded the girls – perhaps more than one. They would not permit her to walk out if she tried.

An attempt to run away would meet with punishment, Arabella was certain. This was a dangerous situation and the only way she might escape her fate was by using her wits. There was a possibility that she might be able to persuade Mistress Elizabeth to let her go. Perhaps if she believed that she had money and could pay for her freedom...

She must be careful not to antagonize her. Tears and tantrums would avail her nothing. Persuasion was her only weapon, and she must use it carefully. For the moment it would be wiser to pretend to go along with whatever Elizabeth suggested and use her recent ordeal as an excuse for not entertaining the guests in a more personal manner.

'I am sure you will find a girl who appeals to you at Mistress Elizabeth's house,' Jack said. 'The last time I was there she had a pretty little thing called Thea – hardly above fifteen and as fresh as a daisy. You should forget about the red-haired vixen, Gervase, and indulge yourself with an obliging nun. 'Tis the best way to forget her.'

'Perhaps...' Gervase's tone was non-committal. He was aware that Jack thought him a fool to continue his search for Arabella, and perhaps he was right. Yet the thought of her abandoned, perhaps in trouble, haunted him, leaving him little rest. 'Yet I do not think I am in the mood for Mistress Elizabeth's goods.'

'They say she has a niece from the country staying with her,' Jack went on. 'No one has been allowed near her and she is there merely to serve wine and make conversation with the guests.'

'If you believe that you are more gullible than I thought,' Gervase said and yawned behind his hand. 'They are all her nieces.'

'But this one is different, so they say,' Jack persisted. 'She is a lady, apparently, and gives herself airs...'

Gervase's eyes narrowed as he looked at his friend. Why was Jack so keen to make sure he accompanied him to Mistress Elizabeth's establishment that evening? 'What are you trying to say? Out with it!'

'Someone said they were going to auction her off to the highest bidder at midnight. Apparently she retires at a quarter to each evening and Mistress Elizabeth has refused all offers for her. But tonight it will be different, and after she has gone there will be an auction, the highest bidder will be the first to lie with her.'

'If she be a virgin in the first place,' Gervase said. 'How long has she been staying with Mistress Elizabeth?'

'She has been entertaining the guests for more than a month now,' Jack said. 'Though they say she was staying in the house before that, but unwell. Mistress Elizabeth guarded her like a dragon until she brought her downstairs.'

'To whet the appetite of her customers, one presumes.' Gervase smothered a yawn. 'Go and bid for the little nun if you wish, my friend, but I do not think I care to waste my money.'

Jack shrugged his shoulders. 'Please yourself, Gervase, but never say I don't try to find amusement for you.'

'Oh, you are a very trying fellow,' Gervase said and grinned at him. 'But I bear with you, Jack.'

'Well, if that don't beat all...' Jack stood up. 'Insult a fellow too often, Gervase, and you might find yourself short of friends.'

He took himself off without a backward glance, and Gervase realized that he had ruffled his friend's feathers a little too often of late. His temper had been on a short rein, and though he had merely meant to mock in his old way, Jack was out of sorts. Perhaps he ought to have gone along with him, if only to watch the others making fools of themselves...

'It is a lovely gown,' Arabella said as she tried on the emerald-green silk evening dress. 'But if you would let me send for my own things, Elizabeth, I would not need to use yours.'

'Plenty of time for that, my dear,' Elizabeth said, her shrewd eyes narrowed. 'When you are settled and happy. Besides, it pleases me to lend you pretty things. Our little arrangement has made my guests even more eager to spend their money.'

Arabella had confronted her hostess with her suspicions after the first evening downstairs. Seeing it was useless to deny what was obvious, Elizabeth had agreed that she arranged for girls to entertain men in whatever way they chose in their rooms.

'The gentlemen pay me and I give the girls

bed and board, and provide their clothes. If they can persuade their gentlemen to give them presents, I let them keep all they get. I am not a greedy woman, Arabella. I look after my girls, fetch a doctor to them if they are sick, and protect them.'

'I do not wish to sleep with any man who is willing to pay for me,' Arabella told her. 'I had one lover – a gentleman of rank – who deserted me. I have family and could return home.'

'But you told me you had none when I brought you here.' Elizabeth looked at her sharply.

'My family are not in London, but my father would welcome me home if I chose to go,' Arabella told her. 'But I am willing to stay here for a while to repay my debt to you by being nice to your guests and making them feel welcome – but it ends there, ma'am. I am not your niece and I am not for sale.'

Elizabeth looked at her consideringly. Arabella had given birth only recently and was not truly ready to entertain men in her room. Besides, men always wanted what they could not have, and it would whet their appetites to be told that they could see and not touch. Arabella was clearly of good family, and that would appeal. If she wore her hair powdered for a start, and then, when it was time, went unpowdered, that red hair would drive them wild.

'Why do you not wear your hair without powder this evening?' she asked Arabella now as she looked at herself in the dressing mirror. 'It would set off that gown to perfection.'

Arabella frowned at her reflection. She had hoped that the powder gave her some protection against recognition amongst Mistress Elizabeth's guests. She had recognized at least two gentlemen whom she had met while in the company of her cousin, but both were foxed at the time and neither had seemed to notice her – and she had retired immediately the night that Jack Meadows came to the club with a friend. His companion had clearly been in his cups, but she was not sure whether Gervase's friend had seen her or not.

The longer she stayed at the house the more likely it was that someone would recognize her, Arabella realized. If she was going to run away, it must be soon. She believed that Mistress Elizabeth had relaxed her guard a little, and somehow Arabella would find a way of slipping out during the party that evening.

She smiled at her hostess, pretending to go along with her. 'Yes, I do believe you are right,' she said. 'I shall leave my hair unpowdered this evening, Elizabeth.'

Arabella knew that one of the girls had a

blonde wig in her room. When everyone was drinking heavily and it was possible to leave without being noticed, she would slip into Serena's room, take the wig and a cloak and then go out of a side door and disappear into the night...

Gervase hesitated outside the house. From the outside it was respectable, with little to distinguish it from any other. Inside, it was very different, the decor in shades of gold and scarlet that proclaimed its function as a high-class whorehouse. Having visited it in the past, Gervase knew the madam well enough. She was not a bad woman by any means; there were many worse that exploited their girls and treated them badly. At least Mistress Elizabeth looked after her young ladies, as she liked to call them, though most were ignorant girls who had no education or any skill other than knowing how to please their gentlemen.

It was half past eleven, and if Jack was right the auction was due to take place at midnight. He was not sure why he had come, whether it was out of a desire to make amends to his friend or merely curiosity.

The doorman recognized him at once, inclining his head respectfully as he stood back to admit him. 'We have not seen you for some time, milord.'

Gervase nodded but made no answer.

He was mildly interested in the girl who was to be auctioned that evening, though he did not suppose her to be anything out of the ordinary and had come merely to please Jack. The girl usually left before midnight and...Gervase's idle thoughts were suspended as he saw her talking with one of the gentlemen. The shock was so great that he could only stare in dismay. He had men searching all over London for her, and she was here!

'I see you changed your mind,' Jack said quietly at his elbow. 'I think it may be worth your while after all, Gervase.'

'Did you know it was her?' Gervase's eyes narrowed to angry slits. 'Be careful, Jack, for if—'

'I swear I was as ignorant as you,' Jack protested. 'I caught but a glimpse of her one night as I entered, and thought something familiar, but she wore her hair powdered that night and I could not be sure. I came earlier this evening.'

'Have you spoken to her?'

'I tried but she pretended not to know me and avoided talking to me by saying that she must speak to her aunt.'

'Is she a party to this auction?' Gervase felt the anger rip through him. For months he had been haunted by his fears for Arabella, and there she was laughing and talking as if she hadn't a care in the world.

For a moment he wanted to take her by the neck and throttle her.

'I don't know,' Jack admitted truthfully. 'She must know the purpose of this place. She isn't a fool, and by pretending to be innocent she is pushing her price up...'

'She was never quite that, though Sylvester took advantage of her nature.' Gervase watched Arabella. She was smiling at someone, and accepting a glass of wine, which she simply held but did not touch, putting it on a small wine table as she turned and walked from the room. 'Excuse me...' He moved to follow her, but was prevented by Mistress Elizabeth, who stopped him by laying a hand on his arm.

'I am delighted to see you here for our special evening, my lord.'

'It is true then? You intend to auction the girl?'

'You make it sound so commonplace,' Elizabeth said with a little pout. 'As a special favour to my gentlemen I have decided that one of them shall have her as their own for this night and for as many nights after as pleases the winner of my little contest.'

'Exclusive rights?'

'Why yes, my lord. I would not expect the kind of price I am asking to be paid for one night of her undoubted charms.'

'What if the buyer wanted to take her away?'

'It would have to be a very special price,' Elizabeth said. 'At least twice or three times what anyone else would pay.'

Gervase nodded. 'If anyone were fool enough to pay such a price for used goods.'

'How can you doubt that she is a virgin, fresh up from the country and a sheltered upbringing by my own dear brother.'

'If you have a brother, madam, which I doubt,' Gervase drawled, 'I dare swear he never spawned that beauty. Nevertheless I may be tempted to bid – but if I do she is mine and I take her with me. And the arrangement would remain private between us. No one would know that I had paid more to take her away. Understood?'

Elizabeth shivered as she looked into his cold eyes. She would be ill advised to cross this man and she knew it. 'Of course, my lord. Excuse me, I must see that Arabella is settled for the night. I would not have her anxious if she hears unusual noises.'

Gervase frowned as she hurried in the wake of her so-called niece, wondering what had prompted him to make the offer. He was a fool to bother, but he would not have Arabella passed from man to man, as she would be once the first had done with her.

Perhaps he would bid for her, and perhaps he would leave before the auction began...

Arabella had the cloak and wig in her room.

She was just about to change into one of her plainer gowns when her door opened and Mistress Elizabeth entered bearing a tray and wine glasses.

'I wanted to have a little celebration with you,' she said. 'Wish me happy, Arabella. One of my gentlemen has offered to take me away from all this and make me rich.'

'He will marry you?' Arabella was surprised, accepting the glass from Elizabeth's hand. 'I thought you were happy here with your girls?'

'And so I am,' Elizabeth told her with a smile. 'But I would prefer to be kept in luxury – what woman would not, my dear?' She raised her glass to Arabella. 'I shall sell my house to someone who will look after my girls, but of course some of them may wish to leave...'

'You will allow those who wish it to leave?'

'Yes, of course,' Elizabeth said. 'I have always been kind to them, but a new owner might not be as lenient. Any who wish to leave may do so, of course. You too, Arabella. In the morning I shall give you the name of a friend who might take you in. She is not in my trade but runs a dressmaking establishment and needs a girl to show off her clothes. That might suit you, my dear.'

'I had not thought...' Arabella blushed as she recalled what had been in her mind. 'You are very kind, ma'am.'

'Wish me well, my dear. Will you not drink a last toast with me?'

'Yes, of course.' Arabella lifted her glass and took a sip. She grimaced as she swallowed it. 'It is bitter...what did you put in it?' A look of horror came to her eyes as she realized the wine had been tampered with. 'You are trying to drug me. I shall not drink any more of that foul stuff. What mischief are you about?'

'It is merely a little sleeping draught so that you do not listen to things you should not hear. Finish it up, Arabella, please.'

'I shall not!' Arabella threw the glass down, the rich red wine splashing over the carpet. 'And I shall leave here...'

'Mowley, get in here! She's going to be difficult.'

Arabella looked at the door as it opened and a large, ugly man walked in. His face looked as if he had been ill with the pox at some time, his skin pitted and scarred, one eyelid puckered at the corners.

'No, you can't make me!' Arabella backed away from him but he sprang at her, gripping her arms and holding them behind her. 'No!' She tried to shut her mouth against the wine as Elizabeth held the second glass to her lips, but Mowley pulled her head back and, as she gasped, wine was poured into her mouth. She spat as much of it as she could out, but she knew that some of it had gone down her throat. 'I shall not...'

But already her head was beginning to spin. As she sagged, Elizabeth's henchman caught her, carrying her easily to dump her carelessly on the bed.

'Shall I strip her?'

'No, leave her,' Elizabeth told him. 'I think the gentleman I have in mind will want her just as she is.'

Arabella fought the dizziness sweeping over her. She lifted her head, trying to call out, to beg Mistress Elizabeth not to do this to her, but she was falling...falling into a black pit that seemed to go on and on for ever.

How foolish she had been to trust that woman! Better that she died in the street giving birth to Harry's son than live to become a whore, at the mercy of any man who was willing to pay for her.

Just before she closed her eyes, Arabella remembered a man who had offered to cover her body with jewels if she would become his mistress. She had scorned his offer so proudly and now she was sunk to this level...The taste was bitter indeed.

Arabella stirred and gave a little cry as she felt the pain in her head. The sheets felt smooth beneath her body, for she was quite naked, and they smelled fresh...like flowers.

She opened her eyes and looked about her, trying to remember where she was and what had happened.

The curtains at the window had been opened to let in the morning light and she could see that a pale sun was shining outside. She pushed herself up gingerly against a pile of soft pillows, looking about her warily. Her head felt as if a thousand drums were beating inside it and for a moment she could not think what had happened. Had she been ill? What had happened to her?

She had been somewhere else last night... At Mistress Elizabeth's bawdy house! And they had drugged her. Elizabeth and her henchman had forced the drugged wine down her throat, because...she was about to be sold to a man!

Arabella saw that a jug filled with water had been placed on the table by the bed, and a glass beside it. She hesitated, then filled the glass and took a sip. It appeared to taste as it should and she gulped at it greedily, glad of its coolness on her parched throat. When the glass was empty she placed it back on the tray and flung back the bedclothes, putting her feet to the floor. As she tried to stand, her head began to swim and she was forced to lie back against the pillows once more.

She would have to stay where she was for

the moment. Those devils had done their work well! She could not escape if she wished – but where was she? Not in Mistress Elizabeth's house. This was a very different place, the house of a gentleman if she were not mistaken.

The room was much larger than the one she had used in the bawdy house, and well appointed with quality furniture in a rich, deep mahogany. The bed sheets were the best linen, the heavy coverings and the hangings at the window were of damask silk, the colours varying shades of dark blue and silver with touches of cream to lighten the effect. It was almost certainly a gentleman's bedroom and she had been brought here for his pleasure.

She had been in no state for seduction last night, Arabella reflected. Perhaps that was yet to come, for no true gentleman wanted to take his pleasure when the lady concerned was in the state she had been in last night.

Hearing the sound of a man's tread outside her room, she stiffened, holding the covers to her breasts. If only her head did not ache so very much, she would give whoever had bought her a piece of her mind. She looked around for something to throw at the man should he come in, but the only thing to hand was the jug of water.

The tension mounted inside her as she

heard the door handle turn, and then it opened very slowly. Oh, what she would like to do to Mistress Elizabeth and her henchman for putting her in this position!

And then she was staring at a face she knew, too shocked to do more than gape as he entered the room and stood looking at her. Her hand strayed towards the water jug and then halted. Gervase Roxbourne was one man she did not dare to throw water over.

'So you are awake,' Gervase said with a frown. 'I must apologize for the way you were treated last night, Arabella. Had I known what she intended...But it seems you are none the worse for it.'

'None the worse?' Arabella felt the indignation rise in her. 'If you knew how much my head aches you would not make such foolish remarks, sir! But I dare say this is all your fault. If you had not abducted me...' She grabbed one of the pillows and threw it at him in a surge of temper. He ducked his head and it landed harmlessly beyond him. 'Damn you!'

'Ah, I see I was right,' Gervase said with an odd smile. 'Whatever has happened to you since we last met, at least your spirit has not been broken. I am very glad to see you in such good health, Arabella.'

'I've just told you I have a terrible headache.'

'That will pass,' he said. 'My housekeeper will bring you a tisane if you ring for her – and I assure you it will not be drugged. If you stay in this house you do so of your own free will.'

'But I thought...' Arabella hesitated as she saw his eyes narrow. 'What exactly did happen last night? I know I was drugged to make sure I didn't try to run away, but I do not understand what happened.'

'You really do not know?'

'I know that I was tricked and then forced into taking drugged wine, but I know no more.'

'You were auctioned to the highest bidder. I bought you on the condition that I brought you home with me.'

'You bought me in an auction!' Arabella gasped, staring at him in horror. 'How could you do such a disgusting thing?'

'You would prefer that I had let Snoddington or Entwhistle buy you instead?' Gervase raised his brows at her. 'I dare say they would take you off my hands if you wish.'

She stared at him furiously, then said, with dignity, 'I would have preferred not to be bought by anyone. She had no right to do it.'

'We are in perfect agreement there,' Gervase told her, his mouth crooking in a smile. 'It is my belief that Mistress Elizabeth and her kind should be more tightly controlled by the law, but while the law makers of our time are amongst her customers, it is unlikely to happen. Indeed, I happen to know that a certain lord put up the money for her in the first place.'

'You were amongst her customers last night.'

'For the purpose of observation only. I went to please a friend.'

'Jack Meadows, I suppose.' Arabella glared at him. 'Did he tell you I was there?'

'He wasn't sure it was you until last night.' His eyes narrowed. 'How did you come to be there? Was it not of your own choosing?'

'I was in trouble and she helped me...' Tears welled up in her eyes. 'I was alone and my child was coming in the street. I had been to the prison to see Harry and...'

'You had a child?' Gervase gave no sign of the powerful effect her words were having on him, his expression unchanged. 'What happened to it?'

'Elizabeth told me my son died soon after he was born,' Arabella said. 'I had a terrible time at the birth and then they gave me something to drink and when I woke...the child had gone.'

'I see...' Not a flicker of a muscle to tell her what was in his mind. 'So Mistress Elizabeth George looked after you and you agreed to work for her in payment.'

'No, I wanted to send for my things, to sell

something to pay her, but she wouldn't hear of it. Then she asked me to a party and said that I should just smile and be friendly towards her guests, but I knew that she had other girls there and that they were supposed to be her nieces. I told her that I would help entertain her gentlemen with smiles and conversation, but that I would not take them to my room. She agreed and I thought...But she was merely pushing up my price.'

'Yes, that was the general idea,' Gervase said, a faint smile on his lips. 'It might please you to know that your price was above a thousand guineas at the auction.' And he had paid another two for the privilege of taking her away afterwards.

'That's not fair,' Arabella said. 'She didn't own me. Why should she be paid all that money?' She was thinking that a thousand guineas would have gone some considerable way to paying Harry's debts.

'It is gratifying that you are so concerned for my pockets,' Gervase drawled. 'However, it was but a trifling sum. The point is that having got you, what am I to do with you?'

'What do you mean?' Arabella flushed and pulled the bedcovers closer around her. 'You said I was free to go if I wished.'

'As you are, of course,' Gervase agreed. 'If you stay it will be by mutual consent for as long as we please each other.'

'As your mistress?'

'Certainly as my mistress,' Gervase replied. 'Had you not been another man's mistress it might have been otherwise, but now I cannot offer you marriage, Arabella. Only my protection, a house of your own, and a generous settlement.'

Might have been otherwise? Had he really been thinking of asking her to marry him before she ran away with Harry? She felt a sense of regret, of loss, as though something precious had slipped through her fingers without her realizing it at the time.

'And if I do not choose to be your mistress?' Her eyes met his defiantly.

'Then I shall give you a few guineas to tide you over and wish you good fortune.' Gervase shrugged carelessly. 'It is entirely your choice, Arabella. I doubt you will find anyone willing to marry you now – unless it be a cit, who has not heard of your infamous past.'

Arabella's cheeks turned a fiery red but she continued to meet his gaze. 'My father would take me in.'

The expression in Gervase's eyes changed suddenly. 'I have no doubt he would had he been able, Arabella – but I regret I must tell you that he passed away almost a year ago. I was with him just before he died and I know that he had not ceased to care for you.'

'My father is dead?' She was stunned for a moment, and then the tears burst out of her and she covered her face with her hands, her shoulders shaking. 'Papa...No...No!'

'Do not cry, sweetheart,' Gervase said in a voice softer than any she had previously heard from him. She felt him pull her hands from her face and then, as she looked at him, his arms went round her. He lowered his head to hers, kissing her lips softly. 'I am sorry I could not have brought you better news, Bella.'

Her eyes were dark with misery as she looked up at him. 'I did not know he was ill...'

'He wrote to ask you to go home, but...'

'I had gone with Harry,' Arabella said and a sob broke from her. 'I am truly punished now.'

'Talk not of punishment,' Gervase said, feeling oddly affected by her grief. 'You could not have saved him, nor would he want you to blame yourself. You were foolish to give yourself to that scoundrel, but it is over now. Forget him and come to me. I will promise to make your life sweeter than it has been this last year or so.'

'My lord...Gervase, I—' She got no further, for his mouth was on hers once more. This time it was not a kiss of comfort, but a hungry, devouring one that took her breath and left her senses whirling into space. She clung to him as the desire suddenly raged in her, her body melting in the heat of their mutual passion, going suddenly limp as he let her go and she fell back against the pillows. She was breathless, shocked by the fierceness of her response as she lay looking up at him. What had caused her to feel that way? He smiled as he saw the expression in her eyes. 'That is very much better, my love. I have waited a long time to see such a look in your eyes and it was worth the wait.'

'W–what do you mean?'

'You know very well,' Gervase said, a smile flickering about his mouth. 'We shall deal well together, my sweet. I dare say you need to recover from your ordeal, and I have business. Take this and buy yourself something pretty to wear for this evening. I have ordered the clothes you were wearing last night burned.'

Arabella looked at the pouch of gold he had left on the table beside the bed. There must be enough in there to pay at least a half of Harry's debts. She tipped her head to one side as she looked up at Gervase.

'Supposing I take your money and run away?'

'Where would you go? There are many more like Mistress Elizabeth waiting for naïve girls like you, Arabella, and most are not as kind as she. And there are worse places than her house or mine. Think carefully, my love, for I shall not rescue you twice.'

She felt the hot colour in her cheeks as his eyes dwelled on her and knew that she would not enjoy seeing Gervase truly angry.

'I was but teasing you,' she said. 'I have not made up my mind to stay with you, but if I go I shall not take your money.'

He shrugged carelessly. 'Take it and welcome,' he said. 'But you will find me a generous protector, Bella. And you may find that your life would be hard with no friends and no lover – but the choice is yours.'

She watched as he left the room, her heart racing. Gervase was a dangerous man and she knew that she had pushed him to the limit. The offer he had made her was exceedingly generous. Had she been bought by one of the other men he had named, her fate would not have been as pleasant.

And yet...Her thoughts were so confusing, so distressing, that she threw back the covers and jumped out of bed, snatching up a robe from beside it. For a moment she swayed, but even as she thought of returning to bed the door opened and a plump, smiling woman entered with a tray of food and a pot of hot chocolate.

'You must not think of getting up until you've eaten, milady,' she said in a mildly scolding tone. 'I am Mrs Bumpstead, the housekeeper here. Milord said that you had a headache and would need one of my tisanes. Eat some of these nice bits and pieces I've made for you, and drink your chocolate. Then you shall have your tisane and the maid will bring you hot water and a clean gown to wear.'

Arabella thanked her, but instead of returning to bed she asked if the tray might be taken to the table by the window, where she could sit in comfort in the elbow chair. 'I shall sit there and look out as I eat,' she said. 'And when I have eaten I shall dress and go for a walk.'

Mrs Bumpstead nodded her head and went out, leaving Arabella to nibble at the dainty morsels that had been prepared for her. She had a lot of thinking to do and she would do it best on a full stomach, and to her surprise she had discovered that she was hungry.

Nine

Sulking would do her no good at all, Arabella decided after she had eaten. She was feeling very much better and had enjoyed the housekeeper's tisane, which tasted of honey and lemons. Getting up, she wandered over to the bed where a fresh gown had been laid out for her, looking at it with distaste. It appeared to be a maid's Sunday best!

Was there nothing better in this house? Her hand hovered near the bell pull and then she changed her mind, walking over to the armoire ranged against the far wall and opening it. As she glanced inside, she saw that most of the garments belonged to a man, presumably Gervase himself, but then she caught sight of several gowns tucked away at the back, one of them of a fashion worn some years earlier, but still more stylish than the maid's, and when she took it out she saw that it was almost her size. The bodice would have to be laced loosely to accommodate her, but otherwise it was perfect.

Arabella tried it on, her spirits lifting as she saw herself in the dressing mirror. A vast improvement on the gown provided, she thought, and tied the lace fichu that had been brought with the dull gown around her shoulders to cover the rather revealing bodice.

As she went downstairs, Mrs Bumpstead gave her a rather startled look, but schooled her features as Arabella gave her a haughty stare.

'I would have a carriage,' she said, meaning that she wanted the footman to hire her one.

'I'll have it brought round immediately,' the housekeeper said. 'His lordship said as you were to have everything you needed, mistress.'

'Thank you. I shall wait in...here,' Arabella replied and walked into a small parlour. Its decor was a pretty combination of varying shades of green and cream, the furniture the same high quality mahogany as in the bedchamber upstairs, and made by one of the best craftsmen in London. She wandered about the room, picked up a gilded mantle clock to examine it and discovered it was French, glanced at a delicate lady's writing desk and chair and ran her fingers over the keys of a spinet. The house had been furnished with taste and care and was fine indeed. She was just studying the contents of a cabinet containing exquisite china when the housekeeper returned to tell her that the carriage was waiting.

Arabella thanked her and went outside. It was a pleasant enough day, the sun just breaking through a cloud-laden sky as she climbed into the carriage with the assistance of an attentive footman. Arabella nodded distantly. It was clear that Gervase had ordered she be treated as an honoured guest and she would behave as if there was nothing untoward in her unexpected arrival at his house.

'Where do you wish to be taken, Mistress Tucker?'

Arabella's thoughts had been wandering but his question brought her back to the present. Where did she wish to go? After some thought she decided on the only house in London that she was sure would receive her.

'Lady Mary Randall, Hanover Square, if you please.'

Once inside, Arabella was able to appreciate the comfort of the marquis's carriage. She had thought her cousin's carriage a vast improvement on the one she had travelled to London in, but this was luxury indeed. And it would be hers to use as often as she pleased if she gave Gervase the answer he wanted – but could she be his mistress when her heart belonged to Harry?

Unless her cousin could think of a plan it seemed unlikely that she would receive a better offer, Arabella mused as she glanced out at the London streets. It seemed an age since she had been in the fashionable part of town, and when she caught sight of an acquaintance passing she lifted her hand in salute, but was dismayed when the gentleman seemed not to know her. Only a year or so ago he had been one of her admirers. Had she changed so much – or was he aware of her lost reputation?

Things had changed considerably since she had left London. A year or so ago she had been an innocent country maiden, of good family and respectable. Now she was a woman that most others would refuse to welcome to their house. She was a little uneasy as she told the coachman to wait and then knocked at the door of Lady Mary's house, fearing that she might be refused entrance.

A woman she had not seen before opened the door, but after glancing at the expensive carriage and then Arabella's costly gown, she asked her into the receiving room.

'If you would care to wait here, Mistress Tucker, I shall ask her ladyship if she is at home to visitors.'

Arabella did not care to be left kicking her heels in the small parlour where strangers were shown, and the moment the servant had gone she ran upstairs and made her way along the corridor to her cousin's boudoir. She knocked and entered just as the maid was describing her to Lady Mary.

'Arabella!' her cousin cried in alarm. 'Where have you sprung from, girl?'

'I left her in the receiving room downstairs, milady.'

'Oh go away, Lisa, and stop fussing,' Lady Mary said. She was sitting up in bed, wearing a fetching pink wrapping gown, a scattering of letters spread around her and a pot of chocolate on the table beside her. 'Come here, Arabella, and let me look at you. I must say that you seem none the worse for your adventures, girl, though that gown is not in the first stare. Where have you been? We were all concerned about you. Lady Spencer was quite beside herself – and the Marquis of Roxbourne had people looking for you for sometime, I believe.'

'It was he who found me,' Arabella said, deciding to leave the details vague. 'I was in some difficulty after Lord Sylvester was taken to a debtors' prison.'

'That rogue!' Lady Mary pulled a face. 'I rue the day I ever encouraged him to this house. Had you not met him here you might have been happily married – instead of which you are ruined. I suppose you realize that, Bella. No decent woman would invite you to her house, my dear. You are so

227

foolish! Did I not warn you? Could you not have married some obliging fool and taken your lover after giving your husband an heir? No one would have been in the least shocked about that and you might have been a wealthy woman.'

'Do you not think that hypocrisy, Cousin? That a young single woman may not take a lover, but a married one may do as she pleases?'

'Whatever you think of our rules, they are there to protect us,' her cousin told her crossly. 'You flout them at your peril. I am sorry for your troubles, but must tell you that I cannot help you now, Bella. I can give you a little money, but nothing more. It would be frowned upon if I tried to take you back into my circle and as I have a new protector – a gentleman of some distinction – he would not care for the association. You have no one to blame but yourself.'

Arabella saw that it was useless to appeal to her cousin. She had not even told her about her sojourn in Mistress Elizabeth's bawdy house, and knew that it would merely set the seal upon her disgrace. Even had she been able to persuade her aunt to help her, someone was bound to recognize her and she would be cast out immediately.

'Thank you, but I have some money,' Arabella said, her head lifting with pride. 'I did not come to you for help, merely to ask how my sister does and if my father was buried properly.'

'Nan is well enough.' Lady Mary's mouth twisted sourly. 'She leads her husband a merry dance, I dare say, but he will tire of her in the end. As for your father, Roxbourne did all that was necessary. You should have married him, Bella. Of course, he would not look at you now. Everyone knows that he hated Harry Sylvester.'

'And he ruined him!' Arabella said. 'If poor Harry hadn't been in such terrible debt he might have married me.'

Lady Mary gave a harsh laugh. 'If you believe that, you have learned nothing,' she said. 'Well, I have spoken fairly with you, Bella, for you were always my favourite – but I shall not see you again. My servants will be told that my door is not open to you in future.'

Arabella inclined her head. Her cheeks stung with a high colour and she wished that she could think of some way to discomfort her cousin, but knew that she had no power to reach her. Lady Mary would probably have refused to see her at all if she had not taken the initiative.

'Then we shall not meet again, Cousin,' she said. 'I thank you for your past kindness, and regret that I have caused you unease.'

'Why could you not have been sensible?' Lady Mary sighed and waved her hand. 'Go away, Bella. You have chosen your own path to destruction and must follow it.'

Arabella walked from the house, her head high. Her cousin was not a cruel woman but she had always believed in making things plain, and the situation could not be rectified. Her reputation was gone, and she must live by her wits in future. If she could not have Harry, she must have another man as her protector. Even if she tried to find work as a governess or a companion, she would be dismissed the moment her reputation was discovered.

She allowed Gervase's servant to help her into the carriage, leaning her head back against the squabs as she gave the order to return to his house. She had no appetite for shopping. Nor was she sure that some of the exclusive seamstresses she had visited in the past would serve her now. They had their reputations to think of and might feel that a woman in her situation was likely to deter their regular customers.

A single tear slipped from the corner of her eye, but she brushed it away. She would not give way to self-pity! It hurt her that her cousin had rejected her, for it meant that she had no one she could turn to, no one she could count as her friend. Nan would delight in humbling her if she went there – and her beloved father was dead.

The carriage had come to a standstill.

Arabella opened her eyes and glanced out of the window. A crowd had gathered in the street, which was why the carriage could not pass. She saw that they were close to a church and heard the bells ring out as a bridal couple emerged to the laughing reception of their friends, who threw dried rose petals over them.

'Forgive the delay, your ladyship,' someone said to her from outside her carriage window. ''Tis the wedding of my daughter Miss Jane Archer to her lord and I fear we are blocking the street...'

'Miss Jane...' Arabella looked more intently at the bridegroom, who was looking happy and sure of himself as his plain, plump bride hung possessively on his arm. 'Lord Harry Sylvester...'

'The very same,' the proud father agreed. 'You may have heard sad tales of him, ma'am, but he is a reformed character now, and my Jane loves him. She had to have her way, and I dare say he will behave himself in the future...'

Arabella sat back against the squabs, drawing down the blind at her window as she felt the shock run through her. Harry's wedding day! He was marrying that cit's daughter for her inheritance! He had sold himself for money. How could he do that when he had sworn that he loved her – would *always* love her?

The carriage jerked as the horses began to move again. Arabella resisted the temptation to look out of the window as they moved nearer to the church. She felt sick, devastated by what she had seen and heard, but also angry.

It seemed that men were all the same. They lied and cheated, using women who were foolish enough to give into their charm. She wanted to leap from the carriage and attack Harry, to tear him limb from limb. Oh, how she hated him! If she were a man she would take a horsewhip to him.

She wanted to die and yet at the same time she wanted to live so that one day she would be able to pay Harry back for what he had done to her. He had ruined her, left her to give birth to his child alone, taken the money she had been foolish enough to give him – and now he had married that wretched girl for her money.

He would make her miserable and it served her right! Tears of rage welled up in Arabella's eyes but she dashed them away. She would not cry for Harry again. He was not worth her tears.

She must accept Gervase's offer. She must become his mistress. She had no other choice. At least, none that appealed to her, and his kiss that morning had made her think that perhaps she might quite like to be his lover. She shrugged off her misery. Since she had no choice, she might as well make the best of things.

Arabella glanced at herself in the dressing mirror. The gown she was wearing now was a dark blue silk over a petticoat of cream and silver. The neckline was more modest than she would have chosen for herself, but apart from loosening the bodice a little so that she could breathe, she had not tried to change it. Her hair was caught up on top of her head in soft curls, one ringlet allowed to fall on her shoulder.

She had no jewels of any kind, but she supposed she looked well enough. Gervase must think her attractive or he would not have bought her in that wretched auction. Nor would he have offered to set her up as his mistress.

Arabella pouted at her reflection. She imagined Gervase would be pleased with her. She had ordered a celebration dinner for them to be served in the small dining parlour and she was wearing the most stylish gown she could find. He would have his answer and must be satisfied.

She was about to go downstairs when she heard the heavy footsteps of a man coming down the hall and braced herself. Her future depended on his not changing his mind about wanting her as his mistress.

'Arabella...' Gervase began as he saw her. 'You went out...Damn it! Where did you get that gown?'

'From the armoire,' she said, startled by the flash of temper in his eyes. Now what had she done to upset him? 'Does it not become me?'

'No, it does not,' Gervase said harshly. 'I gave you money to buy clothes. What did you do with it?'

'I was not in the mood for buying clothes – and I did not know if Madame Suzanne would serve me.' Arabella's head went up. 'It appears that I am not fit to mix in decent society now.'

'You have been to your cousin's,' Gervase said and nodded. 'I'll have her eating out of your hand before she's done – and the seamstress will be delighted to serve you. Take that gown off and put on the dress Mrs Bumpstead provided for now.'

'I shall not wear that dowdy thing!'

'You will take off what you are wearing this minute.'

'No, I shall not.' Arabella set her face stubbornly. 'You may have bought me but you do not own my soul. You cannot make me do anything I don't want to do.'

'Take it off or I'll do it for you.'

Arabella held her breath. She looked him in the eyes. 'I shall not...Oh!' She gave a little scream as he descended on her pur-

234

posefully. 'Don't you dare, Gervase. I shall fight you...'

'Do as you wish, my sweet,' he said and reached out to grab hold of her. 'You shall not wear this dress or any of the others you found in my armoire. I forbid it, Arabella.'

'I hate—' she began, but broke off with a gasp as he ripped the bodice of her gown apart, the silken ties tearing through eyelets and costly material. 'You have ruined it...'

'No, you ruined it,' he said and ripped at it again. 'Better it should lie in shreds than be worn by any other than she.'

'Who was she?' Arabella asked, stung by unreasoning jealousy. He must have loved the owner of this gown very much to feel so strongly about her clothing. 'Tell me! Oh, you are a brute and a beast and I hate you!'

Gervase glared at her. 'All the better,' he murmured. 'But I think we'll put that statement to the test, my sweet.'

Before Arabella knew what he meant to do, he swooped on her, lifting her off her feet and slinging her across his shoulder as if she were a sack of fodder for his horse. With utter disregard for her fists that pummelled against his back, he tossed her on to the bed and then began to discard his own clothes, dropping them to lie on the floor. His body was lean and hard, honed to supreme fitness. She realized that he was a much finer specimen of male beauty than

Harry, who had been a little thicker about his waist and not as vital in certain private parts. Fully aroused, Gervase's manhood was almost terrifying to behold and set a fire burning inside her. Yet still she fought him, fought the desire that was beginning to rage inside her.

'Don't you dare to touch me...' she cried, her breath thready with a mixture of fear and excitement.

'I intend to do more than touch you, Bella. It's time you learned your lesson.'

'I shall hate you.'

'You have always hated me.'

'No, I didn't. I merely disliked you, but I shall hate you now.'

'We don't need this between us...' Gervase took a handful of the delicate silk and ripped it right down the skirt. Arabella was wearing nothing beneath it and he laughed as he saw the soft, pearly pink glow of her skin. 'I do not think a lady would go dressed as you do, my precious – but then you are no lady, are you, Bella?'

'I could not find any undergarments...'

'That is just as well,' Gervase said hoarsely. 'I like things the way they are...' He bent his head to kiss her breasts and then as she tore at his hair gave a yelp of pain. 'So you are determined to fight me, Bella?'

'Don't you—' She got no further. His mouth was on hers, cutting off her protests as he held her arms at her sides, preventing her from taking any revenge on his body as he kissed her until she subsided breathlessly. He raised his head to look down at her as she stared up at him, a smoky passion in her eyes that made him groan with wanting.

'Why fight me, Bella? You know you want this as much as I do – have always wanted it. We were made for each other. I knew it from the start but you...'

'I...don't want to fight you...' she admitted in a choked voice. Her body was submitting, needing the excitement and fulfilment he offered, though her spirit resisted. 'But you were such a brute to me...'

'Yes, I was, but you made me angry. Those things are not for you or any woman but *her*.'

'I shan't touch them again.'

'You will be mine,' Gervase muttered as he bent his head to nuzzle her breasts, his tongue delicately laving the peaked nipples, his teeth grazing her so that she writhed and arched her back as the pleasure began to mount. 'No more talk of fighting, my precious. We shall show them all how to live. Everything you ever wanted shall be yours – jewels, clothes, a house and carriage of your own...They will all envy you, those fine ladies who will not acknowledge you.'

'Just make me happy,' she said softly, her mouth parting in a sigh of invitation. 'Don't hurt me or desert me, Gervase. Make me yours and keep me safe...'

'My sweet temptress,' he muttered, his hand moving to part her legs. 'How I have longed for this moment – for you.'

And then he was on her and inside her, filling her, stretching her, making her cry out as she accommodated the huge throbbing length of him, deeper and deeper until she screamed her pleasure aloud. Never, never had she known such ecstasy as this. Her body fit with his as if it had been made for this one purpose, throbbing like the strings of a harp as he played on her, bringing forth sweet music. It was like a heavenly choir or the rushing wind meeting the oncoming tide of a restless sea. She did not know whether she lived or had died and gone to paradise, and when at last his body jerked and hers rippled with spasms of pleasure, she clawed his shoulder as she cried out his name.

'Gervase!'

Gervase said nothing, lying with his face against her breasts for a few moments, until he rolled away from her, leaving the bed to pull on a dressing robe. He turned and looked at her as she began to take off the ruined remnants of the gown.

'Here, wear this,' he said and tossed her another robe. 'I'll have dinner served in my private sitting room. You need not wear the gown you so despise if you do not wish it. I imagined you would buy something better, but tomorrow we shall put things right.'

'I should have done as you told me.'

'It might have been better.' Gervase grinned wickedly. 'On the other hand...I think it turned out well enough. I am going to bathe and change – and I suggest you make yourself comfortable, my sweet. We shall dine together and then see if we can find other ways to amuse ourselves...'

'Ah, Madame Suzanne,' Gervase said, at his most charming when shown into the seamstress's private parlour the next morning. 'It was kind of you to see us at short notice. As perhaps you can see, Mrs Tucker is desperate. She is the widow of one of my dearest friends and her clothes were lost at sea, forcing her to wear a most unsuitable gown to accompany me here this morning.'

The seamstress's eyes went over Arabella assessingly. She did not for one moment believe his story that Arabella was a widow, for if she were not mistaken she had dressed the young lady before. However, the Marquis of Roxbourne was a valued customer and she would not think of refusing him. Even if the girl were his mistress she would be welcome here, for his name and wealth made all respectable.

'I shall be delighted to work a little miracle

for you, my lord,' she said. 'If you return in two hours you shall see a change I believe you will appreciate.'

'Ah, but I have no wish to leave,' Gervase told her with a smile. 'I believe I shall stay here and watch this transformation. My friend has been away from London too long and may need my advice, you see.' He sat down in an elegant chair that hardly looked able to bear his weight and stretched out his long legs before him.

Madame Suzanne saw exactly. The girl was his mistress and he intended to supervise her clothes. If he was taking such an interest she must be important to him. Lucky girl! she thought, a little enviously.

'Then we shall begin with a few gowns I have made up, which could be adjusted to fit Mrs Tucker's figure, and then move on to a more extensive wardrobe – if that is your wish, my lord.'

'Mrs Tucker lost everything,' Gervase replied. 'We shall need a great deal of your time and attention to repair the loss, madame.'

The seamstress was positively purring as she clapped her hands, urging her girls into action. In the next few minutes a succession of gowns was shown to them, three of which Gervase chose for Arabella to try on. The others were dismissed as not stylish enough, and after some consultation with her head seamstress, Madame Suzanne brought out a magnificent evening gown.

'This was ordered by a lady who has not seen fit to collect it,' she said. 'I will let you have it, my lord, as a special favour.'

'Try it on, Bella,' Gervase said. 'And then we'll look at materials and patterns – but you will need something for this evening, and this may do.'

Arabella would have preferred to choose her own gowns, but she was feeling in a mellow mood that morning, and could not fail to be impressed by the way Madame Suzanne was fawning over him. She half expected the woman to become less obliging when they retired to the fitting room, but was pleased to discover that her respectful manner did not change. It seemed that Gervase's money could buy almost anything.

The gown she tried first was a dark blue heavy damask silk with silver embroidery and a daring neckline that swept low over her full breasts. The birth of her child had left her with even more fullness in that region, though fortunately her waist had returned to its original size, which, when laced, was not much larger than the span of a man's hands.

'We should perhaps add a gauze fichu to give you a little more modesty,' the seamstress said. 'But we shall ask for milord's opinion.'

'I think the gown will do very well as it is,' Arabella said. 'But I would not mind a spangled shawl to wear over my shoulders if I felt a little cool.'

'Ah yes, that would be charming,' the seamstress said and snapped her fingers. A filmy shawl was produced and arranged and Arabella went back to the private parlour to show Gervase the result.

'Yes, that will do very well for this evening,' he said with a nod of approval. 'And the other gowns will do for daywear until Madame Suzanne has your clothes ready. And now we shall choose the materials and I will tell you what I have in mind, madame.'

'You have something special in mind, my lord?'

'Yes. I think it may tax even your talents, madame, but I require a wardrobe of some magnificence for my dear friend. Arabella is to be dressed in the first stare as befits a woman of rank and wealth, but the gowns will follow a certain style that is a little out of the ordinary. I want people to be aware of her charms, but they should not be displayed too blatantly. You understand me? She is not an innocent debutante but a woman of great beauty, as I believe you will agree?'

'Oh yes, my lord – and I understand perfectly.'

Of course she understood. He wanted to flaunt his mistress, to make other men jealous that he possessed such a beautiful creature, but he did not want her to look cheap or like a woman of the night. It was a delicate balance, but Madame Suzanne believed she could manage it – providing Mrs Tucker did not insist on having her breasts too much on display.

'Should I not have some say in my clothes, Gervase?' A militant sparkle had crept into Arabella's eyes.

'I shall leave you to choose your bonnets and shawls, my love,' he murmured silkily, 'and anything else you desire – but trust me in the matter of your wardrobe. I believe you will be happy with the result.'

'The marquis is known for his excellent taste,' Madame Suzanne told her, giving him a simpering look that set Arabella's teeth on edge. 'No lady could fault it.'

Arabella felt tempted to make a cutting reply, but recalled a moment the previous night when she had felt truly happy. Gervase had made love to her so many times, his manner that of a lover rather than a protector, and she suddenly realized that she was lucky to have found such generosity. What did it matter if it pleased him to choose her clothes? He would tire of it eventually and then she could choose others that pleased her more.

'Then I must accept your judgement,' she said and smiled sweetly at Gervase. 'I am sure that I could not do better.'

A smile hovered about his mouth, and she could see the mockery in his eyes. He did not believe in her meek manner for one moment, and would no doubt take her to task over it later, when they were alone. Her heart beat faster at the thought, and she realized that nothing else really mattered other than the time they spent in each other's arms. Clothes were not important, for she was happiest when wearing none at all.

'You were very good in there,' Gervase told her as they left some minutes later, Arabella wearing one of the new gowns he had purchased for her. It was a walking gown of green cloth trimmed with black ribbons – a little severe for her taste, though she had to admit it set off her figure to perfection. The bonnet was a piece of frivolous nonsense concocted of feathers, silk ribbons and straw, and she had chosen it herself. 'I shall have to reward you for that, Bella.'

'Where are you taking me this evening?' she asked. 'You said I needed a special gown.'

'We are going to the opera,' he told her. 'I keep a box there and have invited some friends to join us. Afterwards, we shall have supper at an exclusive club – if the idea pleases you?'

'Oh yes, I love music,' she said happily. 'And it is ages since I went out in company – but...'

'You think that some people may cut you?'

'My cousin assured me it would happen.'

'I think you may find that most gentlemen will be happy to acknowledge you,' Gervase told her. 'Some ladies may be frosty, but we shall not mind them, my love. They will all be envious of you.' He touched a finger to her cheek. 'Now I am going to buy you something pretty to wear with that evening gown. Sapphires and diamonds, I think – though emeralds would set off your eyes. But perhaps just diamonds would be best of all...'

'Oh, Gervase...' Arabella looked at herself in the mirror as he fastened the magnificent diamond collar they had purchased at the Bond Street jeweller that morning. 'It is wonderful. Better than anything my cousin possessed, or any of her friends either.'

'And so I should hope,' Gervase said, a smile flickering at the corners of his mouth. The cost of the necklace was prohibitive but he had been determined to make a state-ment, and the collar of huge stones of the first water certainly did that to a nicety. 'I would expect my...woman to wear rather better jewellery than Lady Mary or any of her friends.'

'It would make Nan so jealous,' Arabella said, eyes shining with excitement. 'You are so good to me, Gervase. I do not know what I've done to deserve anything like this.'

'Do you not, Bella?' His eyes were soft and amused as they rested on her face. She was magnificent that night, more beautiful than he had ever seen her, and he believed that the glow radiating from inside her had not been caused simply by the purchase of new gowns and a necklace that would beggar many men. 'Well, perhaps I can think of something later?'

She felt her heart quicken as she gazed up into his eyes and saw the promise there, and almost wished that they were not going out that night.

'Look at me like that and I may forgo the opera,' Gervase said, a mocking smile on his lips. 'Yet it would be a shame to waste such a toilette. I think we are ready, my love. Let us venture forth and see what delights the world has to offer us this night.'

As he offered her his arm, Arabella gurg-led with pleasure. When he was like this, she could almost believe that he loved her and that she returned his feelings. It was just an illusion, of course, and soon enough she would wake from the dream to reality, but for now she would enjoy being the Marquis of Roxbourne's mistress, for it was proving even more exciting than she might have imagined.

The evening was delightful for Arabella. She could not recall ever having had such a wonderful time. Gervase was attentive to her at all times – he could not have been more so had they recently been married – and she felt flattered and privileged to be with such a charming companion.

She knew immediately they entered their box that she had been noticed, and felt the eyes of both men and women upon her during the first act of Handel's *Rinaldo*, which was the story of the capture of Jerusalem by Christians from the Saracens. She was entranced by the music, especially when Armida the sorceress threatened the Saracen king because he admitted his love for a Christian princess.

Their box seemed to be the prime attraction for gentlemen of all ages during the intervals. They came ostensibly to talk with Gervase and the three friends he had invited, one of whom was Jack Meadows, and stayed, enchanted by Arabella's smile and soft laughter.

'By George, you're a lucky fellow,' she heard more than one gentleman tell him, but they did not dare to say anything untoward, treating Arabella with the utmost respect – almost reverence in some cases. It seemed not to matter that she had lost her reputation, for she had gained lustre as Roxbourne's mistress. She was a beautiful woman with a charming manner and a ready wit, and most were happy to accept her for what she was.

Afterwards, at supper, she was treated to more of the same, and felt almost reluctant to leave all her new admirers. And yet when they were alone in Gervase's room, her heart beat faster and she knew that beneath the glamour and excitement of the evening, she had been waiting for this moment.

'So, Bella,' Gervase said, quirking his eyebrow mockingly. 'I believe the evening was a success for you.'

'Because you made it so,' she said honestly. 'You treated me with respect and so your friends followed suit. It is you they respect, Gervase. They would not be so charming if I were not your mistress.'

He reached out, touching her cheek with his fingertips, an odd, slightly regretful expression in his eyes. 'I cannot give you back what you have lost, my love, but while you remain in my protection you will be treated with respect or I shall want to know the reason why.'

'I should not be received in mixed company, Gervase.'

'There are some who may invite you to less formal occasions,' he said. 'Certainly you will accompany me to the houses of my friends and to the theatre, but I must admit that even I cannot force the entrée into some circles. However, we shall ignore them, my love. We may take a jaunt to Paris or Vienna at some time in the summer, and there I dare say you will find society is freer. I sometimes find English society manners stifling, though in private it is a different matter. You committed the cardinal sin, my sweet, and for that you cannot be forgiven. Others may do worse, but they do not flaunt their vices as you did.'

'I do not care what the old tabbies think of me!' she declared and stuck her head in the air.

'Nor I,' Gervase replied and reached out for her, drawing her close. 'You are mine as I always meant you to be, and for so long as you are faithful to me, I shall keep you safe.'

Did he think she would betray him? Arabella pressed her face against his shoulder as he lifted her in his arms to carry her to the bed they shared. She would be a fool to do so. Besides, there was no one she liked sufficiently, no other man who could compare to Gervase. At least...But she must never think of Harry Sylvester. Harry had lied to her, deserted her, and married another. Surely she did not still care for him?

Why should she when Gervase's loving

was so satisfying? She had all she could possibly want of life. She would be a fool to throw it away for a man who had betrayed her.

The next morning Gervase took her to see the house he had bought for her. It was a delightful Queen Anne cottage by the river and just twenty minutes' drive in a carriage from his own home. She was to have a full complement of servants to run it for her, a carriage and horses, and a settlement of ten thousand pounds. The money was to be placed in trust for her, the income hers to spend as she chose, but if their arrangement ended by mutual consent, then she would be able to break the trust and use the capital as she pleased after a year had passed.

'That is a huge sum,' Arabella said, slightly overcome by his generosity. Had she been his wife she could not have expected more. 'Are you sure you want to give me so much, Gervase?'

'I shall give you much more if you please me,' he said, one finger beneath her chin. 'I see no reason why we should not continue to be happy together for many years, Bella, but I shall not stomach unfaithfulness. Remember that, for if you betray me our arrangement is at an end.'

'Why do you not trust me?' she asked, feeling a little hurt that he had thought it necessary to remind her yet again. 'There is no other I would look at, Gervase. Why should I when you make me so happy?'

'Are you happy, my love?'

'You know I am.'

'And shall you be happy here in this house?'

'Yes...' she hesitated. 'Must I live here, Gervase? I think I may miss you, for I have been used to seeing you each morning as I wake. May I not continue to live at your house?'

Gervase laughed, amused by her confession, which seemed to confirm what he had begun to hope – that she truly cared for him, at least as much as she was able.

'It is expected that we have separate establishments,' he told her. 'But do not fear, I dare say I shall spend more time here than at my own house if you are here. I do not care for that damned place. I inherited it and, though I have done much to lighten the atmosphere, I still dislike it. I believe we shall find true contentment here together, Arabella.'

His house held unhappy memories for him. Were some of them to do with the clothes she had found in his closet? After their return from Madame Suzanne's salon she had discovered that the gowns had been moved elsewhere, and the housekeeper told her they were in a trunk in the attic. No amount of questioning brought an answer to her curiosity about their former owner, for Mrs Bumpstead simply did not know.

'It's a mystery to me as well as you, ma'am,' she said. 'His lordship keeps his secrets to himself – and you're the first lady he has ever brought to this house to stay.'

So Arabella had had to be content with that, for she did not dare to ask Gervase himself. Clearly, the lady the clothes had belonged to was very precious to him. That thought nagged at the back of Arabella's mind, for she did not think he could ever feel as much for her. Oh, she knew that he desired her, was jealous of her, cared for her in his way – but he did not love her. She had forfeited all chance or right to his love when she chose to lie with Harry Sylvester.

It would not be wise to love a man like Gervase, Arabella realized. He seemed to care for her, but he might tire of her soon enough, and this time her heart would truly break.

No, this time she would be wiser. She would hold a little of herself in reserve against the time when Gervase no longer desired her, for if she did not she was lost.

Arabella settled quickly into her new life. Gervase visited her almost every night, even those when she was suffering her womanly flow and could not take him to her bed.

They often spent those evenings quietly, playing games of chance, reading aloud, performing some piece of music, or simply talking. At other times he took her to the theatre, to parties given by his friends, at which she met other ladies who were in a similar situation to her own, and to the opera again.

They also held their own entertainment at Gervase's house. Card evenings and soirées, a small dance, which was attended by some ladies and gentlemen she had not thought would enter a house that she was known to frequent. It seemed that she was being accepted as the marquis's mistress, for their liaison had lasted several months and seemed as if it might continue, and there were many who did not choose to cut such a wealthy man. They spent a few weeks in Paris, and talked of visiting Italy the following spring.

At Christmas they went down to Gervase's country house and he invited a large party of mixed company. Only one lady declined to accompany her husband, who came anyway, for Roxbourne's hospitality was lavish. He excused his wife on the grounds that they had hope she might be increasing, but Arabella knew that it was because the lady would not want to meet her on such intimate terms.

Despite such small pinpricks, she was

happy. Her life was fuller than she could have expected, and when on their return to town her cousin came to visit her, she felt that her cup was overflowing.

'It is foolish for us to be enemies,' Lady Mary told her. 'It would have been so much better if you had married him, Arabella – but there, it is no use to cry over spilled milk. You have been fortunate, my dear, and I hope you appreciate your happy position?'

'Oh, I do, Cousin,' Arabella told her. 'We are both very happy.'

'Then I shall not scold you for past foolishness. Be careful not to upset Roxbourne, Arabella, that is all I would say to you. He is generous to a fault, but they say he makes a bad enemy.'

'I need no warning, cousin. Besides...' She left the sentence unfinished. Her thoughts were private and she would not share them with Lady Mary.

Gervase was still a mystery to her. They shared so much that was good, but there were parts of his life that he held back from her. She still had no idea of the identity of the woman he had loved so much, or where his wealth came from. He spent it lavishly – on her, on his horses, and gave freely to his friends when he was minded to do so.

She had asked him once why he was so trustful of Jack Meadows.

'Do you not like him, Bella?' Gervase had

raised an eyebrow. 'Has he said or done anything to displese you?'

'No, not at all. He is always most respectful,' she replied. 'I think he takes advantage of your good nature, Gervase, that is all.'

Gervase laughed softly. 'Jack knows how far he can go,' he replied. 'There is a debt I owe him, but even that would not save him if he tried to touch you.' The smile died from his eyes. 'You would tell me if there was anything?'

'There is a look in his eyes sometimes,' she admitted. 'But no more than in other men's eyes. He has never said or done anything that you would dislike, I promise you.'

'Jack knows his fate if he did,' Gervase said, his good humour restored. 'What shall I give you as a birthday gift, my love?'

'I lack for nothing,' she told him truthfully. 'You have been so generous, Gervase. I would have your approval, nothing more.'

'Nothing more?' He tipped her chin up with his finger, quizzing her. 'Not even an emerald ring to go with the necklace I bought you at Christmas?'

'If you wish to give it to me,' Arabella said. 'But I am content as I am.'

'You run the risk of sounding too fond, my sweet,' Gervase told her, a wry smile on his lips. 'You will have me thinking you truly care for me if you are not careful.'

'I should be a fool if I did not.'

'Yes...' Gervase looked at her thoughtfully. 'Whatever you are, you are not that, Bella. Should I believe you? Women are ever free with soft smiles and pleasant words when you please them, but seldom mean them. If I were to believe you, I might demand so much more of you, my love.'

'What do you mean?'

Gervase shook his head. 'I might ask something of you that you would not care to give,' he said. 'Perhaps it is best that we go on as we are for the moment.'

Arabella had puzzled over his odd words. What could he mean? What could she give him that he did not already possess? She could think of nothing and in the end gave it up.

Gervase was the one who gave. She had nothing to give but her body and he already possessed that whenever and as often as he chose.

Ten

They had been together more than a year, longer than she had been with Harry, Arabella realized as she opened the gift that had arrived for her that morning with a note from Gervase. He had not spent the previous night with her because he had been out of town for three days on business, but he had not forgotten to send her a gift for this special day.

His note said that he was back in town and would be taking her to the theatre that night and hoped she had a special gown to wear to accompany his small gift: a parure of pearls and diamonds, consisting of a tiara, necklace, matching bracelet and earrings.

Arabella thought of the new gown she had purchased from Madame Suzanne. It was of a deep green silk, trimmed with seed pearls on the bodice and at the hem, and would set off Gervase's gift to perfection. She had so many jewels now that she had begun to tire of them, to long for something more – something that she did not quite understand but knew came from deep down inside her.

She often thought of the child she had lost. He would be almost fourteen months old now, if he had lived, but she must not let herself think of the past. That was over and she had a wonderful new life. Harry was nothing but a memory to her.

It was strange that she had never seen him, though. When Gervase was in London, which was most of the time, they went to various theatres and sometimes an exclusive gaming club, which admitted ladies, providing the lady was accompanied by a gentleman. She had thought they might see Harry at one of these public places, but somehow they never had.

She was pleased that Gervase was home and that she would be seeing him that evening. He had been a little odd just before he went away – secretive. She had wondered if there was another woman, but she had not dared to ask. Gervase did not tell her about his business, and he had sworn that it was business that took him from town. She could only accept his word and pray that he was not tiring of her.

Yet the fear had grown these past days. What would she do if Gervase no longer wanted her? She refused to think of what her life might become. Gervase must still care for her or he would not have sent her such a lovely gift...

'Have you been good while I was away, my sweet?'

Arabella raised her head proudly. 'You should not need to ask that, Gervase. You know that I would not betray you. I am not the one who has secrets.'

Gervase gave a wry smile. 'One day you shall know my secret. I had hoped it might be this time, Bella, but it was not to be.'

'You talk in riddles!' She looked at him crossly. It was all of a piece. He would tell her nothing, which meant that he did not trust her. 'I do not know what to make of you.'

'Do you not, my love?' He raised his brow but went no further.

His refusal to answer her unspoken questions made her feel irritable and a little on edge as they left for the theatre that night. Gervase expected her to trust him, but he would not share his life with her. He said that he cared for her, that there was no other woman he wanted – that there had never been a woman he cared for as he did her – but still he kept his secrets.

Would he have done so if she had been his wife? Perhaps, she admitted. Many husbands kept secrets from their wives. However, she was not his wife, and that had begun to rankle. She had everything she wanted, except that which she wanted most.

Arabella did not know why she wanted marriage so much. Her life could hardly be more satisfying, yet there was a vague dissatisfaction, a need she could not fill.

Gervase glanced at her as he handed her down from the carriage. 'You are very quiet this evening, my sweet.'

'My thoughts are my own, Gervase. You do not own them.'

'What does that mean?' His eyes narrowed suspiciously. What was the matter with her? She had behaved oddly ever since his return. Was she beginning to tire of their relationship?

He had thought to bring her news that would please her, but it had been a false trail and his search must go on. To tell her what was in his mind would be to arouse false hopes, and he would not do that, nor would he tell her yet of his plans for the future. Plans that he had begun to make the night he rescued her from the whorehouse...

Arabella took her seat in their box at the theatre, settling down to watch the play – a comedy that she had looked forward to seeing. The lights had not yet gone down and as she let her eyes wander over the audience she noticed a man looking up at her. He made what she considered a mocking bow, his eyes insolent as they rested on the neckline of her gown, which was décolleté and quite daring. Now she wished that she had worn a fichu with it, realizing that she did not care to be stared at that way. Especially when the man ogling her was Harry Sylvester – and by the look of him he had been drinking heavily.

She averted her head, her cheeks hot, heart thumping madly. Why was it that Harry could still affect her this way? She was no longer in love with him, but his look had made her uncomfortable. She glanced uneasily at Gervase. Had he seen Harry? She could imagine his reaction if he noticed the way he was staring at her!

Fortunately, the lights went down and Arabella was able to concentrate on the first act of the play, which amused her greatly. Indeed, she was so caught up in it that when the lights went up she had forgotten the earlier incident.

Their box was the focus of attention as it so often was, and several gentlemen arrived to join them for a glass of wine during the interval. She stiffened as she heard what Jack Meadows was saying to one of the other visitors.

'That fool Sylvester is here this evening.'

'Drunk as usual, I dare say,' the other replied. 'He finds marriage to that sour-faced cit less pleasurable than he imagined, I think.'

'What would you expect,' Jack said on a

coarse laugh. 'He has been used to finer fare – and the father keeps a tight rein on the money, I believe. Sylvester is like a tame bear on a leading string. No wonder he drinks all the time. I vow I would rather be dead than in his shoes.'

Arabella sipped her wine and looked out at the audience, her heart thumping as she saw that Harry was immediately below their box, looking up at them. He made an elaborate bow and then blew a kiss to her. She looked away immediately, fanning herself to cool her heated cheeks. Then, snatching a glance at Gervase, she saw that he had noticed this latest incident, and his eyes had narrowed to angry slits of displeasure.

Arabella was relieved when the lights went down and most of their guests returned to their own seats. However, her pleasure in the play had been spoiled, for she could not concentrate on what the actors were saying.

Harry was miserable in his marriage! Did that mean he regretted it – that he wished he had married Arabella instead? She remembered his bow and the kiss he had blown to her. She had thought he was mocking her, but supposing he still cared...

What a fool she was to even think it! All that was over. She had a new life now. Harry might be attracted to her in the fine gowns and jewels that Gervase had provided, but he had not cared for her when she was carrying his child. She would be a fool to let him back into her life. Indeed, she did not want him, had found contentment in her life as it was – or would if she could be certain that Gervase was not thinking of ending their arrangement.

She tried hard to dismiss all thought of Harry Sylvester, and when Gervase took her home she kissed him, showing him that she was pleased to have him back home. He seemed a little cool at first, almost withdrawn, but once aroused made love to her as passionately as always, bringing her to a trembling climax so that she screamed his name aloud, her nails scoring his shoulder.

But afterwards, when she would have liked to lie in his arms and talk of what he had been doing while he was away from her, he left the bed, saying that he was returning to his own house.

'But why, Gervase?' she asked. 'I have not seen you for three days. I thought you would stay with me all night.'

'I have things to see to in the morning and must be about early,' Gervase said, frowning. 'I'll take you somewhere tomorrow evening, Bella – and then perhaps I'll stay.'

'Sometimes I think you grow tired of me,' she said, a sulky pout to her mouth. 'Is there someone new in your life, Gervase?'

'Perhaps I should be the one asking that

263

question. Or rather, what is Sylvester to you?'

'Nothing! How could he be?' She sat up in bed, her knees to her chest, hair hanging over her shoulders in gorgeous disarray. 'How could you ask me that, Gervase? You know that is long over.'

'Perhaps.' His eyes were brooding, smoky with doubt. 'Yet Sylvester did not appear to think so this evening.'

'I cannot help the way men look at me,' Arabella said. 'You do not care when others stare at me.'

'But they have not been your lover.' His mouth was a thin, hard line, his eyes cold, sending a shiver down her spine.

'Will you never forget that?' she cried. 'Why do you hate him so? What has he done to you that made you set out to ruin him?'

'It is an old story,' Gervase said, his voice harsh and cold, shutting her out. 'But remember that I should not continue to keep you as my mistress if I believed that you were seeing him behind my back.'

'Believe what you like!' Arabella said and lay down, hunching her shoulder under the sheets. He would always believe the worst of her and nothing she could do would change that.

'What I want to believe is that you prefer me,' Gervase said softly. 'But perhaps I am a fool.'

Arabella lay with her face hidden in the pillows. She felt hurt and humiliated that Gervase should believe her faithless. Harry's bows and kisses had affected her that evening, she could not deny it, but not to the extent that she would risk all she had for his sake. A part of her responded to him still, but there was another part that told her she was happier with Gervase than she had ever been.

'I shall see you tomorrow,' Gervase said.

She made no reply as he went out, and discovered that her cheeks were wet with tears. If Gervase loved her he would trust her, wouldn't he? But she knew that he didn't love her. He merely desired her – and if he no longer wanted to stay all night with her, that must mean she was losing him. He would visit her less and less, and then she would be alone.

'A peace offering,' Gervase said as he presented her with a hatbox the next evening. 'Forgive me for being harsh to you last night, my love. It was merely my jealousy.'

'Were you jealous?' Arabella asked. She opened the box and took out a delicious confection of feathers and ribbons, which she held over her head in front of the mirror before laying it aside. 'It is lovely, Gervase. You spoil me as always.'

'You are worth spoiling, Bella.'

'Am I?' Her eyes were very bright with the tears that she would not allow to fall. 'Where are we going this evening?'

'Jack has asked us to a supper he is giving at the club. I said we would go, but we need not stay long. I would rather be alone with you. I have something I wish to talk to you about, Bella.'

Arabella's heart caught with fright. He was going to tell her it was over, she was certain of it, and she hardly knew how to smile as she slipped her arm through his. Yet she would not let him see how much she was hurting inside. She had always known this day would come – what she hadn't understood was how much it would hurt.

'Then shall we go?' she asked brightly.

'Of course, my sweet. May I tell you that I have seldom seen you looking lovelier, Bella? I dare say you will have a bevy of new admirers this evening, but do not be afraid, I shall keep my temper locked securely away. I do not wish to fall out with you this evening.'

Jack's supper party was a merry one. He had met a new heiress and was considering a proposal of marriage to her in the near future.

'Bethan is a sweet girl,' he told his friends. 'And her father is so very wealthy. I almost think it worth giving up my freedom for the

266

privilege of wedding her.'

'Do you love her?' Arabella asked and he looked at her consideringly.

'Probably as much as I could ever love anyone other than myself.'

'Now that is an honest answer,' Gervase said and laughed. 'I believe our Jack has been caught in the cat's claws at last.'

'Would you marry her if she were not wealthy?' Arabella asked.

'Good lord no,' Jack admitted. 'Couldn't afford it, Bella my love. I'm far too expensive – ask Gervase. He's kept me from a debtors' prison often enough.'

'Only the Lord knows why,' Gervase said, but gave him an affectionate look. 'So you will be a reformed character and there will be no more suppers in places like this?'

'No – not for a while,' Jack said looking a little rueful. 'I dare say Bethan wouldn't like it, and I couldn't bring her here, could I? Not to a place like this.'

His careless words brought a flush to Arabella's cheeks. She turned away, hurt that Gervase had not answered his friend. Surely he could have said something to defend her?

As she glanced across the large dining room she saw another party of young gentlemen, one of whom was Harry Sylvester. She had not seen him at the club before and turned away quickly, her cheeks hot.

'Perhaps we should go, Gervase?'

He glanced at her, saw her distress and nodded, offering her his arm as he turned back to his friends. 'We have a prior appointment. You will excuse us, everyone.'

Arabella clung to his arm as they made their way across the room. All she wanted was to leave quickly. Jack's careless insult had hurt her more than she would have thought possible, and she wanted to avoid contact with Harry Sylvester.

'So...' Harry was on his feet as they approached his table. ''Tis Roxbourne and his lovely doxy. How are you, Arabella, my love? I vow you look even more beautiful than you did when you were my whore.'

Arabella felt as if she had been turned to stone. How could Harry say such things to her? How could he so insult her?

'Stand aside, Sylvester.' Gervase's tone was cold. 'We have no desire for your company.'

'It irks you, doesn't it?' Harry said with an insulting leer. 'That she was mine first. You can't stomach that I had her.'

Gervase let go of Arabella's arm and stepped forward. His mouth was a thin line, his eyes like ice as they moved over the other man with obvious disdain. 'You are a disgusting swine, Sylvester,' he said. 'If I thought you capable I would challenge you to a duel – but I hear you are never sober long enough...'

'Be damned to you!' Harry lunged at him, striking him across the face. 'I'll meet you whenever you like. Marsham and Bellinger will stand my seconds.'

'As you wish,' Gervase replied and named two of the gentlemen that had been at Jack's supper with them. 'My seconds will call on you in the morning, sir. Come, Arabella, the air in here is sour. We shall not stay to breathe it further.'

Arabella felt him grip her arm, his fingers digging into her flesh, hurting her as he almost dragged her from the room and out into the cool night air. She was shaken by what had happened, her stomach sickened with the insults that had been offered her.

She was bundled inside Gervase's carriage roughly, as if he were angry with her, which made her angry in turn. Why had he not defended her – either to Jack or to Harry? He had been coldly insulting to Harry, but he had not tried to defend her reputation, and that had cut her to the bone.

'You will not fight him?' She flung the words at him without thinking. 'He would be no match for you, Gervase. You keep your skills honed. Harry has let himself go...'

'The more fool him,' Gervase replied. 'He challenged me. I would have let it go.'

'Because you agreed with him?' Arabella accused. 'Just as you agreed with Jack.'

'Don't be a fool, Bella.'

'Jack couldn't take his fiancée to a place like that, but it is all right for me to go.'

'That is a different matter. The girl is young and innocent. She would be shocked by some of the behaviour there.'

'And I am not innocent,' Arabella said bitterly. 'That's what you mean, isn't it, Gervase? I committed the unforgivable sin, did I not? Therefore I am nothing, and can be shown no respect.'

'Do not be ridiculous. I have always treated you with respect.'

'Have you?' She turned her face aside, fighting her tears and her hurt. It was true that Gervase had never treated her as if she were merely a whore to him, but he had not defended her when Jack said those hurtful words, nor had he denied Harry's taunts. But how could he when they were true? Arabella felt the sting of regret. If only she could go back to that day when she had allowed Harry to make love to her. If only she could change what had happened.

'Do not sulk, Bella,' Gervase said. 'We cannot change the past. And you need not shed tears for Sylvester. I dare say it will end with honour being satisfied with first blood.'

Arabella did not answer him. When they got to her house she allowed him to help her down from the carriage, but went on ahead, her head high. She did not look at him as she walked upstairs, and once inside her room she locked the door, leaning against it as the tears she had held back ran down her cheeks.

'Bella! Open the door,' Gervase said. 'I need to talk to you. I have something to tell you.'

'Go away,' she said, wiping her hand across her face. 'I don't want to talk to you tonight. Tell me what you have to say another time.'

'You are being foolish. There is no need to be upset. If you will only let me in I shall explain why none of this matters to us.'

'Go away. I want to be alone.'

'So you can cry over that wretch Sylvester, I suppose,' Gervase said, an angry note in his voice. 'Surely this evening told you what you can expect from him? Why won't you trust me, Bella?'

'You don't care about me. You let Jack insult me...'

'Jack wasn't thinking. He accepts you as one of us, Bella, and that is a greater compliment than you know. I shall insist that he apologizes to you in private. It would only have made things worse had I made a fuss this evening.'

Arabella said nothing. She knew in her heart that he was right, but she was hurting too much to be sensible. 'Leave me alone tonight, Gervase.'

'If that is what you want...But I shan't be here tomorrow. I shall see you in two days' time. Try not to be more foolish than you can help in the meantime. None of this is important. Believe me, it will all be different soon.'

He could not have made things plainer. Hearing his footsteps walk away from her door, Arabella threw herself on the bed and began to sob in earnest. He had made up his mind to part from her. No doubt he would be generous. He might allow her to keep the less valuable of her jewels, and the house and settlement were already tied up in her name. She would not be destitute, but she would be alone.

Gervase cursed as he left the house and instructed his driver to take him home. He would have liked to sort this out with Arabella for once and all. It was time they came to a proper understanding. His plans were almost ready now for the new life he planned for them. The class-ridden society of England would be left behind, the prejudice of those who had insulted Arabella that evening forgotten as they sought new horizons.

He had hoped that she would be glad to go with him, that they were close enough to enjoy the adventure he believed lay ahead of them. Yet she still clung to her memories of Harry Sylvester. Even his insults this evening had not cured her.

Once, Gervase had wanted nothing more than to see Harry Sylvester bleeding and dying at his feet. His anger had been such after the discovery of what had happened to his innocent sister that he could happily have horsewhipped the rogue or strangled him with his bare hands. Of late his anger had abated, leaving him only a kind of sadness that his poor Helen had died without ever knowing the happiness he had discovered with Arabella. A kind of happiness he believed would grow stronger over the years, would grow and blossom in the new life he planned for them.

Arabella's feeling of misery intensified as the long night and the following, even longer, day passed. It was certain that Gervase had tired of her and she knew she must accept his decision without tears or recriminations. He had never told her he loved her, never promised her more than he had already given her.

But what was she to do with the rest of her life? Arabella could think of nothing but the empty days and nights to come. Her life had revolved around Gervase this past year and although she had made one or two friends, young women in a similar situation to herself, there was no one she could unburden herself to. Her cousin she knew would have no sympathy, nor would she bother with Arabella once she knew that she was no longer Gervase's mistress.

A visit to her sister was out of the question – Lady Mary had told her that Nan's temper had not improved since the birth of her first child. She could of course find herself a new protector. She knew that was the advice her cousin would give her, but the thought of taking another man in Gervase's place was so awful that Arabella felt sick at the mere idea.

Yet what else could she do? She had not been meant to live alone and would miss the gaiety and comradeship she had experienced with Gervase's friends.

What if something were to happen to Gervase? Amidst her own feelings of misery and fear for the future she was suddenly aware of her fear for Gervase. She did not believe that Harry could beat him in a sword fight, but something might happen...

No, she would not let herself think about that stupid duel! Gervase had told her it was a mere formality, and she was sure that it would end with the pair of them making friends and going off to drink together.

Arabella's conviction did not keep her from a sleepless night, for she had received a note from one of Gervase's friends to say that the duel was to take place in the morning.

After tossing endlessly on her pillow, she rose early and, putting on her cloak, went for a walk in the cool morning air. She had drawn her hood well up over her face, and though she received a few curious stares, no one accosted her and she returned feeling refreshed. She would never have believed it possible, she thought as she went up to her bedchamber, but on her walk she had felt nostalgic for her home in the country. It seemed that life in London had begun to lose its charm for her – or perhaps that was merely because she was feeling so low?

On her return to the house, she found a note from Gervase waiting for her. The duel was over and both men were alive. Arabella closed her eyes, realizing how much she had feared something very different, and then read on.

Gervase had received nothing more than a scratch on his arm, but he was sorry to inform her that Harry was more severely wounded and there were fears for his life.

If that happens, Gervase had written, *I shall have to go to the country for a while, Bella. I shall expect you to accompany me. I have something important to discuss with you.*

She already knew what that was, of course, but why did he want her to accompany him to the country? Duelling was not illegal, though it was frowned upon these days and, when a man was killed, often led to arrest or disgrace for the victor. A speedy release could be obtained by payment of a fine, and she saw no reason why Gervase should wish to avoid that – unless the fight had been deemed unfair.

Had Gervase been determined to kill Harry? Had he done something terrible? Something for which he might be accused of murder?

Suddenly, Arabella's sympathies were all with Harry. She had seen for herself that he was drunk the night he challenged Gervase, and he had said dreadful things, but perhaps it was because he was so unhappy. Perhaps he had been jealous when he saw her looking so well and happy with Gervase...

And Gervase no longer wanted her for himself. Why did he have to kill the only man she had cared for? In her rising anger and distress her thoughts were confused and she forgot the months of contentment she had known with Gervase. All the pain of losing Harry came back to her and she began to imagine that he had been miserable because of her – because he had loved her.

Gervase did not want her, but Harry did – and Harry was dying. Gervase had done it to spite her. It was all his fault. If he had not hated Harry, if he had not ruined him at the card tables, she would have been Harry's wife!

Anger had been simmering inside her all day. It burst out as Gervase walked in wearing his coat with one sleeve loose and a sling to support his injured arm, nonchalantly asking her if she was ready to go to the theatre with him that evening.

'How can you ask that?' she demanded, eyes flashing. 'When you have killed Harry!'

'His condition is better than I thought this morning,' Gervase replied, his expression remote and unreadable. 'I dare say he will live, though he may be obliged to keep to his bed for a few weeks.'

'And that is all you care!' Arabella was beyond reason. He had left her alone all day to worry and fret, and now he behaved as if nothing had happened. 'But then, you care nothing for anyone other than yourself.'

'I suppose that means you?' His mouth had drawn into a thin line. 'I am sorry if you have been anxious over your lover, Bella. When I sent that note I believed he might die – but as I said, I imagine he may live.'

'Oh, I hate you!'

'Yes, I can see that you do,' Gervase replied. 'I had hoped your feelings were rather different, Bella, but it seems that I am wrong. That is unfortunate. I had plans for the future for us both, but clearly you have others. I wish you well of them. I dare say Sylvester may care to take you as his mistress. They say his wife is a sour-faced scold and keeps him on a tight rein financially, but he may find a way of escaping her now and then.'

'He loves me,' Arabella declared, knowing only that Gervase had made her angry and she wanted to hit back at him. 'If you had not ruined him at the card tables he would have married me.'

'It seems you have learned nothing,' Gervase said. 'I am sorry. I had hoped that you might have learned to care for me a little. However, I know when I am defeated. You have this house and your settlement, Bella – and whatever presents I have given you. I think we have nothing more to say to one another.'

'Gervase!' Arabella's heart raced, her knees going weak as she realized what he was saying. 'No...I didn't mean...'

'Oh, but I think you did,' he said. 'I believe we have been happy together at times, Bella, but *he* was always between us. Forgive me, I shall not see you again. I leave for the country in the morning. Goodbye, my dearest. I pray that you may find happiness one day.'

'Gervase...' There was so much she wanted to say, but the words stuck in her throat. She watched as he turned and walked away from her.

And then she fell to her knees, covering her face with her hands. It was over. All the happiness she had known these past months was at an end – and for what? Gervase believed that she still cared for Harry Sylvester. In her distress and anger she had given him that impression, but it was not so. How could it be when she cared for Gervase?

She was beginning to realize how much he had meant to her now that it was too late. Gervase had walked out of her life. He would not come back. Even if she ran after him, begged him to forgive her, he would not come back.

Because, of course, he had never loved her. While she amused him he had been content to indulge her, but now it was over. He no longer wanted her and he had used the quarrel over Harry to finish their relationship.

He had already been planning to end their arrangement before the terrible quarrel that had taken place between him and Harry. She had known it in her heart, and his behaviour now confirmed it. There was nothing she could do to change things. But what was she to do with her life now?

Arabella fought her tears. There was no point in giving way to self-pity. Yet she had nothing else, no one else to fill her thoughts.

For the past year she had thought of no one but Gervase and now he was gone.

A devastating emptiness filled her. She almost wished that she might die, but something within her refused to give up. She could not have Gervase – so she would have Harry if she could!

Harry loved her, she was sure of it. He had regretted his marriage to that pale, sour-faced woman he had married, and wanted Arabella again. She would visit him at his house, and when he saw her he would beg her to return to him. She would forget Gervase in Harry's arms.

But she could not go this evening. It was too late. She would go in the morning. In the meantime she would take a glass of brandy to bed with her to help her sleep.

Three glasses of brandy did not give Arabella the sleep she craved, but the fourth sent her into a drugged sleep that kept her abed until mid morning and left her feeling heavy-eyed and ill.

Her head was pounding and she thought she might be sick, but she drank a pot of strong dark coffee and felt a little better. Then she dressed in one of her most attractive carriage gowns and sent for her coach and horses. She gave the driver his instructions, climbed into the back and closed her eyes. Her head was still aching, but she was determined to go through with her plans.

During the long, restless night, it had occurred to her that she was a moderately wealthy woman. The jewels Gervase had given her were worth a small fortune alone, and the settlement was generous. She knew that she could only use the income unless Gervase agreed to release the capital to her, but the house and its contents were also worth a tidy sum. Would they be enough to lure Harry back to her? His wife was the daughter of a very rich merchant, but both father and daughter were reputed to be penny-pinching and Harry was clearly miserable. Surely he would seize the chance to be with Arabella again?

Her headache had almost cleared up by the time her carriage stopped outside Harry's house. She lifted her head proudly as she went up to the imposing front door and knocked confidently. A young maid-servant opened it. She bobbed a curtsey, looking nervous and flustered as she asked for Arabella's name.

'I am Mistress Tucker,' she said. 'A very dear friend of your master. I have heard that he is ill and I have called to ask after him.'

'Please come in, ma'am,' the girl said. 'I shall go and ask Lady Sylvester if she will see you.'

'Thank you, child,' Arabella said, smiling at her sweetly.

As soon as she was left alone she left the small reception room to which she had been shown and headed for the stairs, knowing that this was her best chance of seeing Harry. If Lady Sylvester saw her she would instantly be shown the door, and having come this far she was determined to see him.

A young footman stared at her at the top of the stairs. 'May I help you, ma'am?'

'I am your master's sister come to visit him,' Arabella lied wildly. 'Pray show me where I may find him, for I am out of my wits with worry and could not wait a moment longer to see him.'

'Why certainly, ma'am,' he said, flushing to the roots of his hair as she smiled at him. 'He is much better today and insisted on leaving his bed, though the doctor forbade it for a week. You will find him in the green parlour – at the end of this hall.'

'Thank you. I shan't forget your kindness,' Arabella murmured huskily and dabbed at her eyes. The tears she had cried for Gervase had vanished for the moment and she was filled with an odd excitement. It was all going to be wonderful. Harry was in love with her. He would leave his wife for her and they would be happy together. She would forget Gervase in his arms.

She ran down the hall and threw open the door of the small parlour, a very elegant room decorated expensively with exquisite French furniture and heavy damask drapes. Everything about it shouted money, though it was perhaps a little vulgar compared to Gervase's home.

Harry was lying on a gilt sofa, his eyes closed, his open dressing robe revealing a heavy strapping of bandages around his chest.

'Harry!' she cried, causing him to look up. 'Oh, my dearest. I had to come when I heard what had happened...' She faltered as she saw the unmistakable look of horror in his eyes. 'Harry...I know I should have let you know I was coming but—'

'Good Lord! What the hell are you doing here, Bella? For goodness sake get out of here before Jane sees you.'

'But you are unhappy with her. Everyone says so. Leave her and come to me, Harry. I have money. We could go away – to Paris, or Italy...'

'Did you not hear me?' Harry's eyes shot to the door. He was clearly nervous. 'Jane will kill me if she sees you here.'

'You don't need her or her money—'

'Damn it!' Harry swore, his face going deadly white as his wife entered the room. 'Get her out of here, Jane, for pity's sake. She is quite mad and I fear she will bring on another seizure.'

'My poor Harry,' Lady Sylvester said, her

283

eyes sparking with fury as she looked at Arabella. 'I suppose you are that...that woman who caused my poor darling so much trouble before? Well, madam, I shall give you one minute to leave my house and then my servants will throw you into the street.'

Arabella watched as she bent over Harry, stroking his hair back from his forehead. He smiled up at her, perfectly content to be made a fuss of, and ignored Arabella completely.

What a fool she had been to come here! Arabella realized what she ought to have known at the beginning. Harry Sylvester cared for no one but himself. He had never loved her. He did not love his wife, but she gave him what he needed – money and a certain amount of freedom. And she clearly loved him.

Lady 'Sylvester had straightened up. She glared at Arabella and then went over to a satinwood side table where a silver bell had been placed. As she picked it up, Arabella turned and walked out of the room. Her cheeks were burning and she felt the sting of humiliation. She had no place in this house. She ought never to have come.

All she could do now was to return to her own house and think about what she was going to do with the rest of her life.

Eleven

'There is a visitor, ma'am. A gentleman,' Arabella's maid said as she came into the salon where Arabella was drinking yet another glass of wine. She had decided to stick to wine because the after-effects of overindulging were not as severe as she had suffered from Gervase's best brandy. 'He was most insistent on seeing you.'

'Tell him to go away,' Arabella said. In the past week she had had five gentlemen callers, all of them so-called friends of Gervase, and all of them with one purpose in mind. 'I do not want to see anyone unless it is Roxbourne.' But of course Gervase would not come. He had told her it was over and she knew he would not change his mind.

She sipped her wine as the maid went away, glancing at herself in the mirror above the fireplace. She was hardly fit to receive callers, her hair straggling about her shoulders, her gown creased and stained with wine she had spilled on the skirt earlier. Her eyes were puffy from weeping, but she had discovered that tears did not help. The only thing that helped her to sleep was wine, and that made her mouth taste foul and riled her stomach. Yet she could not rest without it, and she did not know how to face her life.

'Your maid said you were receiving only Roxbourne,' a voice said from the doorway and she turned to see Jack Meadows enter the pretty salon. 'He won't come, Bella. Once he is finished with someone, that's it. I would have thought you would know that much by now.'

'Who asked for your opinion?' Arabella asked, deliberately rude. She had not forgiven him for his insult. It seemed to her fuddled mind that everything had started to go wrong that evening. 'I do not know why you have come here – you and all the others. I don't want to be any man's mistress. There isn't a penny to choose between you and I've had enough of you all.'

'I dare say you feel that way for the moment,' Jack drawled. 'I think you cared for Gervase more than he realized.'

'Damn him – and the rest of you,' Arabella muttered and took another sip of her wine. 'Why should I care? I have money. I can look after myself.'

'Drink yourself into a stupor, you mean? How long will your looks last if you drown your sorrows in wine day and night?'

'I might as well be dead.'

'But why? Because one man deserted you?

Why not take another in his place? Show him it doesn't matter to you that he went off to the country to sulk and left you to fend for yourself.'

'Why do you care what happens to me?' Arabella's eyes flashed with temper as she looked at him. 'You never liked me, Jack. I could see it in your eyes. And you insulted me the other night.'

'Yes, Gervase told me you took that hard,' Jack said. 'It wasn't meant the way you think, Bella. I don't despise you – and I've always wanted you. I envied Gervase having you as his mistress, but I couldn't compete with him. I don't have his money or his power. Besides, I wouldn't have dared to try and take you from him while he wanted you. Now he has finished the affair it's different. I think we might suit each other, Bella. I haven't as much money, but I dare say I could please you in other ways.'

'I doubt it,' she said, angry that he should imagine Gervase had bought her favours. It was true that he had rescued her from the bawdy house, and that he had given her presents and money, but she had given herself to him so wholeheartedly because ...she loved him. She hadn't known it until it was too late, but now she realized it was the cause of her present misery. 'Go away, Mr Meadows. I do not want to be your mistress. Nor any man's. Tell your friends that if you please.'

'Because you still want him, I suppose?' Jack laughed harshly. 'The stupid fool doesn't know that of course, or he wouldn't have left you. He would give me a hand-some present for that knowledge, Bella – but I would rather have you. At least once...'

Arabella put her wine glass down hastily as he took a purposeful step towards her. Her head was spinning and she knew that she was intoxicated. She had been feeling sorry for herself for days and had been drinking far too much wine in an effort to block out her unhappiness. Now she wished she hadn't!

'Stay away from me,' she warned and held her hands up to ward him off. 'I shall never be your mistress. You are not half the man Gervase is and—'

'Not half the man?' Jack smiled nastily. 'How he would love to hear you say that, Bella, but after I've finished with you he won't touch you. No man will want you again...'

The menacing note in his voice and the strange look in his eyes combined to fill Arabella with terror. She knew that he was going to attack her and she looked about her for a weapon, picking up a fire iron to hold it aloft.

'I'm warning you! Stay away from me.'

'You send me wild when you look at me

like that,' Jack said. 'I would have been good to you if you had pleased me, Bella – but now I want to punish you.'

Arabella gave a little shriek of dismay as he lunged at her. He grasped the front of her gown and tore it, revealing the plump swell of her breasts as they rose and fell in fear. She was breathing hard, terrified of this man she hardly recognized as Jack Meadows. He had hidden his true nature beneath a veneer of charm, but now his jealousy and his bitterness were showing through. He wanted to despoil her because she loved Gervase.

She took her arm back to strike him with the fire iron, catching him a glancing blow on his temple. It was enough to draw blood but not enough to fell him. He gripped her wrist, twisting it until the iron fell with a clatter against the grate and on to the floor, and then he bent his head, his teeth biting at the tender flesh he had exposed. She gave a scream of pain and pushed at him, struggling to free herself from his frenzied attack. He was not mad with love but with hatred, she realized, renewing her struggle. Her back had been to the fireplace, but somehow she had managed to struggle round so that his was now against the heavy stone mantle. Placing her hands against his chest, she pushed with all her strength and sent him stumbling back. And then, somehow, he tripped on the iron fender and fell over sideways, striking his head against the metal.

Arabella backed away from him. She was panting, fearful that he would jump up and come after her. As she reached the door, it opened and her maid entered.

'He attacked me...' Arabella gasped. 'I pushed him and he fell...'

The maid bent over him, reaching out to touch him, and then she saw his staring eyes and the blood oozing from the gash to the back of his head. On the floor not far away lay the fire iron with which Arabella had hit Jack, a trace of blood on its point.

'You've killed him,' the startled girl said. 'You've murdered him!'

'No...' Arabella shook her head. 'You don't understand. He attacked me. I pushed him away and he fell. It was an accident...You must believe me.'

'Murder!' the girl cried and started screaming. 'Murder! Murder!'

Arabella stood as if turned to stone as the girl ran from the room, still screaming. She walked over to Jack, gazing down at him. Surely he wasn't dead? He couldn't be dead? She had simply pushed him and he'd fallen and hit his head. People didn't die from a little accident like that. Yet as she looked down at his face she knew that it was true.

She gasped and drew back, her hand going to her throat. Even her maid thought she had killed Jack. No one would believe her. She would surely hang...

She must get out of here – run away! She rushed to the door and saw that her servants had gathered in the street, a crowd around them. They all turned and looked at her and she read her fate in their faces. They thought she was a murderess and they would take her to the prison themselves rather than see her escape.

'You are sure it is the right child this time?' Gervase questioned his agent thoroughly. He felt a surge of elation. At last it seemed that his search was over! 'The child born in Mistress Elizabeth George's house just over a year ago and sold to a childless couple?'

'Yes, my lord, quite sure,' the man told him triumphantly. 'As you know, the child was sold several times, but the present parents are in Portsmouth and waiting for a ship to take them to the Americas. Another few days and the child would have disappeared for good.'

'God be praised,' Gervase said. 'You did as I asked you?'

'Yes, my lord.'

'And their answer?'

'They said at first that they would not give the child up – but when I told them what you had offered they changed their minds. They want to see you in person, my lord, and then they may give him up to you.'

'Or sell him for the right price,' Gervase said grimly. 'Have you brought them here?'

'They would not come, my lord. They expect their ship to be ready within days. But I did set a man to watch them, and a few more to stop them if they try to take the child on board that ship.'

'You have done well, Salmons,' Gervase said. 'We shall leave this day for Portsmouth, and you shall be well rewarded once I have the child.'

'Yes, my lord. I am well aware of the terms of our agreement.'

'My carriage will be ready within minutes,' Gervase said. 'I shall not forget this service, which is greater than you may imagine.'

Gervase was smiling grimly as he summoned his servants. It looked as if the search was at last coming to an end, but he had been disappointed before. He hoped that this time it would not turn out to be a false trail.

'Come, mistress,' the turnkey ordered. 'It is time for your trial.'

'So soon?' Arabella looked at him in surprise. 'How long have I been here in this place?'

'A week – long enough for a wicked wretch like you to repent of your sins,' he grunted. 'Judge Harding is dealing with your case and many others this morning. He has other more important things to do and so he has had you all brought up at the same time to save himself the trouble of coming back next week.'

Arabella stood up, closing her eyes for a moment. She felt the trembling begin inside her as she recalled the horror of being dragged here by a howling mob. No one had listened to her. They had condemned her as guilty without a hearing. Some of the women had wanted to stone her to death, but the men had insisted that she be brought to the magistrates and then to the prison.

Once she was cast into this filthy cell – which was no bigger than a cupboard, with stone floors covered in damp straw that had rats and mice crawling amongst the scraps of rotten food and human excrement – she had closed her mind to her surroundings. She was either already dead and in hell, or this was all a nightmare and she would wake to find that it was all in her mind, the result of drinking too much wine. But she hadn't woken from her nightmare and now she knew it was all too real.

If only she had not drunk so much wine that fateful day, she might have been able to give a proper account to the magistrate. But he had been too annoyed at having his supper interrupted and had given the order to have her incarcerated without listening to her story. She had huddled into the corner of her cell, hearing the awful sounds nearby – people coughing, weeping, screaming and vomiting – but seeing no one.

It might have been better if she could have talked to someone, but the guard who brought her water and a hard crust of bread once a day never spoke to her. The first words she'd heard in so many days were from this turnkey, who was ordering her from the cell, pushing her roughly in front of him.

'I am innocent,' she said. 'Stop pushing me or I shall have my friends call you to account for your ill treatment of me.'

'Fine friends you've got, mistress,' the man said with a harsh laugh. 'There's none been to see you nor put in a word for you. Even the common thieves have someone to pay easement for them.'

'Lord Roxbourne is away on business,' Arabella replied, her head up. 'When he returns and discovers what has happened to me he will come and find me. He will tell the judge that this charge is ridiculous.'

The turnkey grinned unpleasantly. 'He'd best come soon then, for you'll not last long in Judge Harding's court.' He drew a hand across his throat to indicate that the out-come would be death for her. 'His Honour ain't got no love for women – especially them what murder a good man.'

'But I didn't murder him—' Arabella felt the touch of a hand against hers and looked round to see another woman being brought along the dark passage behind her.

'Ain't no use tellin' 'im, luv,' she said. 'Save it fer the judge – not that it'll do yer any good. Judge Harding is the worst o' the lot.'

Arabella swallowed hard. 'Are you saying he'll hang me anyway?'

'Plead yer belly,' the woman told her in hushed tones. 'You might get transportation then. Otherwise they'll 'ang yer fer sure.'

Arabella knew what she meant. She had heard that women often did it to escape the gallows, opting for the sentence of seven years hard labour in the American colonies instead. But surely the judge would listen to the truth? She had killed Jack but she had not meant to; it had been an accident. Why would no one believe her?

She was hustled into a large room, which was in a different part of the prison. The judge in his robes of office sat at a table at one end and a few chairs had been set out for various officials; the spectators, who had managed to get into the makeshift court, had been herded into one corner and were chattering excitedly to one another.

About thirty prisoners had been brought up from the cells and were being held in a group at some distance from the judge. It wasn't even a proper court, Arabella realized, and tried to protest to the turnkey.

'Quiet, woman, if you know what's good for you,' he told her. 'The judge ain't got much time. We're overflowin' with prisoners, can't take no more of them and this is His Honour's way of gettin' through the work.'

'But it's not fair – nor is it legal...' she began, and received a pinch on her arm for her pains.

'Quiet, or he'll have you flogged and me with yer.'

Arabella subsided. Surely her turn to speak out would come. This was a travesty of justice. She felt as if she were in a waking nightmare, watching as one by one the prisoners were marched out in front of the judge.

'Crime?'

'Petty thieving, your honour.'

'Transportation for five years. Next.'

'House breaking. Took five 'undred pounds of goods from Lord Thrust's London 'ouse, he did.'

'Hang him. Next. Come on, man! I haven't all day.'

Arabella listened in disbelief as the judge

went through the list of accused. One or two tried to protest their innocence but were silenced by threats of a flogging. It was so unfair. How could this judge be acting within the law?

The turnkey had hold of her arm, was pushing her forward to face the judge. She raised her head, looking straight at him, refusing to hang her head in submission or shame. 'I am innocent,' she declared loudly before he could ask her crime. 'I did not murder Mr Meadows; he fell and hit his head. I was defending myself from—'

'Silence!' Judge Harding roared at her, his eyes glittering with fury. 'Turnkey, if you cannot keep this woman in order you do not deserve your job here.'

'Be quiet, woman!' the turnkey said and threatened Arabella with his fist. 'I'll make yer sorry if yer say another word.'

'I will have my say. It is my right.'

'That's it, luv!' a woman cried out in the crowd. 'Give 'er 'er say, 'tis only fair.'

'Be quiet or I'll have you flogged,' the judge said, directing his baleful stare at the woman in the crowd. He beckoned to one of the officials and whispered to him for a moment, then looked at Arabella. 'You were drunk when you were brought before the magistrate. He says you quarrelled with your lover and killed him.'

'That is a lie. Jack Meadows was never my

lover. He wanted to be but I refused him and he tried to force me—'

'So you killed him.' The magistrate whispered again and Judge Harding nodded. 'You hit him with a poker – there was blood on the edge of the iron.'

'I defended myself, but the blow did not kill him. He fell and hit his head on the iron fender.'

'You stand convicted out of your own mouth, woman,' the judge said, his eyes hard and cold as they swept over her with disgust. Arabella flinched, knowing what she must look like, for she had not washed in days and her hair was straggling down her back in greasy strands. 'Give me one reason why I should not hang you.'

'Because I am innocent and in your heart you know it.'

The judge's eyes narrowed. 'You do not plead your belly?'

'I am not with child, sir, and I do not lie.'

He looked stunned for a moment, seeming almost to believe her, then he frowned and shook his head. 'Transportation for seven years hard labour.'

Arabella was too shocked to protest as the turnkey hustled her away. Seven years hard labour! She was to be transported to the colonies, which were, as far as she knew, a wilderness. She had heard people talk of the uncivilized colonists who were always causing trouble, but knew little else of them.

'Yer lucky,' the turnkey muttered as he pushed her from the room, into which still more poor wretches were being hustled. 'He needs to fill a transport ship leavin' from Greenwich within a few days. That'll be why he didn't 'ang yer.'

'Where are you taking me?' Arabella asked, for she had realized that they were not going back the way they had come.

'Yer've 'ad yer trial,' he replied. 'We've got ter get rid of some of yer or they'll 'ave no room fer the next lot.'

'It is little wonder the prisons are so overcrowded if everyone is treated as I have been,' Arabella said. 'If the magistrate had listened to me in the first place I should never have been brought here.'

'They all say as they ain't guilty when they get caught,' the turnkey told her. 'Think yerself lucky yer ain't gallows bait, mistress. He were in a hurry and you upset 'im. 'Tis a wonder he didn't order a flogging.'

Arabella shivered inwardly as she recalled the expression in the judge's eyes. For a moment as he'd looked at her he had known that she was telling the truth, but it had not weighed with him – other than the restraint shown over her insistence on being heard. Three other prisoners had not been so lucky.

Yet she was innocent and she was being

transported for seven years! It was so unfair. She could not believe all this had happened to her in so short a time. But perhaps she was fortunate that her trial had been so swift, for how long could she have survived on the food she had been given in her cell? Some of the other prisoners looked ill and seemed hardly able to stand. At least she was healthy.

Herded together with other men and women waiting in the prison yard for transportation, Arabella wondered how she would fare on the ship taking them to America.

'Cheer up, lass,' a man said as she smothered a sob of despair. 'It ain't so bad. They say it's better over there than 'ere in lots o' ways. A better place, see, once you've served yer time.'

'But I didn't do anything!'

'No, course yer didn't,' the man agreed and grinned at her. 'Most of us are innocent – what's wrong in taking a loaf of bread when yer kid's 'ungry? Half of us ain't done nuthin' much – but I reckon as we'll be better off there once we earn our freedom. They say the colonists are sick of being under British rule. One of these days they'll break free and then maybe we'll be free too.'

'Might as well 'ope fer the moon,' another voice said from behind him. 'They'll want their money's worth, mark my words. Yer bond is fer seven years and yer'll 'ave ter serve it, Nat.'

'Yer a bleedin' cheerful bitch, Peg,' he said, but without rancour. 'I've 'eard 'tis a better place, see, and I'm glad I got transportation.'

'Considerin' what yer done, yer lucky,' the woman called Peg said with a wide grin. 'They oughter 'ave 'ung yer, yer rogue.'

'It were an accident,' Nat said and winked at her. 'Me pistol went orf on its own just when I were taking 'is purse. Bleedin' thing never were reliable. Still, I'm lucky ter 'ave got away with transportation. I expected him to hang me.'

'Are you a highwayman?' Arabella looked at him in surprise. He had seemed such an innocent, pleasant fellow.

'Worst o' the lot,' Peg chortled. 'They've 'ad a price on 'im fer years and he's lucky ter get away wiv it.'

'Now, Peg, yer'll 'ave this nice young lady thinkin' bad o' me if yer not careful.'

'Good thing an' all,' Peg said and laughed good-naturedly. 'Don't believe a word 'e says, luv. You stay along o' Peg. I'll look after yer. I'll bet yer've never been in trouble afore yer topped that blighter, 'ave yer?'

'I merely pushed him away. He was trying to rape me. He hit his head as he fell.'

'Yer poor cow,' Peg said. 'I know what it's like wiv customers. They think they can treat us as rough as they like and it don't matter – but raise an 'and to them or take their purse and see where yer end up.'

'Is that what happened to you?'

'Peg ain't a whore,' Nat said and grinned. 'She's one of the best cutpurses in the business. Watch yer back or she'll 'ave the gown right orf yer.'

'You watch yer mouth or I'll shut it fer yer,' Peg said, but it was clear she liked the man and was enjoying this exchange between them. 'I like yer, lass – what did yer say yer name was?'

'My friends call me Bella.'

'That's a pretty name,' she said. ''Ave yer got any money wiv yer, Bella? Yer can pay fer extra food and stuff if yer 'ave.'

'No – only this ring.' Arabella took a ring from inside her bodice. 'I hid it when I was taken to the prison.'

'Best thing yer could 'ave done,' Peg said. 'When we go on board, you give it to me and I'll bargain wiv the crew ter look after us...'

'Give it ter Peg and that's the last yer'll see of it,' Nat warned her. 'Give it 'ere, lass, and I'll take care of it fer yer. It's too good to give to a sailor. The captain is the one fer you, lass. You might be able to buy yer own bond when yer get there wiv that.'

'Don't trust 'im, Bella,' Peg said. 'I'll treat yer fair.'

302

Arabella looked from one to the other uncertainly. She thought of the two Nat was probably the more trustworthy, but before she could decide they were moved along, parted by the turnkeys who were herding them into carts to drive them to the docks where the ship was waiting to take them to their servitude.

Arabella thrust the ring back into her bodice. She saw Peg watching her with avarice and knew that she would have to think of a new place to hide her ring or she might wake up one day to find it had gone.

Gone as her life had gone, vanished into thin air, leaving her only memories. As she entered the cart taking her away from the prison she searched the faces of the people gathered in the street, hoping to see the one she longed for, but there was no sign of him. But of course he would not be here. Why should he? He had told her it was over. Even if he knew what had happened he would not care.

Women were weeping, calling out to their men, promising to follow them to America. Half-starved children stared at fathers and mothers being carried away from them, wiping their dripping noses on the rags they wore. Men watched from the side of the road, eyes sullen, angry at the fate of those they knew as friends or brothers, unable to do anything, cursing the unfairness of a society in which life was cheap.

Arabella turned as she felt someone move nearer to her and saw that it was Peg.

'I ain't goin' ter steal yer ring, Bella,' she said. 'But if yer sell it yer can 'elp me and I'll 'elp you. It ain't easy in them 'olds and yer'll need someone ter look out fer yer.'

'Thank you for the offer,' Arabella said. 'I shall speak to the captain and offer him the ring as soon as I can. Nat is right – it is too valuable to offer to the sailors and we'll be cheated.'

'As long as yer goin' ter share...'

'Of course I will, Peg,' Arabella said. 'You are my friend, and I know you will look out for me. I'll sell the ring and we'll share the money.'

'That's it,' Peg said and grinned at her, showing a row of blackened teeth. 'You share the money and I'll see as none of them thievin' rascals get their 'ands on it.'

Arabella smiled. She didn't trust Peg for one minute, but it was as well to remain on good terms with her if possible – at least until she knew how things stood on board the ship. She could only protect what she had and hope that she might be able to do as Nat had suggested when they reached the colony.

Until this moment she had hoped that Gervase might forgive her and help her, but now she knew that she had been foolish to hope. There was no one to help her, and if she was to survive she must live by her own wits.

'Gone? Gone where?' Gervase demanded as he looked at the girl who had admitted him into the house. He could see that no cleaning had been done in some time and wondered what had been happening here. 'You had best explain yourself, Rutford.'

'They took her off to prison nearly two weeks ago, my lord – for murder, it were.'

'Murder? Arabella?' Gervase felt a cold shiver down his spine. 'Who was she supposed to have murdered?'

'It was your friend, sir. Mr Meadows.'

'Jack...' The icy chill was spreading through him, echoing something...A dream or premonition he had once had. 'Why has no one thought to let me know? What happened? I want to know the truth, girl – all of it!'

'Mistress Tucker was...drinking, sir. She had been drinking most of the time since you left...'

'And?' Gervase frowned. 'What happened the night Jack Meadows came here?'

'She refused to see him, sir. Sent all the gentlemen away she did, and said she would see only you. But he walked into the parlour where she was without a by your leave and then I heard them arguing and she started

305

screaming, and when I went in he were lying there with blood coming out of his head and his eyes staring. She'd hit him with the fire iron, sir – though she swore he fell and hit his head. There was blood on the iron, plain for all to see.'

Gervase nodded, his expression grim. 'And what happened next?'

'I raised the alarm, my lord – and they took her off to the magistrate and then the prison, so I've heard.'

'And what has been happening here?' He looked at the mess around him. 'Did she not send for her clothes or money?'

'No, my lord – leastwise, I've heard nothing.'

'Send her housekeeper to me. I would have words with her.' He saw the expression in the maid's eyes and frowned. 'Very well, the butler then, or head footman?'

'All gone, sir,' the maid told him falteringly. 'They went the next day – said they wouldn't work in the house of a murderess.'

'But you stayed?'

'I had nowhere else to go, sir – and I thought you might come back.'

His brows rose. 'Did you indeed? Why did you think that?'

The girl flushed and looked nervous. 'You seemed to care for the mistress, my lord, and I thought...'

'Very observant of you, Rutford. I shall see

306

you are rewarded for your loyalty.' He frowned at her. 'Are your mistress's jewels still in her room?'

'Yes, my lord. She had them well hidden. I think someone tried to find them but I didn't tell, even though I knew where they were.'

'And you didn't feel tempted to take them yourself?'

'I'm an honest girl,' Rutford said. 'Besides, I don't want to be hung as a thief.'

'I am glad you have so much sense,' Gervase said, a faint smile in his eyes. 'As I said, you will be rewarded. Would you prefer money or a place with a new employer?'

'Could you find me a new place, sir?'

'I am certain I can,' Gervase said and took five gold guineas from his pocket. 'But you also deserve this. Now, will you show me where the jewels were kept? And then I would like you to pack Arabella's things. I shall have them sent to my house in the country, but the jewels I shall take with me now.'

'Yes, my lord,' Rutford said and bobbed a curtsey.

'And perhaps you can tell me to which prison she was taken?'

'I think it was Newgate, my lord,' Rutford replied. 'But I don't know for sure, for I was not one of those who took her. You see, I wondered afterwards if she had cause to hit him...'

'I am certain that she did. There has been a miscarriage of justice here, but I shall find her,' Gervase said and his mouth settled into a grim line. 'Justice shall be done, you may be certain of that.'

Gervase cursed a thousand times as he made his way to the prison where he had been told Arabella was being held. A shudder ran through him as he thought of her in that dreadful place. She would be at the mercy of hardened villains and rogues, and had no idea of how to protect herself against them.

He had had sharp words with the magistrate who had sent her to the prison, leaving him quivering with fear for his own safety and livelihood. Had Arabella been given a fair hearing she would never have been brought to this place! And what had happened to her since she'd been here?

He knew that a woman like Arabella might suffer many things in prison, rape amongst them. Gervase felt a wave of anger, against himself as much as anyone. Had he rescued her from the whorehouse only to see her reduced to this?

He rang the bell at the gate and explained his business, asking to be taken to the head jailer or whoever was in charge. His obvious wealth and standing commanded respect, and after some hesitation he was admitted and taken to a small room apart from the main building.

The stench of the prison permeated the air, making Gervase's stomach turn – and that was before he had even gone inside the part where prisoners were housed. What must Arabella be suffering?

A man was eating a meal of meat, bread, pickles and ale, a napkin tucked into his neck. He looked annoyed as the turnkey announced Gervase, but when he saw his visitor he tore the napkin away and jumped to his feet. Almost cringing as he saw the expression on Gervase's face, his podgy face assumed a smirk, which was meant to be obliging.

'My lord – sir – what may I do for you?'

'You have a prisoner here,' Gervase said curtly. 'I want to buy easement for her until I can arrange for her release. She was falsely accused and is innocent of any crime. It will go hard with you, sir, if she has come to harm in this foul place.'

'Easement?' The man smiled ingratiatingly. 'Of course, of course. I shall be happy to oblige you. What is the lady's name?'

'Mistress Arabella Tucker. She was falsely accused of murder. It was an accident, as shall shortly be proved.'

'Mistress Tucker...' The head warder shook his head over the name. 'I can't seem to recall...' The turnkey who had brought Gervase to him coughed and shuffled his feet. 'Yes, what is it, Carne? We don't need you anymore. I can handle this for his lordship.'

'Beggin' yer pardon, sir, but the prisoner were taken before Judge Harding last week.'

'Taken before the judge?' Gervase breathed deeply, trying to hold back the rage inside him. 'What happened to her?'

'She...' The turnkey quailed as he sensed Gervase's fury. 'She were sentenced to seven years transportation, me lord.'

'Seven years...' Gervase curled his fists into tight balls at his side. 'How can this be? She was innocent.'

'We had to clear some of the prisoners,' the head warder said, looking nervous. 'It was orders, sir. The judge came and said he would hold a court here – said there was a ship needing prisoners and he wanted to fill it afore it were too late. Don't know what he meant, sir.'

Gervase was only too aware of what the judge meant. The trouble in the American colonies had not abated, despite the repeal of the much hated Stamp Act, and he, amongst a growing number of like-minded men, felt that before too many years had passed, those enterprising men would demand their freedom. Clearly, the policy was to ship as many as possible of the convicts to the colonies now in order to relieve the pressure on the overcrowded prisons. That it would be better to try and treat the causes of so much crime, to make the sentences less harsh and thus avoid overcrowding the prisons in the first place, was obviously something that had not occurred to the worthy gentlemen in Parliament. Yet Gervase knew his reasoning was out of step with most men of his own class, and that was why he had been thinking of leaving England for some time – why he had already taken the first steps towards a new life elsewhere.

'And where will I find Mistress Tucker now?' Gervase asked when he had controlled his anger sufficiently to speak.

'She was taken with a hundred other prisoners to Greenwich,' the turnkey told him, not daring to meet his eyes. 'They were to be taken down the coast to Portsmouth and there be transferred to a prison ship sailing for America.'

The ship that was to have carried the child he had been searching for for so long! Gervase knew a twisting thrust of anguish as he realized that he had been in the harbour close by that ship – might even have seen some of the prisoners being taken on board.

'I thank you for your help, gentlemen,' he said in a measured tone. 'I wish that you had

had better news for me – but take this for your pains.' He tossed a purse of gold coins on to the table before striding from the room.

The prison ship must already have sailed. His own plans were nearly complete, and could be brought forward. But first he would pay a visit to the judge who had so cruelly condemned Arabella to her fate.

Twelve

Arabella bent over double as she vomited yet again. Her stomach felt as if a horse had kicked her, and she wished that she might die. The stench in the hold was indescribable and she knew that both her hair and body were crawling with lice. They were given only enough water for drinking each day, and that was strictly rationed, as was the hard, coarse bread and the thin gruel that was slopped up.

'Give me the ring,' Peg said, bending over her as she moaned. 'If I sell it to Mick he could get us up on deck for an hour or two every day. It's what we both need.'

'Go away,' Arabella muttered. She felt so ill she thought she would probably be dead by the morning. 'Tomorrow. I'll give it to you tomorrow.'

'You've said that every day since we've been on board,' Peg whined.

Arabella lay against the sacking, which was all that had been provided for their bedding, closing her eyes and trying to remember how many days it was since they had been brought to this terrible place. Was it thirty or forty? Perhaps it was even longer. Sometimes she felt that she had been here all her life, but she had marked the days on the wooden strut that she was leaning against and she ran her fingers over them, counting by touch because it was impossible to see in this light. She had been here for forty-five days. More than a month of unendurable hell had passed in a blur of pain and misery. Yet she had endured it because she was determined to survive.

She was no longer afraid of Peg – or of any of the women – though she had been at the start. She had learned to fight for her share of the food and water, and to guard her back. She knew that Peg had searched her when she was sleeping, trying to find Arabella's hiding place, but she had not been able to. Nor had she been able to bully Arabella into parting with the ring. Only the thought of it, safely hidden as they came on board, had kept her alive. With the money she could get from that ring it might be possible to buy her freedom – if they ever arrived in America. Sometimes she thought they would sink during one of the awful storms that had buffeted the ship for the past week, and there were moments of despair when she wished that they would.

She heard the sound of the hold being opened from above and wondered what was happening. The daily rations of food and water had already been given to them. Only once had they been allowed on deck since the beginning of the voyage, and then it was to witness the flogging of one of the male prisoners. Arabella shivered as she recalled his screams. She prayed they were not to be summoned for that purpose again.

'All right, you filthy bitches,' the sailor shouted. 'I want ten women up on deck now. Only the young and fit need come forward.'

There was a surge towards the light, for a visit to the deck was a welcome break for the prisoners and they were all eager, no matter what the reason. Peg grasped Arabella's arm, pushing her through to the front of the crowd.

'Take us!' she yelled. 'We're strong. We can work.'

Arabella felt her stomach heave, but controlled it as best she could. A few minutes in the fresh air would help to settle it if anything could. Besides, it felt as if the rolling was getting less severe and she thought that the storm might have at last blown itself out.

'You two,' the sailor said, beckoning to Peg and Arabella. 'You – the one behind you, you and you – and that four there. Look sharp about it or I might change my mind.'

The women scrambled up the rope ladder to the deck above them, breathing deeply as the fresh air entered their lungs. The sky was overcast and dull, but even so the light seemed too bright and hurt their eyes. Arabella blinked as her head started to spin, but she held on to Peg and they managed to keep each other upright until the dizziness passed.

When all ten women were assembled, the sailor looked them over scornfully. He pulled a face and shook his head over them, scratching behind his ear. 'Filthy, the lot of you,' he said. 'The captain's niece won't want to see you looking like that. You had better wash yourselves. There's water in them buckets, a scrubbing brush and some soap. Give yourselves a good scrub and I'll come and look you over when you've done.'

'What about our clothes?' Arabella asked, and he turned to glare at her. 'We can't do much about them.'

'What do you expect me to do – buy you a new gown?' He leered at her. 'Maybe I could find you something if you were nice to me.'

'Leave her alone,' Peg said. 'We've got money if we want yer 'elp.'

'Money – where is it?' Greed narrowed his eyes to mercenary slits. 'Give it to me and I'll get yer special treatment.'

'Give it to 'im,' Peg whispered to Arabella. 'This is our chance to get out of that place.'

'I've lost it,' Arabella lied. 'That's why I

couldn't give it to you before.'

Peg's face fell, but she seemed to accept the lie. 'Somebody took it orf yer, I suppose. Why didn't yer tell me sooner? I might 'ave got it back fer yer.'

'I thought it would upset you.'

'Lying through yer teeth again, Peg,' the sailor said. 'Just for that you can go below again.'

'That ain't fair,' Peg said and screamed as he grabbed her arm. She looked at Arabella with a desperate appeal in her eyes. 'Bella – help me.'

Arabella felt pity for the woman who had befriended her but she still hesitated and then, as he prepared to shove Peg back into the hold, she knew that she could not refuse to help her.

'Stop!' she cried. 'I've got the ring. We shall want fresh clothes and better food – and you can leave Peg on deck for a while with me.'

'Show me it!' the sailor demanded and Arabella reached into the bodice of her gown, tearing the material so that she could work the ring free of where it had lodged in the intricate stitching.

'I thought I'd looked there an' all,' Peg exclaimed as Arabella produced the ring, and then subsided at a flash of fire from her angry green eyes. 'I would have shared it with you, Bella. You know I would.'

Arabella knew nothing of the sort, but she had nonetheless been glad of Peg sleeping at her back on more than one occasion.

'Show it to me,' the sailor demanded again, his eyes gleaming with greed as he saw the emerald set with diamonds. He knew it was worth more money than he would earn in three years on this damned ship and he grabbed for it, but Arabella drew it back. 'Give it to me!'

'Not until we have the clothes and some food,' Arabella said. 'I want the promise of extra rations for me and for Peg from now until the end of the voyage.'

He could have taken it from her by force, of course, but the captain was strict about stealing from the convicts, and he knew she would get a better price if it were brought to the master's attention. And this one would fight for her property, he could see that in her eyes. She was a right bitch, but she looked fit and spoke better than her companion, which meant she would probably be the one picked – so he had better treat her fairly.

'Get washed with the others and I'll be back,' he muttered. 'They might not fit but I'll get yer somethin'.'

'Didn't I tell yer it would buy us more food?' Peg said triumphantly as he went off. 'Come on, let's get our share of that water!'

The other women looked at them resentfully as they joined the line behind the rough blanket that had been hung up to give them some privacy.

'You might have asked for clothes for all of us,' one of them muttered sullenly. 'That bleedin' ring were worth a fortune.'

'He wouldn't have given everyone the same,' Arabella said and grabbed her bucket. She doused herself, stripping off her rags and scrubbing her skin until it stung. She didn't care that she was naked, all the others were too, and none of them looked much more than bare bones and skin. After weeks of near starvation they were so emaciated that some of them looked as if a puff of wind would blow them over.

Arabella knew that she had lost weight, but was probably in better shape than most because she had been in prison for a much shorter time. She wrapped herself in the ragged cloth that had been provided for drying and waited until a shout told her that clothes had arrived for her and Peg.

They were poor quality and had obviously belonged to a girl of the lower orders, but at least they were clean and looked as if they might fit her. Peg was shorter and would have to gird up her skirt, but she was already pulling the tunic on and tying it around her middle.

'Who did these belong to?' Arabella asked.

'Never you mind,' the sailor replied with a crafty look at her. 'Here's your food. Now give me the ring.'

Arabella handed it over reluctantly. She knew that it was the end of her dream of freedom unless she could find another way to buy her own bond, but she believed that was unlikely. 'What happens now?'

'Captain's niece wants a girl to look after her and the baby,' he said. 'Her last maid took sick and died yesterday. She can't manage the child by herself.'

'I suppose that's where the clothes came from,' Arabella said. 'What did she die of?'

'A fever – but nothing catching,' he told her. 'You ain't likely to die of it.'

'I ain't wearin' them!' Peg cried and flung them back at him. 'I'd rather 'ave me own.'

'Suit yerself. There ain't no more.'

Arabella decided to risk it. If the girl had died of a contagious disease, all her things would probably have been tossed overboard when the body was buried. She pulled on the plain blue gown and discovered that it fitted her reasonably well, except that it strained a little over her breasts. She was tempted to open the fastenings to give herself more room, but decided that it might be better to be cautious for the moment. If she were the lucky one chosen, it would mean she would be out of that stinking hold for the rest of the journey.

The women were ordered to stand in a line and then a pretty but fragile-looking woman came out of the forecastle and nervously approached them. She walked slowly past them, stopped once or twice to look at one of the women and then reached Arabella, who had chosen to stand at the end of the line.

Arabella smiled and bobbed a curtsey. 'Good day, ma'am.'

'Oh...' The woman responded with a nervous smile of her own. 'Who are you, please? What is your name?'

'Arabella Tucker, ma'am.'

'And what was your crime?'

'I am innocent of any crime, ma'am, except that of a woman defending herself against a dishonourable man. I was accused of murder, but he fell and hit his head as we struggled.'

'Murder...' The woman looked horrified and turned away.

Arabella could have screamed her frustration, but just as she was expecting to be turned away, a young man wearing the uniform of first mate came to join the woman. She said something and he glanced at Arabella and frowned, then took his wife by the hand and led her back to where Arabella was standing.

'You are Arabella Tucker?'

'Yes, sir,' she said and bobbed a curtsey. 'The daughter of a country squire in better days. My father had died and I was alone when Mr Meadows tried to persuade me to be his mistress. I refused and he tried...I fought him, sir, and he hit his head on an iron fender. I swear I am innocent. I told the judge so but he would not listen.'

'But murder, John,' the young woman said, gazing up at him anxiously. 'Do you think...'

'She is plainly the best of them,' he replied. 'Be brave, Susan. I am sure this woman would take good care of our son. She knows what would happen to her if she does not.' His bright blue eyes fixed on Arabella.

'Yes, sir. I would be happy to care for your son – and very grateful.'

'Little Johnny needs a great deal of care,' Susan Baxter told her, still looking nervous. 'He cries a lot and runs about if no one checks him.'

'He's a lively little lad of near on eighteen months,' John Baxter said with an affection- ate glance at his young wife. He was not a handsome man, but his features were strong and he looked honest – and clearly thought a great deal of his family. 'Yes, I think we'll give you a try, Arabella – but if my wife complains of you, you'll go back to the hold and you will be flogged.'

'I am sure my mistress will have no reason to complain of me,' Arabella said. 'May I see little Johnny, ma'am?'

'Yes. He is sleeping at the moment – or he was when I left him, but he is teething and has been fretful of late.'

Arabella heard the muttering from the women who were being taken back to the hold but she did not look at them. She had no illusions about the treatment she would receive from them if she were sent back down there. They hated her for being chosen, and for possessing a ring with which to buy the clothes, for they knew that it had given her an unfair advantage. She looked clean and presentable, while they still looked and smelled of the prison. Some women might have looked beyond that, but Susan Baxter was too timid and her husband obviously made the decisions. Arabella looked attractive and her good manners had won her the freedom of the ship and fresh air.

Arabella followed behind Susan as she led the way into the forecastle, where most of the higher ranked crew were housed. Her cabin was the second largest on board, and more comfortable than Arabella had imagined it could be, with a bed, a table and two chairs. There were several sea chests for the family's belongings, and a dressing screen, over which some petticoats had been flung. Other pieces of clothing had been left about the floor, and Arabella bent to pick them up, folding them neatly and laying them on a chest near the child's cot.

Her heart turned over as she saw the child sleeping, his fist against his rosebud mouth. Her own child would have been almost this age now, she thought with a pang of grief.

'How beautiful he is,' she said, and the sincerity in her voice made her new mistress look at her.

'Yes, he is,' she agreed, smiling properly for the first time. 'He is so precious and I have been afraid that we shall lose him on this dreadful voyage.'

'He looks strong and healthy,' Arabella said. 'I am sure that he will be fine, ma'am. I shall do all I can to see that he has every attention.'

'Thank you,' Susan said and sighed wearily. She looked pale and there were shadows beneath her eyes. 'I am not strong, you see. Johnny's birth tired me and I have not yet recovered fully.'

'The journey has been hard for you, ma'am?'

'Yes,' Susan agreed and sighed again. 'I fear my husband and my family spoil me, Arabella. It has always been so. John wanted to wait before making this journey, thinking I might be stronger in a few months, but he has the chance of a good position in Washington and this is his last voyage as a serving officer, so I said that I would accompany him. Otherwise it would have been months before he could return to fetch me and the position might have been lost.'

'That was brave of you, ma'am. I am not sure that I should have consented to such a journey had I been given a choice.'

Susan looked at her gravely. 'If the journey has been hard for me it must have been so much harder for you and the others. I do feel for you, though I may not have shown it earlier. John told me I must not think about the prisoners or I should be ill and so I have tried not to, though sometimes it is impossible to forget.'

'It is not your fault that we were treated so harshly. It is a system of justice that should be reformed, but while those in power abuse their privilege it may never happen.'

'You are an educated girl, Arabella. Is it true that your father was a country squire?'

'Yes, ma'am. We were happy until my mother died and then poor Papa lost his money through gambling and bad investments. He took us to London to find husbands and then...' She shook her head. 'It grieves me to speak of it, ma'am.' She dare not tell this good woman the whole truth for she would find herself being sent back to the hold before she knew what had happened.

'That man who tried to take advantage of you – did you hit him or was it really an accident?'

'He was in a rage, ma'am. I picked up a

poker and dealt him a slight blow, but it did not fell him. He ripped the bodice of my gown and I pushed him. He staggered and fell, hitting his head on the iron fender. My maid came in and screamed for help and everyone was outraged. They all believed I had killed him and I was taken to the magistrate. He was annoyed because he was eating his supper and had me committed to prison without listening to my story. The judge came to the prison a week later. He wanted men and women to fill this ship and, apart from two men he ordered hung, we were all sent here.'

Susan shook her head. 'Yours is a terrible story of injustice and I am sure it is not the only one. That is the reason John was determined to make a new life for us in America. He believes that things may be different there, that the ordinary man may be offered opportunities that could not be found in England – at least he hopes that will be the case.'

'I fear that I know little of the country, ma'am...' Arabella broke off as a wailing sound came from the cot. She saw the look of pain in Susan's eyes and turned quickly to the child, lifting him out and holding him up so that she could look at him. 'What is it, my little one?' she asked. 'Are you hungry?'

'I gave him his food only half an hour ago,' Susan said. 'It is probably the wind – or he

326

may need changing again.'

'Yes, I can feel that he is wet,' Arabella said. 'Where do you keep his napkins, ma'am?'

'In that wicker basket by the cot,' Susan said. 'There are special creams that my mother made for me in her still room. If applied regularly they keep him from becoming sore. Mary used to do it for me...' She looked at Arabella helplessly, as if the thought of changing her son was almost too much for her.

'I shall change him while we talk,' Arabella said. 'You must tell me all the things you would like me to do for you, ma'am, so that I can look after you and little Johnny properly.'

'Oh, how thoughtful you are,' Susan Baxter said and gave her a weary smile. 'I shall lie down on the bed while you take care of the boy, and then you may come and sit next to me and I shall tell you what else needs to be done.'

'I can see that there are some clothes needing to be washed,' Arabella said. 'And the cabin would look more comfortable if it were tidy – but perhaps there is something I could do for you personally, ma'am? Do you have the ingredients to make a tisane – or shall I rub your shoulders to ease them?'

'Oh no,' Susan said, looking shocked. 'Nothing like that, but a tisane would be delightful. You would need to fetch hot water from the galley. Do you think you could do that?'

'Oh yes,' Arabella replied. 'It would be a pleasure, ma'am. I shall go as soon as I have done what is necessary here.'

Arabella took care of the child, who stopped crying as soon as she had made him dry and comfortable. He smiled up at her and patted her face with his tiny fists before yawning and closing his eyes.

Once he was back in his cot, Arabella tidied the cabin, putting all the stained clothes to one side. Then she found a pewter water can and left her mistress to rest while she went in search of water.

Oh yes, she could manage this very well, she thought, feeling the wind in her face and breathing in the salt air. After so many weeks shut away in that dark hold it felt wonderful to be on deck again. Arabella felt herself smiling as she lifted her face to the sky, the warmth of the sun lifting her spirits to new heights. If she was lucky and worked hard, the Baxters might buy her bond when they reached America. She prayed that they would, because then her life in this new world would not be so very terrible.

It would be good to have the care of a child. She could almost pretend he was her own, Arabella thought. And her mistress seemed kind enough, if easily shocked.

For a moment she thought of the life she had left behind. Tears stung her eyes but she blinked them away. She could not afford to be sentimental or regretful. From now on she must accept that she was a servant. Yet there was a part of her that clung to her memories. She would not think of her old life, or of Gervase. No doubt he had forgotten her in the arms of his latest mistress...

'Is the boy well, Isadora?' Gervase looked at the young woman standing beside him as she held the child. She was pretty, though not beautiful, a little plumper than he preferred in a woman, but she had a generous nature. He had been glad of her help on the voyage. 'You do not think you should take him below to the cabin?'

'If it is your wish I shall do so, of course,' Isadora replied. 'But it makes me feel better to breathe in the fresh air, and I think the child must feel the same.'

'Yes, perhaps you are right,' Gervase agreed. 'I dare say I worry too much.'

'The boy means a great deal to you?'

'Yes...' His eyes darkened. 'I have come to feel deeply towards this child, my dear.'

'You knew the mother?'

'Arabella was my mistress for a time.'

'Ah, I see.' She smiled at him. 'Then he is your own.'

'Not of my blood – but yes, the child is

329

mine now.'

'And what of the mother?'

'Who knows?' Gervase turned his gaze seaward. He was standing in the prow of his fastest ship. The *Helen* was his pride and joy, and her captain one of his closest friends. They had been trading with the East Indies for some years now, and Gervase's small fleet of ships was the source of his vast wealth. He had kept it a secret from almost everyone, but he believed that Jack Meadows had guessed his secret.

If it were not for Jack he would not feel this tearing anxiety inside, Gervase thought ruefully. He had believed they were friends, though Jack sometimes took advantage of the debt he owed him. He would never have imagined that he would try to physically abuse Arabella once his back was turned. He had pieced the story together through other friends, men who had also asked Arabella if she would consent to become their mistress and had been refused.

'Jack boasted that he would have her,' Ralph Sommerton had told him – and repeated it to Judge Harding. 'He told us when he was in his cups that she would not refuse him.'

Arabella's pardon was in his cabin. Gervase prayed that he would be in time to save her further humiliation. If her bond had been sold to someone else it might take months to track her down, and to force her owner to give her up.

They were making good time. The ship carrying Arabella to America was old and hardly seaworthy. Gervase's ship should reach Chesapeake Bay almost as soon as the prison hulk – or perhaps even before it if they had fair winds.

He could only pray that it was in time.

The Chesapeake was like a huge lake served by so many tributaries that it was impossible to make them all out. Arabella stared at the beauty spread out before her, wondering if she had died and woken in paradise.

'I never imagined anywhere could be this lovely,' she breathed to Susan as she stood nursing the child. 'Oh, do you see those fish? See the way they leap out of the water – they flash like silver in the sunlight.'

'See the mountains, Bella,' Susan said, as bemused as her servant. 'They are so majestic. The mist above them looks nearly as blue as the water.'

'It is all so colourful,' Arabella sighed, awed by the luxuriant vegetation on the shore. 'I can see houses now. At first I thought there was nothing but forest, but now I can see buildings and people.'

She was aware of excitement. Until now she had been afraid of what they would find in this new land. She had heard vague stories of savage Indians who sometimes attacked the settlers, and of wild beasts that roamed the forests, but seeing the lush greenery and catching the smell of flowers, she realized that it was going to be an adventure such as she had never imagined.

'Are you excited?' Susan asked, and smiled as Arabella held her son up to look at his new country. 'Yes, take a good look at your new country, Johnny darling. I feel excited now. I was nervous, afraid of whether I would be able to cope, but I have felt so much better since you have been looking after me.'

'I have tried to do whatever you want,' Arabella said, giving her a look of gratitude and appreciation. 'Are you certain your husband will buy my bond?'

'He has already tried to,' Susan confirmed. 'But my uncle abides by the rules, and they say that he must allow others to bid for you.' She reached out to touch Arabella's hand. 'Do not worry. I am sure it will be arranged as soon as the bidding opens.'

Arabella nodded, but she was watching the boats being rowed towards the ship. There were men in those boats and they were coming to take their pick of the new arrivals. Suddenly she could not bear to be paraded before them like a horse or cattle.

'Would you mind if I went to the cabin

until it is all over, ma'am?'

'No, of course not. Perhaps it might be best if you were not seen,' Susan said, a slight frown wrinkling her brow. The last few weeks had seen a vast improvement in Arabella's looks and she did not wish to lose her. Anyone seeing her and then looking at most of the other women on board would not hesitate to pay more for her bond. 'It cannot matter since John has already spoken to my uncle and gained his promise that you shall go to no one else. I shall come and tell you as soon as John has secured your bond.'

Arabella thanked her and took the little boy back to the cabin. It was warmer than on deck, where they'd had the benefit of a breeze, but she felt safer. A feeling of impending doom had suddenly come over her as she saw the small boats heading towards the ship. Supposing John Baxter didn't manage to buy her? She shivered as she imagined what might happen to her. It was unlikely she would find a mistress as kind and gentle as Susan – or be employed simply to take care of a child. If the wrong type of man bought her, she might suffer a worse fate than the one Jack Meadows had planned for her.

Arabella sat nursing the child for what seemed an age, her fears growing as the time passed. She knew that the prisoners had started to leave the ship, because she had heard loud cries and some screaming as the women were dragged away from friends and lovers.

She wondered what would happen to Peg and the highwayman. Would they find contentment in this new life, or merely another form of servitude?

Hearing the tread of boots outside the cabin, Arabella stiffened. The door opened and John Baxter came in. She knew at once that things had not gone to plan, for he could hardly bear to look at her.

'Susan asked me to tell you,' he said. 'She is too upset.'

'You were outbid for my bond?' Arabella stood up, feeling the ice spread through her veins. Susan had been so certain it was all arranged, but she had been afraid this might happen. She laid the child in his cot and turned to her former employer. 'That is what you've come to tell me, isn't it?'

'I am very sorry,' he said. 'But I believe it will not be as bad as you might fear, Bella. You have been bought by a gentleman to care for his son. I think his wife is very young and needs a good servant.'

'I see...' Arabella felt the sting of tears. It might have been worse, and yet she would hate parting from little Johnny. 'I must thank you for your kindness to me, sir. May I say goodbye to Mrs Baxter?'

'She cannot face you,' he replied. 'It would cause her too much distress. I must ask you to forgive her.'

'Yes, I understand. I hope that you will find a suitable replacement.'

'I have bought another young woman,' he replied. 'She is not you, Bella, but we shall teach her to do the things you did so well.'

Arabella swallowed hard, fighting her disappointment. 'Must I go up now?'

'Yes, I think so.' He hesitated and then reached out to take her hand, holding it for a moment. 'May God be with you, Bella. I shall pray for you.'

'And I for you and your family, sir.'

Arabella walked from the cabin, her head high. She was very close to breaking down, but pride would not let her. She had known from the beginning that this could happen. She felt the sting of humiliation as she went out on deck. She hesitated, wondering what to do, and then a man dressed in clothes of a sober habit and dark hue came towards her.

'You are Mistress Arabella Tucker?'

'Yes.' Arabella raised her head proudly. 'Are you the owner of my bond?'

'Nay, merely his agent,' the man replied. 'I am to take you to his plantation.'

'Plantation?'

'It's what you would call an estate in England,' the man told her. 'My employer is a wealthy man, newly come to the colonies. He bought the plantation from its former owner and is commissioning a new house there. The builders have been working on it for months. It will be a grand place, so they say.'

'I believe I am to have the care of his son?'

'Aye, so I've been told,' the man replied. 'You can call me Roberts if you like, or Matthew.' He glanced round. 'Have you nothing to take with you – no bag?'

'Nothing but what I am wearing,' Arabella replied.

'Well, I dare say they'll find you something to wear at the inn. We're to stay there tonight and begin our journey on the morrow.'

'You will take me to this plantation?'

'You will ride on the wagon with my daughter,' he said. 'She's a good girl but not capable of taking care of a babe alone. She'll be your helper when you get to the plantation. Her name is Flores.'

'Your daughter?' Some of Arabella's fear melted when she saw the smile of affection in his eyes as he nodded. 'She came with you to fetch me?'

'It was the master's orders. He particularly stressed that she should accompany me. It's a longish journey and he wanted to make sure you arrived safely, I dare say. Perhaps he thought I might be tempted, mistress, but I've happy memories of my wife and no desire to stray from the path of decency.' His eyes twinkled as he looked at Arabella. 'You'll find him a generous master, though he has a temper on him.'

'And his wife?'

'Hasn't got one as far as I know.'

'I was told...' Arabella bit her lip as she broke off. Perhaps he would think her impertinent.

'There was a young lady with him for a while, I understand,' Matthew Roberts said. 'But she came out to be married, to a ship's captain I think. No, I believe the master is a widower. We none of us know much as yet, but he will tell us in his own good time I dare say.'

'What does he call himself?' Arabella asked, but before he could reply Susan Baxter came rushing up to her.

'I couldn't let you go without saying goodbye,' she said. 'And I thought you might like this. It is a gown I seldom wear, Bella. You may need to alter it a little, but I think it will fit you.'

It was a pretty gown of a pale blue muslin, and hardly worn. Emotion stung Arabella's throat as she thanked her and for a moment they embraced.

'I wish so much that you could have remained with us,' Susan told her tearfully. 'But it was not to be. I am so sorry, Bella.'

'It is not your fault. My bond was sold to

the highest bidder.'

'Yes...' Susan looked uncertain, as if she wanted to say more but dared not. 'Yes, I fear it was so, Bella.'

'We should be leaving, Mistress Tucker,' Matthew Roberts reminded her. 'I'm sorry to rush you, but I have several things to do before we leave in the morning.'

'Goodbye, Susan,' Arabella said. 'I shall think of you.'

'And I of you, Bella.'

Arabella turned away, raising her head. The tears were very close but she would not let them fall. She must face the future, whatever it held for her. And so far she had not been ill-treated. Indeed, she rather liked the man who had been sent to fetch her. He seemed honest and easy-going, and if he were in charge of the plantation life might be pleasant enough.

She wondered about the man who had bought her bond. Why had he chosen her from so many? She had hoped that by hiding in Susan's cabin until the bidding had finished she would be safe and that John Baxter would buy her bond easily. Indeed, Susan had thought it a certainty. So what had gone wrong?

There was no point in worrying about something that could not be changed. Arabella accepted the hand offered her by Matthew Roberts as she climbed into the little boat that was taking them to the shore. She could see now that there were several fine houses and remembered that some of the colonists were wealthy men.

Her new owner must be very wealthy if he was building a fine new house on his plantation. She could only hope that he was a gentleman in the true sense of the word and that all he wanted from her was that she assume the care of his child.

'You are very pretty,' Flores Roberts said as she greeted Arabella. She gave a little giggle. 'I thought you must be pretty or Mr Winston would not have told Papa that he must be sure to bring you back with him.'

'Mr Winston – do you know his first name by chance?'

'I think it is George, but I'm not sure of that bit. I've seen his initials on his writing box but my father just calls him sir.'

'Are you certain that you heard right?' Arabella was puzzled. She did not know anyone called Winston and wondered how the gentleman had known she was on board that particular prison ship. 'Are you sure he did not tell your father to buy a presentable young woman for the care of his son?'

Flores shook her head and laughed. She was pretty herself, about fifteen years of age with curly dark hair and mischievous brown eyes. 'They did not know I was listening,' she said. 'Papa would be cross if he knew I had listened at the door, but it is the only way to find out what you want to know.'

'Yes, of course it is,' Arabella replied, for she had done it herself as a young girl. 'But it would be frowned upon if you were discovered, Flores. Perhaps you ought not to make a habit of it.'

'Life would be so dull if one did only what one ought,' Flores said with a pout. 'Anyway, I know what I heard – and you were mentioned by name.'

Arabella felt cold at the nape of her neck. If she had been asked for by name then Mr Winston must know her. He had perhaps been at her trial and heard her condemned – and yet Matthew Roberts had told her the house had been commissioned months earlier. How could a man who had been in England at the time of her trial have started to build a house here months before?

It was a mystery, though, as she realized a little time later, he could have been on a visit to England for some reason. She shuddered at the thought of anyone making a voyage of that duration for any reason other than necessity, though of course it must be very much better as a paying passenger than as a prisoner.

'Well,' she said, smiling at Flores, 'I suppose it must remain a mystery until we reach the plantation and meet Mr Winston.'

'Oh no, you won't meet him – at least not at once,' Flores told her. 'He was here with us until after your bond was secured, and then he left on a business trip to Washington. It may be some weeks before he returns.'

'I see...' Arabella felt disappointed. She would have liked to know the identity of her mysterious new owner, but it seemed she must wait. 'Then where is the child?'

'He is upstairs in our chamber,' Flores told her with a smile. 'Little James is so beautiful, Arabella. I adore him already. Isadora has been looking after him until this morning, but she went with her husband when their ship left for the West Indies.'

'May I see him, please?'

'Yes, of course. I am glad you have come. He is a very good little boy but I am nervous of looking after him.'

Arabella's heart was racing as she followed the other girl up the stairs of the inn to the chamber where her employer's son lay sleeping. When they went in she was surprised to see an elderly black woman sitting by the cot. Arabella had heard tell of people with skin like polished ebony, but until this moment she had never seen one. The woman was waving a straw fan over the child to keep away the flies and the heat.

'This is Torah,' Flores said and the old woman gave them a toothless smile. 'She belongs to the plantation and Mr Winston asked that she help with James until you arrived.'

'Belongs to the plantation?'

'The massa he done buy me,' Torah said and nodded, her plump chins waggling. 'My ole massa he sell me cheap in the market place 'cause he say I ain't no use to no one no more, but Massa Winston he say he gonna take me home with him and keep me until I die. He ses as I can help him in lots of ways and he's gonna give me a piece of paper that ses I's a free woman, but I can still live in his house 'cause he likes me.' She grinned at Arabella. 'He's a wicked one that Massa Winston but I reckon I wishes I was twenty years younger.'

'I'm glad he bought you,' Arabella said, for she had taken a liking to the old woman at once. 'But I think it is a wicked thing that you should have been sold at all.'

'You mustn't say that!' Flores looked horrified. 'People don't like abolitionists here, Arabella. You must be careful or you will be in trouble. I heard my father telling Mr Winston that the other day. He wanted all freemen on his plantation, but my father told him that he would upset his neighbours too much. So he said that he would treat his own people as he thought fit and be damned to his neighbours – but my father warned him to be careful.'

342

Arabella bent over the cot. The child was asleep, but so beautiful that her heart turned over as she looked at him. He had dark lashes that lay against his rosy cheeks, but then he opened his eyes and looked up at her and she saw that his eyes were blue.

'Hello, my darling,' Arabella said and reached out to touch his tiny hand. He grabbed her finger, holding on to it tightly and trying to nibble at the tip. 'Are you hungry, my precious?'

Something inside her was responding to him, making her want to hold him in her arms and cuddle him. She had felt a warm affection for Susan Baxter's child, but this one had an immediate and strong pull on her heart strings. Smiling, she picked him up, breathing in the warm baby smell and holding him to her breast. He gave a chuckle of delight and pulled at her hair.

'Mama,' he cooed. 'Mama.'

'He calls everyone that,' Flores told her. 'I think Isadora taught him to say it on the voyage here.'

He must be the same age as her own child would have been, Arabella thought as she held him up above her, dangling him over her head and hearing his laughter. And he had called her Mama. She knew then that she was destined to love him.

Thirteen

The journey to George Winston's plantation had taken several days to complete. The wagon was covered over by a canvas sheet and more comfortable inside than Arabella had expected – perhaps because it was so good to be on firm land again, and to eat in the fresh air, away from the foul stink of the ship. Even in the better cabins there had been no way to ignore the stench from the holds, which was probably why poor Susan Baxter had felt ill so often.

The voyage was beginning to seem like a nightmare now. Arabella was blossoming in the warm sunshine, enjoying the sights and smells of her new country – and the food was beyond anything. It might just be that she had forgotten what it was like to eat good food, she knew, but everything she was given tasted wonderful.

They stopped once in the middle of the day for food and drink, but their main meal was at night, when they gathered round the fire and ate meat roasted over a naked flame, with cornbread and peas from tin plates. The food was prepared by Torah and a young black man. He told Arabella that his name was Samson and that he had also been bought by Massa Winston, who had promised him that in time he would be free.

'What will you do when you are free, Samson?' Arabella asked him, but he shook his head.

'Don't rightly know, Miss Arabella. Ain't never been free. I wus brought here on a slave ship from Africa when I was a babe and I cain't remember what it was like there.'

'You couldn't go back there, could you?'

'No, ma'am, wouldn't seem right somehow. I might go north one day, but I got to earn my freedom, so Massa says. He expects me to work for him for a year and then he'll set me free.'

Her bond was for seven years. Would George Winston expect her to work for him for seven years – or would he set her free? At the moment it did not seem as important as it had on the ship. She liked the people she had met since being bought by her new owner, and the life they seemed to expect at the plantation did not sound so very bad. Besides, she had fallen deeply in love with her master's son, and something told her that she needed to be with this child, to love him and care for him.

'We are on Mr Winston's land now, have

been for some time,' Matthew Roberts told her that afternoon towards sunset. 'I've been here only a few times, and I wasn't sure until this moment, but I believe the plantation is one of the largest in Virginia. But we are almost at the house now – not the new one they are building, but the original house.'

Arabella felt a shiver of excitement as she looked about her. She had seen men working in the fields a short time earlier. Most were black, except for a white overseer, but she had become used to the sight of dark-skinned men and women on the journey here. She thought she might never grow accustomed to her surroundings, for they were so different to the gentle English countryside with huge trees, bright colours and lush forests.

As the house came into view, she sat forward on the buckboard of the wagon, eager to see her new home. It was a small house, long and low, the roof sloping over the bedroom windows. The walls were whitewashed and partly covered by creepers that were heavy with yellow blossoms with a soft perfume that she thought might be jasmine.

The wagon pulled to a halt and Samson came to help her down. Arabella stood looking at the house for a moment, then turned as Samson put the sleeping child into her arms. He woke as she took him, gurgled with laughter and then wriggled impatiently. She put him down on the dry grass and he immediately sat down hard on his bottom, but pulled himself up again by tugging on her skirts. Knowing that Master James Winston was a very independent young man, Arabella waited for him to right himself. She offered her hand, which he accepted with a quaint dignity, and then toddled beside her up the path to the house.

A woman, who was plainly the housekeeper, opened the door at their approach. Her first words of greeting identified her as an Englishwoman. 'I am Mrs Saunders,' she announced importantly. 'Mr Winston's housekeeper. I came here from his...from England to be with him. My family has worked for his for many years and he asked me if I wanted to come. He sent me on ahead of you to get things prepared. You'll find everything as neat and right as I can make it, Mr Roberts. Of course it's not what we're used to, but the new house is almost ready and we shall be more comfortable there.'

She turned from him to Arabella, her eyes dwelling on her face for a moment. Arabella fancied there was a hint of disapproval in her eyes, but it was quickly hidden. 'You'll be Mistress Tucker I dare say. You're here to take care of the master's son I understand.'

'Yes, ma'am,' Arabella replied. 'That was the reason Mr Winston purchased my bond.' She raised her head proudly, determined not to be cowed by the housekeeper.

'So I've been told,' Mrs Saunders said and sniffed. 'Well, I'll get one of the girls to take you upstairs to the nursery in a moment. Let me look at Master James. A lovely boy – just like his father.'

'Do you have some milk for him?' Arabella asked. 'We bought some at a farm on the road but it was finished this morning.'

'Of course, there's milk in the cold pantry,' the housekeeper said scornfully. 'The master's son will not go short of anything in this house.'

'If you would show me where the pantry is, I would prefer to see to his needs before we go upstairs.'

'You are to be waited on by Flores and myself, that's what the master said.' The housekeeper looked at her consideringly. 'But start as you mean to go on, I always say. I'll take you to the kitchen and you can see for yourself where things are.'

'Thank you,' Arabella said and smiled at her. 'I am sure we shall deal well together, Mrs Saunders – if you give me a chance.'

The housekeeper nodded but made no comment. She was not harsh or unfriendly, but Arabella realized that she was keeping her distance, reserving judgement. She certainly wasn't as friendly as Flores and Matthew Roberts or the other servants, but she was finding her way in a new land, as Arabella also must.

She followed the older woman to the kitchen, which was at the back of the house and cool, the pantry reached by going down some stone steps. The walls had been built of stone so that the temperature remained cool even in the heat of the day, and the milk when it was poured into a cup was fresh and delicious. James drank half of it thirstily, and Arabella smiled as the house-keeper offered him a small biscuit to accompany it.

'We shall go up now, I think,' Arabella said. 'But later I would like to speak with you, Mrs Saunders. I need to know your routine so that we do not interfere with it, and to understand how things are run here.'

'If you are willing to be guided by me, mistress, I dare say we shan't fall out.'

'I certainly hope that we shall be friends,' Arabella replied with a smile of relief. 'This is a new life for all of us, ma'am, and we should strive to make the most of it.'

Once again the housekeeper nodded but made no comment beyond summoning a maid to take Arabella upstairs to her room, which was a part of the nursery provided for the child.

'She's a sharp tongue on her,' the girl said

in what was plainly an Irish accent. 'But she's not bad as housekeepers go.'

'Did you come here of your own free will?' Arabella asked.

'I came because my daddy died,' the girl replied. 'My brothers were a wild lot and always in trouble with the English. They were about to be arrested but we ran away and took a ship for America – and I ended up here. I was here before the new master came.' She smiled at Arabella. 'I'm Maura O'Mara – Maura to you, if you like.'

'And I'm Bella to my friends,' Arabella said. 'What do you do here, Maura?'

'I'm a bit of a cook and a bit of a seamstress,' she replied. 'But to tell the truth, I do a bit of anything they ask me so I do. As long as they feed me well I don't mind what I do – I had enough of starving in the old country when times were hard.'

Arabella nodded. She had learned what it felt like to go hungry in prison and then on the ship, and she hoped she would never have to experience it again.

The nursery wing was furnished with plain heavy pieces made of American oak. But there were rich hangings at the windows and around the bed, which was plainly for her use, and a large armoire had been provided for her clothes. She smiled as she thought of the dress Susan Baxter had given her; it would get lost in that great thing, she thought, and went over to look inside. To her surprise there were several gowns hanging there – not the silks and satins she had once been accustomed to, but good quality dresses of light-blue homespun that would be ideal for wearing in the rather warm climate.

'Is someone already sleeping here?' Arabella asked Maura.

'The gowns are for you,' Maura replied, her cheeks pink. 'The master gave orders that you were to be supplied with a few good dresses because you would have nothing with you.'

'There is no need to be embarrassed, Maura,' Arabella said. 'I came out here as a convict and Mr Winston bought my bond. I was convicted of murder and my sentence is seven years penal service.'

'But surely you were innocent?'

'Did Mr Winston tell you that?'

'No – but he told Mrs Saunders and she told me. You're to be treated the same as any of us, Bella. Mr Winston doesn't hold with owning men or women, thinks it a sin he does, though he hasn't had the time to set all his slaves free yet. He bought them with the plantation, you see, but I've been told it's his intention to have all freemen working here.'

'He sounds...an interesting man.'

'I've not met him yet,' Maura told her. 'Mr

Roberts did all the negotiating over the plantation, and it was he that hired me, so it was. We've most of us to meet the master yet – apart from Mrs Saunders, and she's worked for his family since she was a young girl.'

'I wonder when he will come here,' Arabella said, her curiosity aroused. 'Flores Roberts told me only that he had gone to Washington on business.'

'He's a rich man, so Mrs Saunders says – and an important one if she is to be believed. I dare say he'll be making friends and meeting other important folk. He doesn't have to come here much at all unless he likes. Mr Roberts will do all that is necessary. The master will likely live in Richmond, so he will, and visit us when he thinks about it.'

'Yes, perhaps,' Arabella said. 'And yet if he doesn't plan to live here – why should he build a fine new house?'

'In the old country the English sometimes built fine houses, but they didn't choose to live in them very often,' Maura said with a wry twist of her mouth. 'There's no telling with them – the rich ones, that is, saving yourself, Bella – and that's the truth of it.'

Arabella smiled inwardly. She had taken to the Irish woman, just as she had to Flores and Matthew, Samson and Torah. Mrs Saunders was a little more difficult – but she was not unfriendly, merely reserved. If the rest of Mr Winston's household was as friendly, life here could be very pleasant indeed.

Arabella found that life at the plantation was even more pleasant than she had imagined. She had expected that she would have a mistress who would tell her what her duties should be, but soon discovered that she was allowed to do as she pleased. Indeed, it soon became plain that the care of the child was to be left to her discretion. Flores Roberts helped where she could, and Torah was a wonderful source of information when it came to easing teething problems and sore bottoms.

'I done birthed all my ole massa's childer,' she told Arabella. 'Nursed every one of them till they was big enough to run free, and I reckons I knows a little 'bout easin' their troubles.'

'It was very clever of Mr Winston to find you and bring you here,' Arabella said one night when James had been crying with his tooth. 'That stuff you gave me to rub in his gum helped him sleep, and it tasted nice too.'

'I knows childer,' the old woman said and grinned at her. 'And the massa, he see me cryin' my eyes out that day, and he say to me, "Ain't no need for you to go cryin' like that, Mammy, 'cos I'm gonna buy you and look after you." And if I can help his boy then I's happy, Miss Bella. Massa a good man and I likes him.'

'I think he must be a nice man,' Arabella said. 'And I am glad he brought you here, because I wouldn't have known what to do for poor James.'

'If I's right, you gonna see for yourself pretty soon,' Torah told her and smiled. 'Massa Roberts he done tole his daughter that Massa comin' home soon.'

Arabella nodded, but had an uneasy feeling deep down inside her. Everything had been so pleasant these last two weeks that she was sure it had to change. George Winston just couldn't be the paragon his servants believed. Even in Paradise there had been a serpent and she was afraid that in her case it would turn out to be the master...

'Arabella!' She heard someone call her name and turned, shading her eyes against the hot sunshine to look at the man walking towards her. It was midday, the sun beating down on the earth, the air sultry and uncomfortable, making her clothes stick to her. For a moment she didn't recognize the man who had called to her, but as he got nearer she realized who he was. 'It is you, isn't it? You look so different and yet I was sure it was when Maura was tellin' me about you just now.'

'You're Nat – from the ship,' she said, her eyes going over him with appreciation. He was wearing clean, serviceable working breeches and a grey shirt, his dark hair cropped short, his eyes twinkling. In his prison dirt she had known that he must have been handsome once, but now, recovered from the voyage, clearly fit and well fed, he was a fine figure of a man. 'You look well.'

'I feel well,' he told her. 'It was a hard fight to get here, Arabella. I thought I might not make it for a while – but as you see I survived and I've landed on me feet. Mr Winston bought my bond, but he's promised I'll work for wages as if I were free and that if I serve him well he'll help me to get on.'

'You said it was a land of promise and opportunity, Nat,' Arabella said. 'And it seems you were right.'

'Aye, I was. You look blooming yourself, lass – are they treatin' you well?'

'Yes. I've been very lucky. I was picked to be a child's nurse on the ship and now I'm here. Do you know what happened to Peg or any of the others?'

'Peg was bought along with several others,' Nat said. 'I don't know where she went, other than in a boat with six of the other women.'

'I hope she finds a good place – but I doubt if there are many as good as this one.'

'We're both lucky to be here,' Nat said. 'Well, I'd best go and see to Mr Winston's horses. That's what he pays me for and I don't want to lose my place.'

'Is he here?' Arabella's heart quickened. 'I was told it would be soon, but I wasn't sure.'

'Aye, he's here – gone up to the new house to see what they've been up to I dare say.' Nat grinned at her. 'He'll be lookin' for a wife when it's done, I reckon. There were plenty after him in Washington, I can tell you. Him being a titled gentleman.'

'Titled?' Arabella suddenly felt breathless. 'I thought he was simply Mr George Winston.'

'Now where in the world did you get that from?' Nat's eyes twinkled. 'His name ain't George – and Winston is only one of his names. He's got a string of them. He might choose to go as plain Mister out here, but he's a marquis – a real blue blood if ever there was one. But he ain't like them I've seen afore, I can tell you. Right bastards most of them if you ask me – but this one is different. Odd sense of humour sometimes, but decent when you get down to it.'

Arabella's mouth felt dry and somehow she knew. She knew who Mr Winston was. She turned and walked away from Nat. Surely it couldn't be true? It was her imagination, her mind playing tricks on her – but somewhere deep down in her memory she recalled seeing a letter in Gervase's drawing room once when they stayed at his country house. There had been a lot of names at the heading, and now she thought she recalled seeing Winston amongst them.

Why had it not occurred to her before? But she had never dreamed that Gervase would be here in America. Would he have followed her halfway across the world? No, of course not. The man who had purchased this plantation had been planning to come here for many months – perhaps even years.

How could it be Gervase? And yet the man who had bought her bond had known her name. He had told his agent that he was to bring her back without fail. Why should a stranger have done that? It seemed highly unlikely. But if her owner was really Gervase ...Somehow it all fitted together. Gervase had bought her from Mistress Elizabeth George. And now he had bought her again.

She felt the sting of humiliation wash over her. Why had he done it? Was it so that he could mock her, flaunt his power over her – but why? Oh, if only it wasn't true! She did not think she could bear it if Gervase owned her bond. But what could she do? She was tied to him for the term of seven years whether she liked it or not. She turned and went back to the house, her intention to walk down to the river forgotten.

Mrs Saunders tutted as Arabella walked into the house. 'So there you are, Arabella. The master was here a few minutes ago asking to see his son, and you not here to greet him. I sent you to fetch me some eggs from the hen house, not to stand talking all day.'

'I'm sorry if I was longer than necessary,' Arabella said. 'It was so hot and I thought I should like to walk for a while. Did...did Mr Winston see James.'

'Aye, that he did, and he's taken him out to see the horses. He'll be back in an hour or so and you'd best be here then or I'll not vouch for you again.'

'I shall go up to the nursery now. I have some sewing to do.'

Arabella ran up the short flight of stairs to the rooms beneath the eaves. In the nursery itself one wall sloped sharply to the ceiling and she had to watch that she did not bang her head there. She picked up her mending basket and began to work on the tiny shirt she was making for James, her mind working furiously. Gervase had been here – would be here soon – if it was he, of course. But she had a growing conviction that it must be him.

Her heart was racing and she felt uneasy. She recalled the night they had quarrelled and parted. He had told her he had something important to say, and she had believed he was about to tell her their affair was over. Could he have been about to tell her of his plans for a new life? Had he been going to ask her to come out here with him?

She pricked her finger and cursed, sucking it so that the blood should not stain the fine linen she was working on, and then suddenly she became aware of something and looked up. Gervase was standing in the doorway watching her, an odd expression in his eyes. She put down the needlework and stood up, feeling breathless. She had known it had to be him, but now she was shocked and nervous.

She curtsied to him but in the manner of a lady to a gentleman, her head held high, her eyes proud. 'Good day, Mr Winston. I trust you found James well and happy?'

'You do not seem surprised to see me, Arabella. Do I take it you had guessed who Mr Winston was in reality?'

'Until this day I had no idea,' she replied. 'But when I was speaking to Nat a few minutes ago he said something that made me suspect it.'

'And you are still here?' Gervase raised his brows mockingly. 'The old Arabella would have gone off in a temper I believe.'

'The Arabella you knew died some months ago, Mr Winston.'

'You know my name well enough – use it.'

His eyes narrowed in displeasure. 'What are these gowns you are wearing? They are not what I ordered for you. I brought all your belongings with me – why have you not been given them?'

'Perhaps your housekeeper did not think them fitting for a servant.'

'Do you imagine I brought you here to be my servant?' Gervase glared at her, his anger as much with others as Arabella. Clearly he had not made his intentions plain enough. That would be rectified!

'What else, my lord? You have bought me twice over now – why should you not use me as you wish?'

'As I wish?' He moved towards her, his eyes gleaming with what she knew was a mixture of anger and passion. 'You know how I would use you if I had my wish, Bella. But you are free to choose. Be my mistress if you will, or remain my servant if it soothes your pride. You will do what pleases you as always.'

'As I please?' Arabella gave a harsh laugh. 'You know that I am bound to you for seven years. How can I leave here?'

'Would you leave if you were free?'

'Perhaps...' Her eyes flashed with temper. 'Why should I want to stay? You must have planned this for months before you left England. Why did you never mention it to me? Oh, pray do not trouble yourself,

360

Gervase. I know the truth well enough. I knew it that last night before you quarrelled with Harry Sylvester. You had tired of me and meant to leave me.'

'Was that my intention? I thank you for telling me.' A smile touched his mouth. 'Well, it is a cruel fate that brings us together once more is it not, my sweet? Since I need a mother for my child and you need a home, I dare say we may rub along well enough.'

'What are you saying?'

'Only this...' Gervase took two strides towards her, pulling her roughly into his arms and kissing her so hungrily that she was shocked. 'I find I still want you, Bella. As you say, you are mine, and I shall have you in the end – in my bed, in my house, where I choose.'

'You said that I was free to choose,' she gasped, pressing her fingers to her bruised lips. She was trembling, shocked because he had lit a fire in her.

'I lied,' he said. 'You may have a time to consider your position, Bella, but I shall not wait too long.'

'Gervase...' She watched as he turned on his heel and left the room without a backward glance. His kiss had left her shaken, aching for more. She wondered why they must always quarrel. Why could they not simply be kind and good to each other?

Both knew that an invisible bond, which had nothing to do with the one he had bought, bound them so tightly that neither could break it. 'Oh, Gervase, my love, forgive me...'

'Forgive me, Mistress Tucker,' the housekeeper said, her hands folded before her. Her expression was stony but she could not meet Arabella's eyes. 'I did not exactly understand his lordship's orders. He told me to see that you had clothes befitting your station and I...'

Arabella had thought Maura's embarrassment over the gowns was because she had arrived on a prison ship with nothing, but now she guessed that the Irish girl had known they were not the gowns that had been intended for Arabella.

'You did not think that the silks and satins in the chests were meant for a woman who had come here in the belly of a prison ship?' Arabella smiled. 'As it happens I agree with you, and I shall continue to wear the gowns you provided for me – at least for the moment.'

The other woman looked at her oddly. 'We never met, but I knew that you were his mistress in England. I was away at my sister's house looking after her during her last illness when he brought you to the country – but I knew your name, and I knew he cared for you.'

'Why do you say that?'

'The master never brought his mistresses to the country house,' Mrs Saunders replied. 'He gave you the room that had belonged to his sister – though I was told her London clothes were packed away after you wore one of them. And the remainder of her things were burned after she died by the old master.'

'His sister...' Arabella stared at her in astonishment. 'Those gowns belonged to Gervase's sister?'

'Aye. Thought the world of her, he did. If Gervase ever loved anyone it was Miss Helen. It sent him near mad with grief when he knew what had happened to her, what that rogue Sylvester did to her, and her but an innocent child. If I could have got my hands on him I'd have killed him myself. It was wicked, and the way her father treated her no better.'

'You mean Harry Sylvester? Did he seduce her?' Arabella felt the shock run through her as the housekeeper nodded. She felt sick to her stomach. 'No wonder Gervase hated Harry! I cannot blame him after what you have told me. What happened to his sister?'

'Her father sent her away in disgrace. She died after having the child, and the child died soon after of neglect, so they say. When his lordship heard of it he was in a blue rage for weeks. I thought his grief would send him mad or that he would kill that rogue for sure, but Sylvester would never fight him until that last time, and his lordship is too honourable a man to send his servants to thrash him. There's a good many others would have done it, miss, and so I tell you!'

'Yes, I believe you,' Arabella said. The tale was harrowing and had made her want to cry. 'I...thank you for telling me. I wish that I had known this a long time ago.' If she had known how wicked Harry was, she might have been more sensible.

'It was hushed up at the time. His lordship didn't want Miss Helen's name dragged through the mud or I dare say he would have thrashed Sylvester in public.'

Why had he not told her? She understood now why he had been so angry to see her wearing the gown – why he had hated Harry and warned her not to trust him right from the beginning. If only she had listened! If she had never believed herself in love with Harry, how different things might have been.

'You have made it easier for me to understand many things, Mrs Saunders. I am grateful to you.'

The housekeeper nodded, relaxing slightly. 'I hope that there need be no unpleasantness between us, Mistress Tucker.'

'No, of course not,' Arabella said. 'But you

may call me Bella if you wish. Nothing has changed.'

'I thank you for the offer, miss, but I beg to differ. His lordship knows his own mind, and I believe you will find that he intends a great many changes.'

Arabella left James sleeping in his cot one afternoon three weeks later. Torah was sitting by him, keeping a watch as she often did, and Arabella was free for an hour or so. Whenever she felt that she could leave the child, she liked to walk in the sunshine, to explore the estate. Once she had walked up to the new house to watch the men at work on it. Clearly it was intended to be a grand mansion, with many windows, and steps leading up to the imposing colonnade and front door. Most of it was ready but the walls were receiving a final coat of white-wash and the sound of hammering could still be heard from inside.

Gervase had been there, discussing something with the master builder, so intent on his purpose that he had not noticed her. She had done nothing to attract his attention, for she knew that if he wanted to see her he would come to her.

In the three weeks since his return she had seen him at a distance as she walked, some-times with James, sometimes alone, and she knew that he had visited his son several times when she was out. Had he deliberately chosen those times? She was uncertain whether he was avoiding her or she him; she only knew that there was a part of her that longed for him while another resisted.

If she had truly been free to choose, would she have left him? Sometimes her pride made her want to be free, but she knew that she was bound to Gervase – and to the child she loved as if he were her own. So if she did not wish to leave, why did she fear giving herself to Gervase again? Was it only pride, or something more?

She was standing by the river that fed the plantation when she heard the sound of a horse's hooves. She knew that the rider had dismounted but did not turn her head, sensing without looking that it was Gervase. 'Nat told me you come here,' Gervase said as he came to stand beside her. 'He likes you – did you know that?'

She turned to look at him, her heart catching. How strong and vital he looked, wearing riding breeches and an open-necked shirt. His skin had taken on a healthy glow since he'd come to this country and it clearly suited him far better than the life he had led in London. Her heart was racing and her mouth felt dry as she turned back to look at the river.

'He is a rogue but I find him amusing company,' she said. 'But you need not glare so, Gervase. He is merely a friend – as Matthew and Flores and all the others...'

'You have found a life for yourself here?'

'Yes.' She lifted her head, gazing into his eyes. 'I am content, my lord.'

'It is better if you call me Gervase,' he replied, his expression giving nothing away. 'I have no use for empty titles here – nor ever did, if truth be known.'

'They meant something in England.'

'But not here,' Gervase said. 'This is a young country, Bella, and we shall not always bend the knee to England. Why should we pay their taxes? We do not need them, or their laws. We shall form our own.'

'Become an independent country?'

'Why not?'

'I see no reason why not,' Arabella said. 'That is why you planned to come here, isn't it, Gervase? Because you were tired of the old ways – of the injustice and the corruption? You wanted to be free of it, to find a new life here.'

'Yes,' he admitted. 'England had become too small for me, Bella. I felt stifled there and I believed that a man might be able to breathe in this country. There is so much space, so much freedom – and equality. Here a man may rise on the back of his ambition. In England, class and birth is all and the poor have little chance of acquiring anything more than they were born with –

unless they rob or cheat. 'Tis little wonder that men like Nat take the law into their own hands. Here he will have a chance to make something of himself.'

'He was lucky not to hang,' she said. 'As was I...You have not forgotten that I was accused of murdering your closest friend?'

'Jack saved my life, but he was not always a friend to me,' Gervase replied. 'He took advantage too often and I sometimes felt that I should end the association, but being of an indolent nature, I did not.' He shrugged his shoulders.

'There is nothing indolent about the man who dreamed of this and made it happen,' Arabella said and laughed huskily. 'You would have me believe you something other than you are, Gervase. You kept up your friendship with Jack because you were grateful to him for saving your life, and despite his faults you liked him – as I did most of the time.'

'You don't hate him?'

'I wish that none of it had happened.' She looked him in the eyes. 'Why did you never tell me the truth about Harry Sylvester?'

'Would it have made a difference?' His eyes were gently mocking. 'I have not forgotten the girl I propositioned at that inn, Bella. I do not believe that she would have listened to anything I had to say.'

'I was terribly insulted,' she said, her eyes

bright with laughter. 'At least, I knew that I ought to be insulted – but in truth I was excited. You were the first man who had ever dared to speak to me that way. My father's neighbours were so polite and so boring! You made my blood race but I was angry with you for thinking me a whore.'

'I was foolish to think money could buy you. I have learned my lesson the hard way, my love.'

'But you *have* bought me, Gervase – twice.'

'I bought you once to save you from being sold to the highest bidder at that infamous auction,' he admitted. 'But that is the only time, Bella. I do not own your bond. You were given a free pardon by the judge who so carelessly condemned you.'

'A pardon? But I was told...' She stared at him in bewilderment. 'I don't understand, Gervase.'

'I planned it that way,' he said. 'I was afraid of what you might do if you knew the truth. I feared that you might hate me after all that had happened, and I blamed myself for leaving you to the wolves. When I left you I was too angry to consider, but I should have known what they would do. You were alone and vulnerable, but I did not expect things to develop so quickly, and I intended to return as soon as my plans were complete.'

'You meant to return?' All the rest meant nothing. Her heart beat so fast that she could scarcely breathe. 'I thought that I should never see you again. You said it was over...'

'I know what I said, Bella, but once my temper had cooled I knew that it could never be over between us. You are a part of me, the heart of me, and I could no more live without you than the air I breathe. I should have returned the next day and told you how I felt, but my pride would not permit it. I thought it would do you good to have time to regret – at least I hoped you would regret our parting.'

'Gervase...' Her throat felt tight and she was close to tears. 'Of course I regretted it, but you seemed not to care. I thought I was just...just...'

'Just a mistress I could discard when I was tired of you? That is my fault, Bella – but I was too afraid to let you see what you meant to me. I loved you, but I did not trust you. I thought you would betray me with...' He broke off, a look of pain in his eyes.

'With Harry Sylvester?' She blinked away her tears, realizing for the first time how much she had hurt him by giving herself to the man he hated. 'I was such a fool to think that Harry was the man for me. So young and silly that I could not tell the dross from the gold. And when you quarrelled with him

I defended him despite myself. In my heart I knew the truth by then, but I thought you meant to leave me and I wanted to strike out, to hurt you as you were hurting me.'

'Then we were both fools,' Gervase said, the mockery leaving his eyes. 'Can we start again, Bella? Can we go back to the beginning, when I promised to cover your beautiful body in jewels if you would consent to be mine?'

'And I told you to go to the Devil!' Arabella gurgled with laughter. 'Oh, how I wanted to hit you that night, Gervase. You seemed so arrogant, so sure of yourself.'

'I had always found women too quick to fall into my arms,' he admitted. 'At first I saw you as a challenge – as a citadel to be breached – but then I began to realize that you meant much more to me. When I saw you flirting with Sylvester I wanted to snatch you away from him and put you across my knee. And I wanted to kill him.'

'Why didn't you kill him, Gervase? They told me you could have done so easily if you wished.'

'Because I thought of you, Bella. I knew that I had no right to kill the man you loved. That I had no right to deny you the right to choose.'

'If you had killed him I might never have known the truth,' Arabella said. 'I was beginning to forget him until that night, but I didn't know for sure until it was too late.'

'Know what, Bella?' His eyes were intent on her face.

'I wasn't sure that I loved you,' she said, gazing up at him. 'It was only after you left me that I realized my life was empty without you. I even went to see Harry, but it wasn't him I wanted. There were plenty of others to take your place had I been ready to accept them – but I couldn't stop crying. I drank too much wine and then Jack tried to force himself on me. I didn't kill him, Gervase. I struck him with a poker, but it did no more than draw a spot of blood, and that made him furious. He hated it when I told him you were twice the man he was, and was determined to punish me. We were fighting and I pushed him away and he fell.'

'I know, my love,' Gervase told her. 'I never believed it of you. Why did you not send for me at once? Surely you knew I would help you? Had I known sooner I might have saved you the horror of that terrible journey here.' His eyes moved over her, seeming to caress her. 'I was so afraid that you might suffer more than you could bear – that you might die.'

'Have you not heard that the Devil takes care of his own?' She looked up at him mischievously. 'As usual I was lucky. I sold a ring and bought clean clothes, and because of that I was the one picked to look after

Susan Baxter's son. It almost broke my heart when they told me I was not to go with her but to a stranger. I had fallen in love with her son and I did not know what I would find here.'

'But you care for James?' He looked at her oddly. 'I have seen you with him about the plantation. It seems to me that you are fond of him.'

'I adore him,' she said. 'How could it be otherwise? He looks like you, Gervase. Who was his mother?' Gervase threw back his head and laughed, and she pouted. 'It is not so very funny to me, though I shall not be jealous of her. We are together now.'

'We have similar colouring and I suppose he could be taken for my own blood,' Gervase said. 'And I've done nothing to abuse that notion. Indeed, he is mine for I have adopted him legally – but have you not guessed, Bella?'

'Guessed what?' She stared at him and then began to tremble. What could he mean? He was looking at her in such a way. 'What should I have guessed? My child died...' Her hand crept to her throat as she saw the answer in his eyes. 'Gervase...how can it be?'

'Mistress Elizabeth had sold babies before,' Gervase said with an angry look in his eyes. 'I knew it and wondered if your child had also been sold. She was reluctant to tell me, but a threat of prison and a hefty bribe got the truth from her. However, when I tried to find the couple who had taken the babe it was more difficult than I had imagined. It seems the child was sold on three times before my agents traced him, and we were only just in time. The new parents were about to leave for America and if they had we should never have found him.'

'Is that why you went away on business that last time?' Her eyes were misted with tears. 'Why did you do it, Gervase – was it only to please me?'

'A part of it was to please you, but my father left my own sister's child to die of neglect. I didn't want that to happen to your son, Bella.'

'Oh, Gervase.' Tears were trickling down her cheeks and she was helpless to stop them. 'Gervase, my love...I don't know how to thank you, to tell you what this means to me.'

She gazed at him in wonder. How she had misjudged him! Only a very special man would trace the child of a man he had good reason to hate, take that child and adopt him as his own son. He was a man she could respect, a man she could trust with all her heart, a man she could love for all her life.

'You can thank me by becoming my wife, my darling Arabella.'

'Your wife?' She stared at him in surprise.

'But you can't...You can't marry me, Gervase. You have your position in this new world to think of. Even if you no longer use your title, you are a man others respect and listen to in important matters. How can you marry a woman who came here in a prison ship?'

'I shall marry her because she is the woman I love,' he said and reached out to draw her close to him. 'I shall marry her and hold a grand ball at my new house, and I shall invite all the people I know. Those who choose may come, the others may stay away.'

'But, Gervase...'

He hushed her with a kiss. 'Would you have your son grow up thinking his father would not wed his mother?'

'Gervase...' she began and he kissed her again, so deeply this time that she melted into his body, feeling the desire ripple through her, making her gasp and arch herself against him. How could she resist when she wanted him so very much?

'You are mine, Bella,' he murmured against her throat as he kissed the soft white flesh at the hollow between her breasts. 'I shall never let you go from me again.'

'But Gervase...'

And then she could no longer even think of resisting as he took her down to the soft dry grass, and there in the privacy of a

375

clump of scented bushes, made her his own once more. Their loving was sweet and hungry, driven by the need that had grown in them during the months of their separation, made sweeter still by the knowledge of the love that bound them.

'What were you saying, wench?' Gervase said much later as she lay still in his arms, her body curving into his as if it fit by some divine purpose. 'Some nonsense about my standing in the community being lost if I wed you? I would have you know that I am already considered a leading light in Washington circles by those who hope, as I do, for an independent nation state for Americans. My knowledge of English law is perhaps rather more than you might imagine, and I have been told my advice will be invaluable when dealing with the imposition of new and unwelcome taxes.'

'They will all know that I am a wicked wench,' she told him, reaching up to stroke his cheek with her fingertips. 'You should marry a good woman, Gervase, of unblemished reputation. I am sure all your friends would give you the same advice.'

'And die of boredom within a sennight,' he said and grinned at her. 'Only you, my love – my wicked, wilful wench – could keep me from straying. Only you can give me the happiness I have never known. Only you complete me.'

'Then I suppose you must have your way,' she said and laughed throatily. 'I have it on good authority that you were stubborn even as a lad and I dare say you will never change.'

'Would you want me to?' he asked and laughed as she shook her head. 'Nor I you,' he murmured. 'Nor I you.'